Praise for *The Other Side of the Ocean*

"J.D. Netto's timely and illuminating story captures the longing, joy, and heartache of being young, an immigrant, undocumented, queer—and in love."

—Alex Sanchez, LAMBDA Award-winning author of *Rainbow Boys* and *You Brought Me the Ocean*

"I absolutely loved this moving story that celebrates the courage it takes to love openly and live authentically in an uncertain world, offering readers humor, heart, and ultimately hope."

—Isaac Fitzsimons, LAMBDA Award-nominated author of *The Passing Playbook*

"J.D. Netto's *The Other Side of the Ocean* is a poetic and candid must-read queer coming-of-age story. Braiding humor and emotion, Matt's voice pulls readers into his life as he grapples with his first gay love and finds his place in the world as a young undocumented person. Honest and immersive, you won't want to put this book down."

—Robin Gow, LAMBDA Award-winning author of *Dear Mothman*

"This story is pure magic. Heartwarming and hopeful, I couldn't stop turning the page."

—Emily Rath, *New York Times* bestselling author

"A deeply moving story that sheds light on the reality of so many undocumented teenagers in America."

—Sasha Alsberg, #1 *New York Times* Bestselling author of The Androma Saga and Breaking Time duology

"*The Other Side of the Ocean* is as heartwarming as it is timely. This sweet romance will sweep you off your feet."

—Matthias Roberts, author of *Holy Runaways* and *Beyond Shame*

THE OTHER SIDE OF THE OCEAN

INSPIRED BY TRUE EVENTS

ALSO BY J.D. NETTO

HENDERBELL
Henderbell: The Shadow of Saint Nicholas
Whispers in the Dark

THE BROKEN MIRACLE
The Broken Miracle: Part 1
The Broken Miracle: Part 2

THE ECHOES OF FALLEN STARS
Immortal Crowns
Gods and Mortals

J.D. Netto

THE OTHER SIDE OF THE OCEAN

INSPIRED BY TRUE EVENTS

JAB Books

The Other Side of the Ocean
Copyright © 2025 by J.D. Netto
Published in 2025 by
JABberwocky Literary Agency, Inc.

All rights reserved.

This is a work of fiction. Names, characters, businesses, places, events and incidents are either the products of the author's imagination or used in a fictitious manner. Any resemblance to actual persons, living or dead, or actual events is purely coincidental.

Cover art by J.D. Netto
Interior design by Christy Admiraal

ISBN 978-1-625677-19-8 (ebook)
ISBN 978-1625677-20-4 (paperback)

JABberwocky Literary Agency, Inc.
49 W. 45th Street, Suite #5N
New York, NY 10036
http://awfulagent.com
ebooks@awfulagent.com

Dedicated to my mother, whose courage, joy, and determination have been a constant source of inspiration. And to every immigrant who dared to face the impossible in pursuit of their own American dream—this one is for you.

1
SECRETS

September 2011

I was in the living room when Mom answered her phone and sat on the porch. She stayed there after she hung up, alone with the sunset. I didn't bother interrupting. She eventually came inside and spilled it. Her friend's husband had been detained by ICE. There had been no word on him since. No phone call. Nothing.

I tried imagining what that felt like. One moment you're working, the next you have cuffs around your wrists and ICE is dragging you to prison until your fate is decided. Sure, overstaying your visa and-or crossing the border was against the law. Some people did it to commit crimes. Others to dream. Deportation stories were like legends in my house. You'd hear about them from parents who had heard it from their friends, but they were these tales that happened to people other people knew. It had never happened so close to us.

No matter how much I wanted to pretend—how much I wanted to dream—the most fucked-up part was that my family and my best friends weren't exempt from meeting the same fate. When it came to my friends, we lived an illegal life because other people had made choices for us when we were young. And now we had to make the best with what we got—which wasn't so bad, aside from the whole no-paper thing.

Sometimes I felt bad about complaining that I lived in America. So many people risk their lives for a chance at the so-called American Dream. But mine was neither a dream nor a nightmare. It was limbo.

I stared at the white ceiling of my bedroom, hoping it'd turn into a canvas displaying a way out of my undocumented reality. I thought about it often. How I couldn't have roots in the place I had spent the last ten years; how my dreams were limited to a piece of paper; how there was no light at the end of the tunnel from the place I stood. And now, I was doomed to think about this secret identity more often.

My family's undocumented truth wasn't something I went around advertising. A lot of people didn't really understand what that adventure meant. Blame the movies or the media. Every illegal person had a different story, but a whole lot of people assumed we had all swum across a river, crossed a desert, and ended up here to become criminals. Little did they know that, to some, that was the price to pay to have a shot at a life beyond oppression.

I was six when the family and I left Brazil and flew over the Atlantic, tourist visas in hand. My parents sold whatever we had after we lost our store. I somewhat understood what staying here meant at the time. I hoped things would work themselves out eventually. Well, I was still hoping.

I ignored my undocumented thoughts whenever they knocked. I'd lose my shit if I let them hang out for too long. Which I did sometimes. I'd then spiral. My let-me-Google-any-immigration-loopholes obsession followed. The last time I fell down the rabbit hole, I came across all these articles talking about immigration reform for kids like me. The famous DREAM Act. Its fate had been a roller coaster ride as wild as my own. From being introduced over a decade ago to being brought to the US Senate last year and obviously failing because apparently kids like me—Dreamers, as the press liked to call us for dramatic purposes—were political pawns for whichever party. I mean, how many times can you ride the same roller coaster in a row before you puke everywhere?

My own roller coaster had a few loops and drops that led me to my big internal debate: to stay undocumented or to go back to the place that served as the setting for what I called "The Great Franco Family Debacle."

I finally got out of bed, showered, and got dressed in the first thing I could find in my closet: jeans, boots, an Abercrombie t-shirt, and a jacket. If my mom were home, she'd tell me not to go to school with my hair wet. Fall was here and the cold could give me pneumonia—or so she'd say. Mom was awesome. I actually enjoyed our talks and the effort she made to be a part of my life regardless of how much she had to work.

I always questioned her whenever she casually mentioned the dangers of living in the cold weather. Why Framingham, Massachusetts, then? Why not Miami or LA? Her argument was that the cold would give us thicker skin. To me, she just wanted to escape anything mirroring our lives back in Fogo Dourado—even the everlasting tropical weather. Even though I was young kid at the time, I still had vivid memories of Dad rolling down the steel doors of the store for the last time; Mom crying on the sidewalk; all the gossip and criticism.

When I was a kid, I'd watch American movies where the family gathered for a lavish breakfast before the kids jetted off to school. When my parents told us we were moving to America, I thought that we'd live like that. My life couldn't be more different. A bowl of Fruit Loops was breakfast for my sister and me most days; Pop Tarts were also accepted. No fancy pancakes or bacon on weekdays. Parents started working before the sun was out and sometimes were home early enough for dinner.

My sister was already in the kitchen, eyes glued to her phone as she whirled the cereal in her bowl with a spoon.

"We should skip," she said, her backpack on the chair beside her.

"Laila, I actually enjoy shop week." I grabbed a bowl from the cabinet. "That was the whole reason why I decided to go to a technical high school. It's already Thursday, anyway. And today I get to draw shit, eat junk, and listen to music. It really isn't so bad."

"Mom already told you not to say 'shit' in front of me." Her phone screen was still more interesting than my face.

"Like you don't hear worse at school." I poured the cereal and the store-branded milk into my bowl and reclined on the edge of the table. Laila was thirteen but looked much older. Her face had gone from being round and plump to chiseled and long in a matter of months. No more styling her brown hair in pigtails. Now her shoulder-length locks draped in front of her face or in a bun.

"We could tell them we got deported," she suggested with a smirk, finally looking at me. "She got so emotional over what happened to the Moreiras yesterday."

"What a nice thing to say before seven a.m.," I said.

"I can't wait until it's my turn to go to a tech school next year." She disregarded my comment.

"If we're here by then." I munched on some cereal. "I hate this whole ping-pong game they play with us. They decide to stay, to leave, to hang for a little longer. A decade later and we're still going through this shit."

"Ah!" She raised a finger. "There it is again."

"Well, this situation deserves the word. It's shit. Shitty."

"Seriously." She dropped the spoon on the edge of the bowl. "Like, hello, can I plan on going to high school next year or should I just, I don't know, curl into a ball, and stay in my room listening to sad music? My Portuguese is practically nonexistent. Should I take Portuguese classes online? You, at least, speak it a little bit."

"Um pouco," I said. "Mas não suficiente. Anyway, on the bright side, I did read this thing online about Obama and what they were planning for immigration—"

"Matt," she interrupted, holding her hands in the air like a traffic cop. "Just stop. You always do this. You want to see the good in this whole thing. I get it. That's how you cope. I cope with sarcasm. And it's okay. But stop doing this to yourself. Let's just enjoy today, okay?" Her brown eyes returned to the phone as she crushed her cereal with her spoon. "At least if we go back, Dad won't be on your case about going to school for art anymore."

"Right," I mumbled. "Such a plus. He'll want me to take over the business he plans on reopening after it destroyed the family. Because that's what I've always wanted to do with my life. Que merda."

"Saying 'shit' in Portuguese doesn't exempt you from Mom's request," Laila said snidely.

The hissing of the bus pulling up in front of our house was her invitation to leave before I could contest her snarky comment.

"See you later." She grabbed her backpack.

"Still can't believe they pick you up in front of our house!"

"I'm one of the lucky ones," she said as soon as she closed the door behind her.

I dumped the rest of the cereal down the drain, put on my headphones, and left the house only after pressing play on Linkin Park and Jay-Z's "Numb/Encore."

Things weren't so bad once I stepped out of the house and tucked my undocumented thoughts into my secret imaginary drawer of unwanted things. I loved my friends. I loved where I lived. I loved art and Halloween and every cheesy holiday celebration there was.

A couple of my neighbors had already decorated for spooky season. Pumpkins, ghosts, and skeletons crowded the front yard of a few homes. One of the neighbors had even built a cemetery. Some would say that September was too early to decorate. I neither confirmed nor denied that fact, because if it were up to me, I'd decorate for Christmas on the first day of fall.

The bus arrived. I dozed off and woke up when we stopped in front of the concrete façade displaying the silver letters spelling out "Joseph Ferguson High School." Our mascot was proudly displayed next to the words, a unicorn inside a triangle.

I grabbed my phone to check my messages and accidentally opened my front camera. My brown eyes gave me too much credit; people would think I was high before 7 a.m. I rustled the front of my brown curls over my eyebrows. I'm not that cool—just tired.

Three messages. Fa—or Lesbian One—had sent a quote in the chat: "Focus on the positive and your day will be brighter. See the negative and your day will be fucked." She sent these occasionally. Ignore the ones she considered good and there'd be hell to pay.

Diana—Lesbian Two—had replied with a heart emoji.

Pedro, aka Manga Boy, simply said, "The positive today is the bell ringing at three. Bro, I already want my bed again. To com sono."

Our chat was called the Forbidden Fortress, named after our own friend group, established back when we met at Woodrow Wilson Elementary. I was never a fan of group chats, so back when we started ours, I requested that we each have epic names. Manga Boy was a tribute to Pedro's undying love for all things anime, manga, and hentai; Fa and Diana called themselves "Lesbians One and Two" on the daily already. They said it was a modern-day tribute to Dr. Seuss's characters. I was Elder Wizard because Fa insisted my soul was old and my mind too complicated. She actually gave me one of those cheap wizard costumes you buy at party stores for my birthday. I had expected a second gift, but no. She claimed I needed to embrace who I truly was, and the costume was a start. I never wore it.

I was the first to arrive at our exclusive table in the cafeteria. Exclusive because, since freshman year, no one else had joined us. It was far enough from all the others but not too far from the vending machines and the food aisle. It also faced the floor-to-ceiling window that provided a view of the football field. The table had been named after our group chat.

After grabbing a bagel with cream cheese and a boxed chocolate milk, I paid the vending machine a visit, bought an apple pie, and returned to the table just in time for the rest of the members of the Forbidden Fortress to arrive.

Fa had picked a pretty modest sweatshirt today. All it said was "Magic Is Around You." Her curly hair was up in a messy ponytail and her black jeans had holes on both her knees. She was a brown curvy girl and wanted the world to know how proud she was of her figure. "The original babe from Rio," she'd call herself sometimes.

Diana had her hair in a single braid falling over her right shoulder. She wore classic Diana color tones. She was like a coffee mug on a foggy fall morning, always wearing browns and oranges, even in the dead of summer. Even her braces were orange. She had insisted on getting them last year to fix her front gap. I always thought the gap was her thing, like, her signature. But she wanted to get rid of it.

Pedro had his usual band t-shirt. Red Hot Chili Peppers was his choice for the day. His once-white Converses were now a mixture of mud and doodles. He'd had a shaved cut since last year. According to him, the five minutes he used to spend on his hair in the morning were now five extra minutes of sleep.

"Somebody didn't wait for his friends." Fa hugged me. "Sacanagem, Matt."

"I was hungry," I said after she let me go, my arms now around Diana. "Please tell her it's too early for lectures."

"She already came for Diana and me on the bus." Pedro fist-bumped me. "She said something about…" He rolled a finger in the air, showing Fa that he needed assistance remembering.

"How you all need to be more in tune with your spiritual selves," Fa added, rolling her eyes. "Listen, people. You all need to listen, okay? You really do."

"Thank God I have you to realign my chakras." Diana pecked Fa on the cheek. "Without you, my spiritual self is like a caffeine addict minus the coffee."

"You're lucky I'm patient, babe," Fa added with a smile. "I'll make the goddess of the sea an offering for all of you on New Year's. I promise."

"You're too kind." I dropped my mouth open. "Can she also bring us green cards?"

"Good one," Pedro said with a laugh.

"I'll ask her." Fa clicked her tongue and winked.

They all marched their way to the food aisle. I didn't miss Fa and Diana lacing their fingers. I wish I had enough guts to take the blow like they did last year, to own up to what I thought would be an inconvenience to people around me.

Many from my parents' generation in Brazil still held on to their anti-queer religious beliefs like anchors. Blame religion. Blame homophobia. Blame whatever. Not that we didn't have a lot of the same in many places in America. Fa and Diana coming out to their Brazilian conservative families who lived here was a big deal. They were sort of forced to do it after everything that happened to them.

When they posted a picture with the rainbow flag last year, Dad began bragging to some of his friends about his son hanging out with lesbians. You'd think he was doing it because of how progressive he was. That wasn't the case. He actually asked me if I had ever considered hooking up with both of them. I'd always ignore his comments. But it was harder to ignore his questions about the girls I was seeing. No, Dad. No girls. Tons of gay porn, though.

I hoped people thought I was just picky when it came to dating. The truth, however, was entirely different. I was eleven when I downloaded an illegal copy of *Brokeback Mountain* on the internet after watching the trailer. Heath Ledger and Jake Gyllenhaal as sexy cowboys made me feel all sorts of things, including fear. I related to Ennis insisting they keep their love a secret. Not because I was ashamed of it. I just didn't want to add that hard truth to the pile of another one. Who knew what could happen after I stepped out of my safe gay closet?

My family wasn't really religious. We were Catholics, but we stopped going to mass after moving here. Some people who attended church were somewhat okay with the gays. I knew where Dad stood on that spectrum. No son of his would ever be a "viado." He made that very clear when one my cousins in Brazil came out last year.

When he told Mom, she nodded and made no comment. She never talked about it. Not with him. Not with me. I assumed she also saw gayness as a sin. Whenever we were out and we saw a gay couple, she'd go quiet or get serious fast.

I knew who I was. I had always known, but the not knowing how people would handle my truth kept me from living it. But I was getting tired of hiding so much of myself. Whenever I saw

Fa and Diana flaunting their love for the world to see, I wondered if I'd ever have anything similar. Would I ever be as brave?

"You heard what happened yesterday at that fabric store downtown?" I asked when they returned to the table.

"The ICE raid?" Pedro asked, pounding the bottom of his wrapped straw on the table until the plastic burst. "Yeah, Dad told me. It's on the Brazilian newspaper today. They were fast about printing that story."

"Foda," Fa said, slicing her bagel with a plastic knife. "I got so scared for my mom and aunt. Even scarier to think we'll join the undocumented club soon. I think I need a sweater that says, 'Undocumented and Proud.'"

"Great idea, Fa." Pedro shook his head. "Wear that after you're eighteen while driving somewhere and you'll be out of here in no time."

"Funny to hear everyone talking about driver's ed and college." Diana sipped from her orange juice. "The other day, these girls in Algebra were talking about the Art Academy in Boston and how they have this amazing graphic design program. I just listened. What was I going to say? 'Hey, this girl born in São Paulo but raised here can't go to college because, well, tuition for illegal people costs a fortune?' It sucks to have grown up here, know nothing but this life, and yet also know it'll soon be taken from us. I was two when they brought me over. Two."

"One of the people arrested is friends with my parents," I revealed. "His wife called yesterday. I didn't ask a lot of questions."

The air around the table grew heavy, like we had all walked into a dark forest or got locked in some dark tower while waiting for the arrival of an imminent monster.

"This is too heavy to start our day with." Fa clapped. "Did. We. Not. Read. What. I. Sent. This. Morning? Can we focus on the fact that today we're doing conté drawings in class?"

"My fucking favorite," I said. "I love when I say 'conté' to people and they have no clue what I mean. Then I say 'charcoal' as if they should've known what that word meant all along. It makes me look smart and trilingual."

"I'm so glad we finished that corny assignment," Diana said. "Coming up with our own cereal boxes? Not interested."

"Your character did look like a stripper on a spaceship," Pedro said. "I actually read this hentai about a dragon and a fairy getting it on and—"

"Don't listen to him, babe," Fa said.

"Hey, I liked the story," Pedro confessed. "I wanted my cereal character to look like Sailor Moon holding a peni—"

"I beg you to never finish that sentence," Diana said. "My ears are too precious."

I never took my time with these three for granted. My childhood years in Fogo Dourado were lonely as fuck. Once I started second grade, my artistic abilities were associated with being a fag or a sissy—and no one wanted to be around one of those.

The Forbidden Fortress had been the only true friends in my life. We started talking after we realized we were all Brazilian kids being raised here. We shared the common trait of a very rusty Portuguese. Our undocumented truth brought us closer. Pedro's thing was drawing his own mangas. Fa loved calligraphy and anything related to the zodiac and witches. Diana loved landscapes. She created these colorful pieces with colored pencils.

A lot of things brought us together. But I carried an extra weight— something unrelated to papers or immigration status. So much of who I was had to be hidden. I wondered how it would feel to let that part of me be on full display. Maybe I'd be given the chance to feel. To forget. Or even to breathe.

2
THE UNEXPECTED

September 2011

The visual arts shop was a vast space. Its walls were covered in art and the drafting tables were splattered with different paint colors. From watercolors to conté pieces, it was like walking inside an art gallery. And I loved every minute of it.

Mr. H claimed having different art styles on display inspired the subconscious mind. The smell of coffee was always there to greet us, drifting from the computer lab where we'd eventually migrate as juniors next year to learn graphic design.

"Morning to the four amigos," Mr. H said, reclining on the edge of his desk. The man was brave in his outfit choice of the day: denim overalls covered in paint blotches and a blue beret.

The drafting tables had been arranged in a circle, and right in the middle was a table with a bowl overflowing with what I assumed was some bizarre abstract art: plastic fruits, a matchbox, a candlestick, old books, a comb, and yarn strings.

"Can we ever get a live model for one of our projects, Mr. H?" Pedro blurted out when he spotted the bowl. "Maybe, I don't know, some really hot people. Not a bad idea, right?"

"Are *you* going to pay these really hot people?" Mr. H eyed the clock on the wall.

"This doesn't inspire me at all." Pedro sneered at the objects as if gazing at a monster.

Even though the desks had been rearranged, we could still identify which ones were ours. The surfaces of the desks displayed years of accumulated ink and scribbles. We had each added our own flair to the overpopulated canvases. Those had become our identifiers.

I sat at my desk first, facing the bowl dead on. The rest of the Forbidden Fortress's desks had been scattered throughout the circle. Pedro was the first to drag out the desk beside me so there'd be space for his. Fa and Diana did the same, sitting to his right. Mr. H watched the scene without a peep. His face spoke volumes, though: it's too early for this shit.

The door opened. Neb, the religious kid whose every breath and step was about his congregation. His red hair was combed back, looking even more vibrant against the green tones of his plaid button-down. He wore his usual black Converses, which he had converted into a canvas for white crosses and Bible verses.

He didn't greet anyone as he headed to his desk, which happened to be in front of me, luckily to my left so we wouldn't have to stare at each other dead in the face.

He always sat properly, like he was attending a very fancy tea party or something. His parents had named him after King Nebuchadnezzar. I Googled that king once and it always made me curious as to why they had named him after someone so cruel.

He was all right when he wasn't trying to convince the entire world that the Bible was one hundred percent factual. One time he told me listening to non-Christian music was the cheapest way for me to buy a one-way ticket to Hell. Ha—I actually struggled to hold a snigger that day. He had these big eyes, like two round fishbowls, and whenever we talked, they widened even more. We chatted here and there while at school, but I always had this feeling he judged everyone who wasn't a part of his coven.

I wondered if he also judged the other students and how most of them lacked any real interest for the arts. Eighty percent of the kids in this shop weren't here because they knew what they wanted from life. On the contrary. They picked art as an excuse to delay their decision. Their lack of interest and commitment was like a billboard plastered on a highway. The display: we're fucking scared to decide what we want to do with our lives.

The other students who were hanging out in the hall darted inside when the bell rang. Mr. H walked to the middle of the circle as they took their seats, leaving an empty desk beside Neb.

"Are we expecting anyone else?" Fa said.

"Curious much, Ms. Andrade?" Mr. H smirked.

"Always," she replied proudly.

Pedro nudged her with an elbow and said, "It's a seat for your ghost buddy. Can't you feel his presence?"

"I do hope a ghost haunts your ass soon," she whispered.

"Language," Mr. H said.

"No, seriously." Pedro pointed at the empty desk. "What's up with the extra desk?"

"We have a new student joining us," Mr. H tucked his hands in his pockets. "Guess he's running late."

"We have a new student joining us on a Thursday?" Pedro asked. "They do realize they could've stayed home and enjoyed a long weekend, right?"

"Amazing advice, Mr. Santana," Mr. H said. "It truly shows how dedicated you are to this class." He clapped. "All right, let's start the day, everybody. Your subject is on the table in front of you." He grabbed one of the apples and tossed it up in the air. "Your piece should have as much detail as possible. I want shadows and depth and everything else you can give me. But that's not all!"

An expectant silence lingered. Mr. H loved his dramatic moments.

"The most interesting drawing will be awarded a donut box from Dunkin' Donuts tomorrow," he revealed.

Ooohs and ahhhs echoed like a choir. Mr. H put the apple back and continued, "But don't give me stick figures, all right? You have until the end of the day tomorrow to finish it."

My phone buzzed in my pocket.

Manga Boy: Win this one for all of us! I require four Boston creams.

"We *will* put our phones away, right, Mateus Franco?" Mr. H was across the room at this point, holding his iPod and staring like I was a criminal who had just broken out of jail. He slid his glasses to the tip of his nose and squinted his eyes before pressing play. Nelly's "Just a Dream" came on.

The sound of the door opening called my attention as I pulled my art box out of my backpack.

He walked—no, strutted—like the world was his. One of the straps of his backpack was around his shoulder, the other hanging loose like a swaying keychain. His messy hair was like a tangled dark yarn, and he had this dimple on his chin—a sudden target for my eyes. My heart pounded faster when we looked at each other for a few seconds, the hint of a smirk popping on his face.

He turned left and walked to Mr. H's desk, handing him a

note. Mr. H glanced at the yellow paper and lowered the volume of the music before it reached the chorus.

Everyone stared at dimple boy.

"Everybody, I'd like you to meet James Alberte, a Framingham High transfer."

"It was about time you joined the good side," Neb said, eyeing him like he was the next victim of his let-me-preach-to-you-for-hours routine. "Those people have nothing on us."

"Joseph pride!" I blurted out with a fist in the air. Why the fuck did I do that? Everyone's stare hurt more than barbed wire. How did I know? When I was a kid, I crawled under one while running away from a stray German shepherd and in return got a gash on my calf. The physical pain of that memory was no match for my current embarrassment. The other three members of the Forbidden Fortress were in disbelief at my action.

"Mr. Alberte, you may sit next to Mr. Hamwinter there." Mr. H pointed at the empty desk next to Neb, clearly suppressing a laugh at my comment. It was only when he walked toward the chair that I noticed that James and I would be facing each other.

He strolled to his seat. I had been so taken by the guy that it took me a while to realize that he'd have to sit in front of me—like, right in front of me. It would be really tough not to stare. What would people say? I mean, the bowl was also in front of me. It could be used as an excuse in case anyone asked.

"Hey, neighbor," Neb said.

"Hey." James got his art box from his backpack as the music resumed. "Is this the usual class setup?"

"Just for still-life days," Neb replied. "Hope you enjoy visual arts."

Mr. H explained to the new kid the assignment and the prize.

The bowl and the new kid competed for my gaze—the new kid winning by a mile. I tried to keep my eyes on the bowl as much as possible, but the dimpled chin called me like a cursed mermaid in the ocean. Kill me now and don't bring me back from the dead.

I was no virgin, but suddenly I sure as hell wished I was. My first experience had been shit. Sixth grade. I went over to his place. We were both in the closet. The kisses were awkward, and the sex was even more strange. I knew where to put it, but I don't think he got as ready as he thought he was. I didn't care, but things went south from there.

James struck me as a guy who would know. Maybe it was just fantasy. Fuck. I had undressed him, and he had only just arrived. I knew one thing. He was pretty good at his craft. He had an outline of the jumbled still life in less than an hour. At one point, I thought he had noticed the staring. He smirked as soon as I caught sight of him. I could've sworn he had waved at one point. Maybe he was wiping eraser dust off his table. Who the fuck knew? All I knew was that if I kept going at this pace, the donut box would remain a desired prize.

Outlining my drawing was normally a fast process, but today it was like pulling thorns from an ass that had crushed a cactus. Ass. Because of the dimple. The dimpled chin made me think of one. I wanted to draw the dimple. Then I thought about his ass.

Fa had already started shading her drawing by the time the lunch bell rang. Diana had decided to add pops of red on hers. Pedro wasn't as far ahead, but he was definitely being more productive than I was. His style had the same clean lines mangas did. At one point, the Forbidden Fortress was worried about me being so behind. Little did they know I had made my own personal progress: imagining James's ass for the last three hours.

We didn't rush to the cafeteria when the lunch bell rang. We knew our table would be there. That's how things were done here. You picked a table in the beginning of the school year and it was yours until the end.

The four of us grabbed our food and headed to the Forbidden Fortress. James sat at the table across from ours with Neb and a few other kids I called Neb's Minions. Thankfully those people were in Neb's academic classes and not in our shop. I wouldn't be able to stand a class with a dozen people like him. They were all in different grades but went to the same church.

Pedro talked about something. I pretended to listen. I nodded and agreed while practicing a thousand ways to stare at James in the most unnoticeable way possible. A punch on my shoulder destroyed my plan.

"What the fuck, Pedro?" I almost crushed the boxed chocolate milk in my hand.

"Tá aqui?" Pedro's jaw hung like a swing.

"Obviously. You see me, right? Fuck, dude. That hurt."

"You hear about this new zombie show?" he said. "Everyone's talking about it. It was inspired by this anime from the eighties."

"No, I haven't," I said. "But I will turn you into a zombie if you do that one more time."

"What are you looking at?" Fa turned around and nodded. A grin appeared on her face when she saw James.

"I feel sorry for him," Diana said with puckered lips. "Corralled into Neb's group on his first day. What a sad choice. He'll have earned a degree on theology by the end of the day."

"Corralled…" Pedro mumbled. "Fancy word."

"I actually read the books on our summer list…"

Diana's words were mumbles. James locked eyes with me. Shit. Did I have food hanging from the corner of my mouth? Had he noticed the staring? Maybe he heard Diana's comment? No, that couldn't have been it. Diana was the most soft-spoken out of the four of us.

Despite my insane thoughts, my eyes remained on his. There was a part of me that wanted to turn away as fast as I could, but I couldn't ignore the other that was curious about dimple boy. I wanted to see who was going to be the first one to break contact, but none of us did after a few seconds. I smirked. So did he. My cheeks burned. I held my ground. He scratched the corner of his lips and was about to say something when Neb bumped him with an elbow and managed to steal his attention again.

James was doomed to be at Neb's Corner for the remainder of the year if he didn't act fast or if somebody didn't rescue him. I debated on whether to go there and invite him to our table. But no one had ever joined the Forbidden Fortress since freshman year. And no one invited you to a different table like that. That's not how it worked.

The bell finally rang and we all flocked back to class. The rest of my school day was a fuck-fest. I couldn't concentrate on the bowl. Even the confused students seemed to be ahead of me. James' frown, the way he stared at his paper, and the way he pressed his lips while drawing were more interesting than the assignment.

The final bell rang. A fucking relief. Fa, Diana, and Pedro left through the back door, since they were all hitching a ride with Fa's mom. The three of them lived on the other side of town.

James followed me as I walked down the hall by myself. No big deal. I turned toward the stairway leading up to the entrance. He was still behind me. I slowed down my pace as we neared the exit. We walked side by side at this point.

"Running from something?" he asked.

"Time," I mumbled. "I mean, you know, time is limited."

"Okay…" He frowned. "Scared you'll miss the bus home?"

"Yeah, that was definitely it."

"Which bus are you taking?" He opened the door and stood ahead of me so I could walk by him.

"Forty-nine. You?"

"Same!" he said. "Good to know one person on the ride home. My parents insisted on dropping me off before they left town this morning."

"Don't get too excited," I said. "Not a lot happens on forty-nine."

"Well, you're on forty-nine." He shrugged. "It can't be that boring."

I felt a laugh coming on, but I snorted instead. "My name is James," I blurted out, my cheeks burning like a toaster. "I mean—Mateus. Jesus."

"So, James, Mateus, or Jesus?" He fixed the straps of his backpack over his shoulder. "Or all three?"

"Mateus," I said as he followed me into the bus. "Mateus Franco. People call me Matt. Easier to remember."

Those sitting down had their headphones over their ears and their eyes on their phones. James followed me until I stumbled upon my usual seat. It was six rows away from the very last seat. He sat beside me as if there was no vacancy around us.

"I thought you were going to save me during lunch." He dropped his backpack between his legs. "Can't believe you left me to the vultures like that."

"You needed saving?" I scratched my head.

He scoffed and continued, "Neb's stories about his church trip to LA last summer are not that interesting. And I love how these kids go on very expensive mission trips. And you knew I needed saving. Come on. You saw me."

"I did." I smiled. "He told you about the Tyler—"

"—Perry encounter," we both finished the sentence together.

"Twice." James held two fingers in the air. "Which, as controversial as this will sound, I think was a lie. No pictures because he left his camera? Why even mention them?"

"Next time you need to be rescued, hold up two fingers like that as a sign and I'll swoop right in."

"Will do." He grabbed his earphones from his backpack.

"You're pretty talented," I mentioned. "Saw your drawing from my desk."

"You, too," he said. "So, are you doing it for the donut box, or do you actually see a future in art?"

"Doing it for the food now," I said. "And plan on doing it to put food on my table as well."

He smiled, arming his ears.

"What're you listening to?" I asked, hoping the conversation would continue. I wasn't ready to let him escape into whatever musical universe he was heading to.

"Hans Zimmer…" The way he said my favorite composer's name as if I wouldn't know him crushed my heart for a second. "Know him?"

"*Know him?* He's only the king of movie scores. I listen to his stuff when I'm drawing. He's composed the most iconic themes."

"I know! I feel the same way about him. So what's your favorite art style to draw?"

"Conté, but not what we're drawing now. Not a big fan of random objects tossed inside a bowl. I like faces—especially eyes. The way the light hits them, the secrets behind them…"

"Why?"

"A face can tell an entire story in a matter of seconds. And eyes are great at telling secrets."

"What do mine tell you?" he grinned.

My legs had been chopped off. I knew that for a fact. I couldn't feel them. He must have known, since he chuckled.

"Want to listen with me?" He held up one of his earphones, the question an obvious way to fill the awkward silence. "It's a playlist I put together the other day. I call it 'My Escape.'"

I gave in to his request, recognizing the song immediately.

"The theme to *Inception*," I said.

"Enjoy." He closed his eyes and rested the back of his head on the cushioned seat.

I *was* enjoying this moment. Not because of the music, but because of him.

He didn't make a single effort to let me walk out in one piece when the bus stopped. He kept his legs in the same position, keeping the space tight between his knees and the seat in front of us. My calves brushed his knees as I walked out. Thank God my jacket hung below my waist, otherwise the rising mountain south of me would've been the hero to have saved forty-nine from its boredom curse.

3
HOW CAN WE STAY?

September 2011

The tip of the sketch pencil grazed the paper as I listened to Hans Zimmer's *Inception* soundtrack. I had been sitting on my bed with my back against the wall and my headphones over my ears since I got home from school. I had one of my books on drawing anatomical poses in front of me. My plan was to practice those poses, but the dimpled chin and the messy hair forced me to draw his face from memory. My cheeks actually burned when the lines and strokes finally resembled him.

I grabbed my phone and looked for him on Facebook. There were a handful of accounts under his name, but he wasn't anywhere to be seen. I probably scrolled for a good minute before I heard the footsteps creaking up the stairs. I would recognize them anywhere. Mom was home. My room was always a mandatory stop before she went into hers. Thank God she always knocked. Barging inside a sixteen-year-old's bedroom without a knock could result in seeing things no mom should ever see.

"Come in!" I shouted, sliding my headphones to my neck.

"Oi, filho," she said. "Just saying a quick hello."

"And I say hello back," I said with a pencil in my mouth.

"Good day?" She realized she still had her name tag pinned

to her white button-down. "Oh, that's why I kept feeling a little prickle driving home." She snapped it out.

I bit down on the pencil. It had been the most memorable yet confusing day of the school year so far. But voicing my thoughts now would trigger a conversation I didn't want to have.

"Pretty ordinary." I chose safety over danger. "Yours?"

"Tranquilo. I'm going to get dinner ready. Your dad left the room since he got home?"

"Don't know." I held up my sketchbook and waved it at her. "Been busy. He's probably been asleep since he got home from work."

"You better wash those smudgy hands really well, Mateus." She stabbed a finger my way. "You're chopping the salad tonight."

"Mom, Laila can do that today," I protested. "Come on. I really want to—"

"Anyone can do it." She widened her eyes. "But *you're* doing it tonight."

Mom worked long hours, but she was always ready to cook the family dinner when she got home. She never complained about her job, no matter how exhausting her day had been. She had been a housekeeper when we first moved here. At the time, even though her shift started at seven a.m., she got dropped off at her first house at around four-thirty because we only had one car and Dad had to start his shift at Nogueira's Marble and Granite around five. To pass the time, she bought an English course from a store downtown. She used to listen to the CDs while waiting for her shift to begin. That's how Mom learned English. She got a job at Mass Scientific as a catering manager two years ago. Dad bought himself a copy and listened to the CDs in his car when he drove to work. He struggled with learning the language more than Mom.

My sister and I picked up the language a lot faster. I was

fluent in less than a year. Obviously, I had to be the one to speak on the phone whenever they needed something back then, since Laila was too young. "Mateus, I need to talk to the cable company." "Mateus, I need to speak to the phone people. The bill is wrong." "Mateus, Mateus, Mateus, Mateus."

I slid my headphones back on and decided to take advantage of the few minutes I had before I had to join Mom in the kitchen. I worked on his eyes, trying to catch the light as they stared. Then the eyebrows, but getting them to resemble their actual shape was a doozy. With the pencil back in my mouth, I gazed at the face of the stranger that had inspired me today, wishing the pencil was a little fleshy southern part of his.

The smell of cooked rice and garlic made me realize that a few minutes had turned to almost an hour. I closed my sketchbook and darted downstairs. Laila was in the kitchen, squeezing a few oranges into a pitcher while Mom stirred the beans.

"Look who decided to leave his cave," Laila said. "Hello, caveman."

"Ha-ha. Mom, did you knock?" I asked.

"You were so focused in your drawing," she said. "I decided to leave you be and make the salad myself."

"Done drawing. I can make it."

"Perfeito," Mom said.

"We need music, though." I approached the iPod dock in the corner. "The silence in this room is killing me."

"Don't play those depressing songs you like," Laila said. "Anything but those, okay?"

"My music isn't depressing," I said. "It's not my fault all you want are beats and synths."

"You have no right to insult Deaf, Jam, and Life." Laila held up an orange. "Those men write and produce their own music. And they're so gorgeous."

I shrugged as if I had never noticed how good-looking they were. I obviously had. They had even showed up in a few dreams that required a fresh pair of underwear after.

"They still sound like something you'd hear in a movie from the early nineties," I said.

"All right, kids." Mom held up a wooden spoon. "Eu escolho a música." She waved the spoon like a wizard casting a spell. "My sertanejo playlist. Now. Thank you."

Sertanejo equals Brazilian country music. I didn't mind the new stuff, but Mom liked the old-school sertanejo. Leandro e Leonardo and Rionegro e Solimões, to name a few. I didn't even protest. If I hadn't barged into the kitchen, I would've been left in my room with my sketchpad until dinner was ready.

I pressed play on the playlist. An acoustic guitar riff joined the conversation. The song sounded like it was being played on an old vinyl record.

Every good Brazilian knew that rice and beans were an essential part of a meal. If a meal didn't include those, then we were having a mere snack. You were allowed to switch up your protein, but those two were the Royal Family of Brazilian cuisine. Mom made beef with onions tonight—one of my favorites.

"Any word from your friend, Mom?" I grabbed a knife from the cabinet drawer.

"Julia called me when I was driving back from work." Mom stirred the rice. "She finally spoke to Mauro at the detention facility. He'll have a court date soon and then he'll be off—lettuce and tomato are in the fridge."

"That sucks," Laila said as I grabbed the stuff.

"She's devastated." Mom watched me reach for a chop board in the cabinet. "It's not like they have a choice to stay now. God, I can't even imagine if…"

Her words were a blur in my ears as a question hit my lips.

"Are we thinking about leaving again? I mean, you guys said that we have the money, and…"

She raised the lid of the cooking pan to check on the rice. "We're running out of options, Mateus." Steam spread above the stove and then disappeared. "Things are getting harder. I know your dad and I keep saying we're going to move back now that we paid off the debt and have enough to reopen the store. We stay because we feel we can save more so we can be more secure when we go back. But things are getting harder for people like us. I'm lucky that people cover for me at my job, but God knows how long that will last. There's talk of a new system that can check your papers during the job interview. If that's true, then very soon, people at my job will be verified. And if the same thing happens to your father, then I am not sure how we'll manage to stick around. And, honestamente, if we keep living with the mentality that we can always save more, then we'll be stuck on this undocumented Ferris wheel forever."

I cringed at the thought of going back to spend the money they made on the damn store. It failed once. The store was the reason we ended up here. Why do it again? Pride? Going back was one thing—one I didn't really like. But going back and making the same mistakes again? That was just stupid.

"We've got Obama running the house," I said. "Come on, something is bound to happen. Democrats love us."

"Promises and promises, Mateus." Mom's eyes were distant. "Remember the DREAM Act? Look how that turned out. It's all politics, filho. You should know that. Your grampa was one. Not in the same capacity, but one thing I learned is that an empty promise can get you far in the voting game."

"Dad is probably happy." While I chopped the lettuce, Laila sat at the table, looking at the tips of her hair. "God, these are brittle."

"Happy that these people are being deported?" Mom frowned.

"Happy that he has even more reason for us to leave." Laila retorted. "That subject always comes up. He's always the one saying that it's time to pack up and go."

"It sucks loving a place you never wanted to move to," I said. "And then, boom, you build an entire life and yet you can't belong to it."

"Listen, kids. I want to stay," Mom said while I transferred the chopped lettuce into a bowl. The tomatoes were next. "I like it here. I love our lives. But I also have to face facts. This is the land of the free, but we are free *with* conditions that don't apply to the majority. That's how it is for people like us. You two are safe because you aren't eighteen yet, but soon, it'll be your turn to drive without a license and get paid under the table and live an undocumented life. And that will always count toward your records in the States. It's bad enough that your dad and I have that under our belts. If we leave, your dad and I won't be able to apply for another visa for ten years. And even when we can, there's no guarantee that we'll get it. If we go back home now, you won't have any illegal presence. You might be able to apply for a change of status—"

"And have our entire lives uprooted in the process," I said. "We aren't leaving with a new plan. You want to leave and go back to the old one. And the old one was the reason we left. I don't get it."

"Meu filho." Mom's eyes glistened. "I wish we could turn to you and say that we can move to São Paulo, or any of the big cities down there, and have financial security when doing so. We don't know any of the big people. I'm sorry, but it's the best we've got."

I'd hear everyone in school talking about driver's ed and how they were getting their permits and stuff. College? Me? A distant dream. Dreamers like me could still attend, but undocumented people in Mass had to pay a "nonresident fee." In other words, undocumented kids like me paid three times as much. We didn't have that kind of money. I also didn't qualify for scholarships. But to me, it was worth the risk. I didn't want to take a chance of coming home and seeing an empty fridge and pantry. I didn't want to go back, build a life, and uproot it all over again. I had spent ten years building this one. My Portuguese was rusty as fuck. I'd lose a school year as I tried to pick it up again. And Laila. God, I felt sorry for her. She understood some, but her accent was thick.

"Your English has improved so much, Mom." I tried to change the subject while tossing the tomatoes into the bowl.

"I've been reading more," she said proudly. "Watching *Friends* also helps."

"Ross is so cute!" my sister said.

"You and your sister need to work on your Portuguese," Mom said. "Lose your gringo accents when talking. Say 'guarana.'"

Laila and I repeated the word, rolling our R's more than we needed to. I laughed it off, going along with the joke. But I hadn't had much of a choice when I was simply thrown into a classroom full of English-speaking people. My brain was like, "Well, you don't need Portuguese right now to survive. You're safe at home, not so much out here." So it slowly tucked my Portuguese into a drawer.

"Your turn, Mom." I put a hand on her shoulder. "Say the word *shit* in three, two…"

She quickly grabbed the wiping cloth hanging on the handle of the oven and smacked my hand. "Me respeita, rapaz. We should start going to mass so you can clean that dirty mouth," she said behind a laugh. "Go tell your father to come down, I'll finish the salad. Se não, vamos comer amanhã."

I rushed up the stairs. The door was slightly open. Dad's snores were like a motorboat treading through water. I knocked three times, interrupting his private soundtrack.

"Janta tá pronta, Pai."

We all had our plates ready at the table by the time he wobbled his way into the kitchen, rubbing his bloodshot eyes, wearing a white shirt he had brought with him from Fogo Dourado and shorts. The shirt had two holes on the back, but he refused to throw it away. It had been a gift from one of his last customers before he closed the convenience store. He treated it as an ancient relic.

He usually got home around six and slept until dinnertime. There were no days off for him. Not because Nogueira's Marble and Granite had never offered them; it had just become a habit in the last eight years.

I often wondered if he worked as much as he did and stayed in their bedroom for as long as he could because of how depressed he was. We still had it pretty good, despite our situation.

"Good day?" Mom asked, walking to the stove to fix him a plate.

"Normal," he replied.

"Ah," I raised a finger, "English."

"That word is the same in English," he said, his accent much thicker than Mom's.

"Still," Laila said. "You got to say it right."

He repeated the word, rolling his tongue so the "R" was deeper.

"Good job." Laila held up two thumbs.

"It's not like I have as much time as the rest of you to study," he said with a vacant stare. "Still, I do my best."

He had a hard time with his R's and L's—especially when they were next to each other. He couldn't pronounce "world" for his life. He sat at the table and continued, "They still want me to be showroom manager. Amanda offered me the position again."

"Are you going to take it this time?" Mom set his plate and sat beside him. "It's the third time she offers. It's better than carrying slabs all day. If you keep going at this rate, you'll end up at the hospital sooner or later."

He tapped his fingers on the table, readying himself for whatever was about to come out of his mouth. "I might take it. I've been thinking about us leaving in a year," he said as if he had been simply talking about the weather or something as ordinary. "Save more money. Buy a house in Fogo Dourado and finally reopen the business."

"A year?" Mom's stare was proof his timeline hadn't been shared with her. "I think we need to talk about this first."

That was so Dad. Not much of a talker. I had no memory of Dad ever sitting me down for a long conversation. Hell, I had no memory of Dad ever having a long conversation with us as a family at any point. The heteronormative sex talk? Mom. He always seemed to be in a hurry to leave. Back in Fogo Dourado, he'd spend as much time at the store as he could. In America, he'd always take the extra shift. He was always tired. Always sleeping. Never around.

"Surpresos?" he asked as if stating the obvious. "You can't expect us to stay for much longer. Look what happened yesterday. We've paid off the debt. We've got enough to leave and reopen Magazine Franco."

I avoided the store's name at all costs. While the word "magazine" in English was about a book with a glossy cover, in Brazil, that word was also used for stores. They were like CVS, minus the medication. You could buy toys, groceries, candy, and all sorts of paraphernalia. I had always found ours to be as chaotic as this conversation.

"And you decide to just drop that information like a bomb? We don't get a say in this decision? Great parenting, Pai. We aren't one of your employees. You work as much as you do and stay locked up in your room for as long as you can and then you walk in here and say stuff like that like it's no big deal. You and Mom have had a life in Fogo Dourado. Laila and I haven't. And whatever little life we had back then was taken from us."

The corner of his lips trembled. He grabbed the fork and the knife from the table and continued, "You two can start over. Your mother and I did it with two kids. It's time to go back to a country where we have basic rights. This life of no license, no papers, no this, no that, and carrying slabs and installing them and working without papers…" He blew a puff of air. "It's exhausting, kid."

I debated on whether I should contain what I had to say. Would he care about my opinion? Would he shrug it off and carry on as if I had never said shit? I didn't care.

"Why spend the money you two earned on something that already failed once? Magazine Franco?" The tone of my voice rose with every word. "We'll be back here only to start all over again."

"Matt," Mom whispered. "Chega."

Dad was angry and disappointed. His fleeting eyes proved he debated which feeling he'd rely on to continue this talk. I still didn't care. He did this all the time—acted like a war plane and dropped these bombs and expected us to be okay with his explosions. "We were forced to come here. We built a life here. My Portuguese is terrible. Laila's even worse. And now we're being forced to leave," I continued. "You just keep making these decisions and you never ask us what we think. *You* borrowed money from people. *You* took out the loan when the store was already going to shit. *You* spent that money—"

"I can still buy you a one-way ticket and have you back tomorrow if you keep talking like that, kid," he said.

Was it suddenly summer? Because my body was fucking hot. "Do it. At least I won't spend all my money trying to prove myself to people who could care less."

He beat the table with a fist.

"Mateus Franco!" Mom's face was flushed. Laila had a devilish smirk on her face, the kind that screamed she loved what I had said but was relieved she hadn't said it.

Dad burrowed his eyes into Mom's in disbelief. He resumed his meal, withholding some strong-worded argument.

"Say you're sorry," Mom insisted. "Agora."

Dad got to make choices. So did I. "I'm going to my room." I darted out of the kitchen. I felt their eyes burning on my neck until I vanished up the stairs.

I locked the door and sank into my bed, facing the ceiling. The screensaver from my computer cast blue and green lights around my room.

When I was younger, I thought the people knocking at our door were Dad's friends, until I realized they were people trying to collect what they were owed. Before Dad took out the loan, he borrowed money from all these people. At one point, to hold them over a bit longer, my father was giving them our groceries.

One time I got in a fight with a woman who explicitly said she wanted her money by the next day. I asked for more details. She shared without any remorse. That was the day I found out about the debt and the loan and our failure as a family. Mom was furious. She knew about the loan, not about the people he owed. A fight broke out between my parents that night. I blamed myself for my big mouth.

We had to move houses three times before coming to the States. Not because we enjoyed swapping homes like dirty underwear, but because we had to sell those houses to pay off the people we owed money to.

How could I be okay with leaving? I'd go home to a place where I was born but didn't belong; to a language I understood but barely spoke.

I used to stay quiet around the shit Dad said. But it had gotten a lot harder to hold back my words in the past few months. I was sick of him acting like everything was normal—like everything he put our family through was okay. Seeing him boss us around like our thoughts didn't matter only made me want even more distance.

4
SO MANY SECRETS

September 2011

"You said that to your dad?" Pedro asked, clutching his backpack as if someone would have ever wanted to steal that old thing.

"I did." I sipped from my boxed chocolate milk.

"Parents are interesting creatures," Fa said. "They do whatever the fuck they want and act like we have to be okay with it. Foda."

"They're people, too, Fa." Diana scowled. "Look at my mom. She married a psycho. God knows why. Thankfully she split when I was too young to remember any of the drama. And it wasn't like my dad wanted to be in the picture after. And then he died. It's sad, really. I don't even remember him."

"Our guardians are meant to teach us in this life," Fa said in the most Fa-ish way possible, a voice destined to be on a meditation podcast. "They also become the main reason why we reincarnate to pay our debts in the next one."

"I honestly want to be a bug the next time I pay this place a visit," I said, watching Pedro flap the Pikachu keychain on his backpack with a finger.

"Think they're really set on leaving in one year?" Pedro looked at me with his puppy eyes.

"Who the fuck knows?" I shrugged. "And if they do, I just can't imagine a life back there. Who was I before I was eight? Fucking nobody." I shivered. "It sucks. The not-knowing part. It's like you never belong. Any of your parents wanting to leave as well?"

"Nah," Pedro said. "But Dad is willing to marry a random woman for papers at some point. He met this girl who said she'd marry him for ten grand."

"At least he has that option," Diana said. "It's not like the gays would be able to take advantage of that now."

"Not only do we have to wait for papers," Fa added, "but we also have to wait until gay marriage is a thing nationwide. It's the perfect drama flick, I swear."

"Think it'd be hard to move to California?" Pedro folded his arms over his backpack, resting his chin on his hands. "Didn't they come up with their own DREAM Act there?"

"Yes." Of course I knew the answer. My countless hours of DREAM Act research came in handy during these types of conversations. "All it does is allow us to get financial aid for college and stuff."

Pedro sighed. "Better than nothing, right? I mean, we'd at least have a lot of sunshine…"

Pedro's voice faded in the background as I spotted James and Neb holding their trays with food, walking toward the table they had sat at yesterday. Neb's shirt displayed a pretty self-righteous statement, "Salvation Is Here." Ha, the nerve. He deserved a medal for that one. Hopefully he wasn't trying to compete with Fa on a bold shirt-slash-sweater statement competition. The girl would drag him down.

James sat on the same seat; Neb next to him. James glanced at me. I stared back. He tilted his head to the side and smirked. The apple in James's hands stole his eyes away from mine. Neb and his minions chatted as James unwrapped his apple out of its plastic blanket.

"That would suck," Fa said loudly. "Right?"

"What would?" I asked, sipping from my boxed chocolate milk, hoping they didn't notice my distraction.

"Kangaroos going extinct," she said. "That'd be bad karma for all of humanity."

"Oh." I nodded. "Totally. No one wants that. They are so cute. And their babies."

"Palhaço." Diana slapped my hand.

"What? What?" I protested. "Personal space, Diana Melo."

"We weren't talking about kangaroos." Pedro rolled his eyes. "You weren't even listening. I was pouring my heart out here."

"Okay." Fa pointed at him. "No need for all the drama, Pedro. We aren't auditioning for a play."

Diana looked across the table, spotting James. "I feel bad for him."

We all followed her eyeline. Thank God James was too busy pretending to listen to the minions to notice our staring.

"Why do you feel bad?" Pedro asked.

"Come on." Diana rolled her eyes. "The guy is clearly bored out of his mind. Oh, well."

"Did you read *Zodiac Daily* today?" Fa's question was an order for everyone to turn around and discuss the newsletter she forced us to subscribe to. I disobeyed the order, keeping my gaze on him.

He noticed me and smiled. He held up two fingers. The sign. Fuck. He needed saving.

Should I save him? Maybe going over there would be the same thing as waving a huge neon sign telling people I was gay. Maybe I was just in my head too much. I mean, kids did that, invited other kids to join their table.

"Mind if I invite James to sit with us?" The words jetted out of my mouth.

The three of them were quiet.

"Kids, I can't read minds." I rolled my eyes. "Is that okay?"

"No one has joined the Forbidden Fortress since it was founded." Diana twirled the tip of her braid between her fingers.

"I know," I said. "Time for a change, right?"

"I think it's great." Fa tried to hide a smile. "We need some fresh blood."

"Okay, vampire girl," Pedro said. "Dude, totally cool. Invite him over."

"Yeah," Diana said. "Go rescue the new white kid."

"I mean, we rescued you in third grade when you were fresh out of Fogo Dourado." Pedro smiled. "Helped you learn English and all. It was cute."

"And for that I'm thankful," I said with a smirk. "But this time, a Brazilian is saving a white boy." I slapped my hand on the table way too hard as I got up. I stood frozen for a second and played it cool, pretending like that had been the plan all along.

Walking toward Neb's lair felt like social suicide. James smiled when he saw me getting closer. He folded his arms and leaned back, proud of what I was about to do.

The entire table fell quiet once they noticed how close I was.

"Hey—" I coughed. "Hey, Ja—" Saliva had decided to take an unannounced trip down my throat. "Jesus Christ." The coughing lasted a few seconds. "Hey, James." I finally managed to say.

"Morning, Matt." The smirk on James's face deserved a frame.

"Matt!" The way Neb said my name in an excited tone sparked an urge to run away. "What… what are you doing here?"

"Didn't mean to interrupt." I blew out a puff of air. "Just wanted to see if James wanted to sit with us today."

"That'd be kind of great," James replied literally half a second after I was done speaking. He turned to Neb and said, "See you in class?" He gently bumped a fist on his shoulder.

"See you." Neb dragged the words as James got up.

I felt the minions' eyes burning my neck as we walked to the Forbidden Fortress. I didn't need to look to know they observed us like prey. And so did the Forbidden Fortress. Curiosity attacked from both sides.

"That was quality content." Fa puckered her lips and nodded. "God, I should've recorded that."

"If by quality you mean awkward, sure," Pedro said.

"Matty, Matty." Diana clapped. "That was… wow."

"Shut up," I said while sitting down.

"Let me tell you," James said, sitting next to me. "I'll take awkwardness over that whole talk of Bible camp. They wanted me to play the tambourine for the band. Like, really?" He burst out laughing. A contagious act that ran through all of us in seconds.

"Yeah, Neb can be…" Diana rolled her finger in the air. "Um, just—"

"A lot to take?" Fa smirked. "Doesn't stop talking? Thinks he knows everything there is to know about the universe?"

"Jeez, are you a mind reader?" James laughed. "Speaking my thoughts out loud like that."

"Oh, mortal human." Fa cleared her throat and laid her hands flat on the table. "I am much more than that."

"Dude, choose your next words carefully," Pedro suggested with a smirk. "She probably already knows what you're going to say, but still."

"Is she, like, the guru of the group? Should Matty and I be concerned?" My heart raced when I heard him call me "Matty." People close to me called me that.

"I don't know if I'd call her a guru." Diana pecked her on the cheek. "But we can definitely call her awesome."

"You two are way too cute." James's eyes glistened. "I swear."

"Didn't see you on the bus this morning," I said. "Everything all right?"

"You. Two. Are. On. The. Same. Bus?" Fa articulated every word like a pre-school teacher teaching her students how to read. I was no mind reader, but I knew the question whirling in her head: why was the Forbidden Fortress not informed?

"We are," James replied. "Forty-nine. And parents insisted on dropping me off again," he revealed. "They claimed they wanted to spend more time with me, since they were leaving. Said the same thing yesterday. Said the same thing at my old school. They leave town for days because of work. So I think they do this crap because they feel bad about leaving. Dropping me off is more about making them feel good."

"Join the parents-need-to-get-their-shit-together club." Pedro raised his boxed chocolate milk in the air. "Now there's a shirt that would sell."

James repeated the gesture, air-toasting Pedro with nothing in hand.

"Aren't you hungry?" I asked.

"Had a big breakfast at home," James said.

"Why Joseph?" Fa crossed her legs and used her hand as a resting spot for her chin. This was the demeanor she took when she was either a) curious or b) more curious.

"Needed a fresh start," he said. "Sometimes stuff happens, and you can't really stick around." A heavy breath.

"You should really lecture our parents," Diana said. "And aunts."

"Aunts?" James asked.

"Dad died in Brazil when I was young," she revealed. "Live with my aunt and Mom now. Been here since I was five."

"Sorry to hear," he said. "Is that where you're all from?"

"Yep." Pedro said. "Minas Gerais here. Been here since I was three."

"Rio," Fa said. "Age four."

"São Paulo," Diana said. "Age five."

"Goiás here," I said. "Or our own version of Texas. And age eight."

"I won't even pretend like I know where those places are." He shrugged. "But I'm sure you can show me on a globe."

"I can." I held up a finger. "These three aren't so great at geography."

"Stop exposing us in front of the new kid." Diana giggled.

The five of us walked to class together. He got along really well with them. Like, extremely well. I imagined what things would be like if James joined the Forbidden Fortress as a permanent resident. I'd have to practice hiding my flushed cheeks every time he looked at me. Then I wondered if that was a skill someone could learn.

For the first few hours, this morning's events mirrored yesterday's—aside from the fact that Mr. H played an 80s playlist he had proudly curated. James sat next to Neb, Fa and Diana sat beside each other, Pedro was next to me, and the bowl of randomness was dead center. And my eyes locked with James's every time I stared at my subject. Maybe I was high from all the conté shavings—if that was even a possibility—but a part me suspected he wanted me to notice that he was staring back. At least that's what I got from the smirks and smiles. His dimpled chin practically begged me to keep on looking.

But I had to win that donut box today. I had to avoid the stare trap at all costs. I was way behind on this assignment.

In one of the one thousand times James's hazel eyes found

mine, he pointed at me with his conté-smudged finger. I shrugged in confusion. He repeated the gesture. I gave him a thumbs up, pretending to understand what he meant. He walked over to Mr. H to the sound of "Billie Jean," bopping his shoulders to the beat. Everyone stared at him.

My gaze returned to the bowl until I heard something hauled across the room. I followed the sound. Everyone did. James dragged his drafting table in my direction, like the Titanic announcing the iceberg with a horn. I jumped up and helped him carry it, as the rest of the Forbidden Fortress made space. I pretended like I had known that this was what he had gestured for.

"Welcome to the cool kids' corner," Pedro said with a fist in the air.

My phone buzzed in my pocket as James organized his art supplies. It was a message from Neb. He'd gotten my number freshman year when he tried to invite me to one of his church meetings. We had never had an actual conversation since then.

Neb: Careful, Matt. He might be wayyy too interested in you.
Me: ...
Neb: The stories I heard are concerning.

I glanced across the room, Neb texting like he was in a competition.

"Mr. Franco!" Mr. H was at his desk, glasses on the tip of his nose. "Care to share what's so entertaining on your phone?"

"Just a text from my mom." I waved it in the air.

"Put it away, please."

I remained focused on my drawing and the bowl. At least I tried to be. What the hell was Neb talking about?

The lunch bell rang, and I decided to stay in shop to catch

up on my drawing. James insisted on keeping me company. As if that would help my progress. He was the reason for my delay. The others decided to leave me to the hounds since today was Friday, aka pizza day in the cafeteria.

James leaned more toward an abstract style, adding pops of bright colors mixed with dull shades. I preferred realism, trying to make every object, line, and texture resemble the subject.

"We have to eat something," James said. "We can't just hang out in shop on an empty stomach."

"The only selection we have is the vending machine by the door," I said.

"Then let's see what's on the menu," he suggested.

"Have you been to *that* vending machine?" I asked. "It's not a buffet, I'll tell you that much."

"Beauty is in the eye of the beholder." He made his way to our only source of food in class. "Any preference?"

"Surprise me," I said, heading to the bathroom in the back of the shop to wash the conté smudges off my fingers. I returned to a pack of tiny donuts, two Cokes, and two small bags of chips on my desk.

"Will these do?" he asked, fingers already smeared with chocolate.

"Absolutely." I took a seat and smudged the corner of my hand on my drawing. "Oh, fuck."

"The reason there's no point in washing your hands when you're working with conté," he said proudly, showing me the smudges on his palms.

"I don't know about you," I said snidely. "But I want to avoid the possibility of a stomach bug."

"From conté smudges?" He scrunched his nose.

"You never know."

"I read this article one time that said that tapeworms are

actually good for you," he said with a serious face—breaking into a loud laugh before I was able to contest.

"You're something else." I tore the bag of chips open, Neb's random message flashing in my mind. "All right," I started. "Give me three things you like about this school already."

He chuckled and scanned the empty shop. "It's only my second day here, but I can say that—" he held three fingers in the air— "the company is better." One finger down. "The food is exquisite." Two down. "The music is the best I've heard in weeks."

"Fair answer."

"Tell me three things that make you you?" He dumped a mountain of chips on his hand.

"Okay. Deep question," I said. "One: Brazilian food—"

"Wait, Brazilian food makes you who you are?"

"Of course. It's the best thing out there."

"I'll say that those cheese ball thingies—"

"Pão de queijo!" I held up two fists in the air, waving them like I had just won a marathon.

"Yes." He snapped his fingers. "Those. I won't even try to repeat those words to avoid any embarrassment. Those are the most amazing thing I've ever tasted."

"My dear James, if Brazilian food was a monarchy like Brazil used to be, cheese-bread would still be its ruling queen," I said.

"Can't disagree with you on that, despite my lack of knowledge of Brazilian cuisine," he said.

My cheeks burned. Fuck. "Two." I cleared my throat to compose myself. "I'm a pile of confusion. Three: I try to see things in a positive light even when others tell me not to."

"Being a pile of confusion is not so bad," he said.

"Oh, yeah?"

"Owning up to the fact you're confused shows that you're

ready to sort your shit out," he said. "The problem is being so confused that you think there's no way out."

A hint of sadness took his eyes.

"Speaking from experience?"

"Aren't the both of us?" He crumbled his empty bag of chips and opened the donuts. "Sometimes things happen…" I stretched my hand after he gestured me one. "They happen, and you have to leave places and people. No matter how much you want to fix things, you realize some things aren't meant to be fixed. They are meant to be left behind. You try to find the good. You even tell yourself that things can go back to the way they were. But everything is dust."

"Dust?"

"It can be blown out from things, swept into a garbage can. Our lives can be wiped away with a cloth and no one would remember us," he added. "So yeah, dust. Disposable. Too small to matter."

"And what does one do to avoid becoming dust?" The donut was still in my hand.

"One owns up to the secret they think the world can't handle," he answered. "When you own your story, you take control. You choose the narrative instead of letting others write it for you. Kind of liberating, really."

His eyes reflected pages and pages written by his life. Eyes were my thing, but his were suddenly my obsession. I wanted to read what they had to say.

"What's your story?" I took a chance. "…your secret?" Our eyes locked in the same way they had the first time he sat across from me yesterday. I didn't waver. I didn't give in to my heart's uneven beating. I stared dead center.

"I could ask you the same." He smirked. "Lunch tomorrow?"

"Huh?" That was the only thing I managed to say. I hadn't been expecting a full-out lunch invitation.

"Unless you have some very important commitment on a Saturday," he said. "Perhaps a kingdom to advise? Hobbits that need your attention?"

I laughed and asked, "Where?"

"Dos Slices Pizza on Route Nine?"

"Sounds good," I said. "But I still think—"

A few students swarmed back into class. The bell rang seconds later. The donut was still in my hand, the chocolate melting over my fingers. I guess that's what happens when you hold onto something for too long. You damage it.

5
TWISTS AND TURNS

September 2011

He won the donut box, and I wasn't upset one bit. Staring at his face was a lot more entertaining than gazing at that weird bowl creature. The Forbidden Fortress made their jokes about how lazy I had gotten with this assignment. I went along, but never told them James was the culprit behind my crimes.

I finally got James alone again when we hopped on the bus. He became pretty popular on the ride back home, since he decided to share his prize with a few of the other kids. I wanted the donut hype to die down. Not because I was jealous. I just wanted to talk to him. Just the two of us. Yes, we were going for lunch tomorrow, but I wanted to talk now. It felt like such a waste of time to entertain the donut vultures.

The donut hype went away after I ate the last Boston cream. That's when I found out he was obsessed with DevianArtBook, this website where artists from all over the world posted their stuff. If you knew DevianArtBook, then you were serious about your art career. That's how that website was seen. I never felt like my stuff was good enough to post. Not yet, at least. He insisted that I should at least try to post something to make my way to the top viewed artists. But I wanted my DevianArtBook debut to be perfect.

I asked him for his phone and typed my number in as my stop was coming up. I saved it under Elder Wizard.

"Wow," he said. "Can I call you this from now on?"

"As long as we're not in public," I said with a laugh.

"See you tomorrow."

"See ya," I said.

He did the leg move again. He kept them in the same place, so my calves brushed his knees. Fuck, James.

I asked Mom to drive me to Dos Slices, but she had to cater an event in the afternoon. Dad became my designated driver. I honestly thought this was Mom creating a situation where Dad and I could talk about what happened at dinner the other night. Dad was the kind of person to brush shit off, tuck it in a drawer, and hope it wouldn't stink up the house.

Dad and I hopped in his purple matchbox-shaped van a few minutes after Mom left for work. Things were always awkward when it was just the two of us. Dad and I never really had one of those deep, life-changing talks. Ever. Mom was the designated talker. There was this void when Dad and I were alone. I tried to dig deep into my brain so I could find things to talk about with him. I hated a lingering silence.

He opened his mouth. He was ready to speak. I was ready for the lecture about my behavior at dinner. I was even ready for another speech about how I was going to throw my life away if I continued to attend Joseph.

"Any girls in your life?" he blurted out, eyes on the road.

I was half relieved and half shocked. I clutched my seatbelt, looked out the window, and said, "Not really. Too busy with school. Also, no point in getting a girl now if we're leaving."

"Não, não," he said with a nod. "No need to be so serious with her. Kissed one yet?"

"Sure," I replied with a wave. It wasn't a lie. I had kissed three girls in middle school and one freshman year. Every experience was more average than the other. I was to blame. I'd known I liked boys since I was a kid, but I insisted on giving girls a try so I could feel more "normal." How did I know? The thighs on the soccer field were always more appealing than the girls on the bleachers. There was no big grand moment where something came down from heaven and crowned me with a gay flag. I just knew what I liked and moved on with my life.

But when the other kids started associating my art with being gay in a way that made me feel weak and less than they were, I figured that being gay was like being sick with a very contagious virus. I didn't want to cause a pandemic. So I learned to chisel myself to what people around me liked. I wanted to make them feel at ease. Nobody liked to be around a contagious kid.

A few of the boys at Joseph joked once that they had to stay away from me in gym and not drop the soap. Pedro was straight, and even though he didn't know I was gay, we got along really well—proof that boys with different tastes could be really good friends, unlike those accusing me of wanting their butts for sex. As if they were attractive enough.

Dad, on the other hand, probably suspected. These have-you-kissed-a-girl questions popped up here and there. Maybe he knew he had a gay son. What if he had some sort of secret sensor that could pick up gay waves in his offspring?

"I know you think leaving is a bad decision," he said. "We came because there was no other choice."

"I remember." My arms folded over my chest. "Trust me, I remember every person who knocked on our door asking to get paid. There was the guy who threatened to take the house and the woman who wanted a car you and Mom had just bought—"

"You and your sister will have more opportunities there," he said. "You can be a doctor or a lawyer, Mateus. Get a job that gives you…" He spent a few seconds trying to find the word in English. He eventually gave up, "segurança."

"I may just stay behind," I mumbled absentmindedly.

My words surprised him. I had never mentioned the possibility of staying by myself. He looked at me like I was a criminal. But in the staring, he missed a stop sign—but neither of us missed the police car stationed near the bushes off the road. Its lights lit up.

I remembered this week's ICE tale. Dad kept driving for a few more seconds, probably wishing the cop had just lit up their lights to drive a little faster. But no, it was right behind us. Dad pulled over.

The side mirror displayed the red and blue lights. At first glance, one would think there was a very patriotic Christmas tree behind us, but the police officer walking our way was definitely not Santa.

Dad took a second to compose himself enough to press the button to roll down the window. He clutched his hands on the steering wheel, trying to hide their trembling.

"Good afternoon, sir," said the officer in a thick Bostonian accent.

"Hello—" Dad cleared his throat. "Hello, officer."

"You missed a stop sign back there." His thumbs clutched to his belt. He was one of those very tall and intimidating cops with the glasses.

"I know," Dad said with a nervous smile. "Sorry. I got… um… distraído…"

The cop's sunglasses weren't big enough to hide his frown after Dad ended that sentence in Portuguese.

"And who's in the car with you?" The officer pointed at me.

"My son," Dad replied.

"License and registration, please."

Dad reached into the glove compartment. We both knew there was a registration in there, but unless the Elder Wizard here had actual magical powers, there would be no license to show. He got the piece of paper and handed it to the officer.

"No license, officer."

"Expired?" The officer scanned the registration.

"No. Just not able to get one." I felt the pain in Dad's affirmation.

This was it. The police officer would ask him why. He'd tell him we were undocumented. Dad would be arrested. Who the fuck knew what would happen after? Life would change. What would it be like to go back to Brazil after Dad got deported? That would be so humiliating. Not if we kept it a secret. But then, Fogo Dourado wasn't the friendliest town toward gay people. What would that look like for me? Maybe I'd marry some girl and I'd pretend to be straight until I died. I'd never see my friends or James again.

He handed the registration back to Dad and stared at me for a few seconds. He seemed conflicted, but things were clear. We missed a stop sign. We got pulled over. No license to show. No papers. Jail.

Mom would call the few people we knew. She would tell them about Dad's arrest and how we needed money so we could cover our expenses until we moved back. Maybe there would even be a headline in a local Brazilian newspaper about us. I would walk inside the Latino store on Franklin Street and find us on the front cover.

"Tell you what." The officer pointed at the road. "You're going to drive away and I'll wait until you're out of sight, all right? Try to find a way to get this sorted, please."

"Okay," Dad mumbled.

"I never saw you," said the officer.

"Okay," Dad repeated, pale as fuck.

"Just keep an eye out for any stop signs you see, pal."

The officer stayed outside of his car as we drove away in silence. I didn't bother breaking it. There was nothing to say. And whatever I did say would only make it worse. He was driving me somewhere. None this would have happened if I hadn't agreed to lunch with James.

He dropped me off without a word and I watched him be on his way.

I scanned the white bold letters on the façade, spelling out "Dos Slices." Beside it was a pizza-shaped neon sign. Through the window I saw James on a bench in the waiting area by the entrance. He tucked his phone inside his pocket when he saw me. His dimpled chin and smile were a much-needed distraction.

"Happy Saturday," he said when I walked in. "Happy you made it."

"Yeah." I shrugged.

"You okay? Looks like you've seen a ghost."

"Dad stuff," I said. I wasn't lying.

"All right." He raised a hand, eyes circling the room. The hostess spotted him and quickly approached. "We're ready," James said.

She grabbed two menus and led us to a round table in the back. Dos Slices' brick walls were decorated with pictures of New York City. Right next to our table was a big stop. Shit, maybe this was the universe sending me a sign. Stop whatever this is or your heart will hurt even more when you leave this life behind.

"Going to tell me what's really on your mind?" James blurted out over the rock song playing in the restaurant after the hostess walked away.

"Sometimes I wish I was my dad," I blurted out. "Other times I wish I was my mom."

"Can't say I was expecting that answer."

"More like, I wish I was in charge of my life," I said. "If I were them, I could've avoided so much shit. I don't mean to unload, but holy fuck. It's like you're in the audience watching a movie about your parents and you can point out every moment that could've led to something different."

"I can sympathize with the feeling," he said. "In my case I wish I was still me. I just want a do-over."

Our waiter showed up with some silverware wrapped in white napkins. We ordered Cokes and she left us alone again.

"How's the weekend so far?" I asked, trying to steer clear of deeper subjects.

"Parents are away a lot. So, loud music and video games."

"You probably like having a house to yourself so often," I said.

"Hey, it's fun." He chuckled. "It can get pretty lonely sometimes. Lunch with you is also keeping my mind away from thinking about my first academic week at Joseph on Monday."

"Oh?" My brows arched up. "Think on a positive note. It's not like it's your first day again."

"Isn't it, though?" he asked. "Don't you, like, have a whole new class? New people around you? I mean, I was lucky with you and the others—"

"And you also won the donuts," I mentioned.

"See? Great first two days." He laughed. "But what if this week there's no one there to save me when the conversation is boring? What if I'm dragged into another meeting of the apostles?"

My heart started acting weird. It wanted to jump out of my chest and sit at the table and join our conversation. No one had ever made it beat so fast.

"Take it from me." I tried to hide the trembling in my voice. "Academic week is… tedious. I won't lie. But you're still at Joseph. So you know next week will be better, because we'll be back in shop and you'll be with your four amigos again."

"Shop week is so freeing." Talking about shop week seemed to lift a weight off his shoulders. "Academic week reminds me of stuff I had to…" He made this thin sound through his teeth.

"You can finish that sentence if you want."

"Scared to finish it," he said.

"Scared of me?"

"Scared of what I had to go through, actually." A nervous chuckle. "I know the story has an okay ending, but it's still uncomfortable. It's not exactly pizza conversation. Thinking about it is like walking through a ghost, knowing it's right next to you. Haven't thought of the ghost that much since Thursday."

Of course I did the math in my head. The ghost had been somewhat absent since the day he met me.

"I just needed to be in a place that could help me forget Framingham High." His words were loaded. "A departure from regular school. I don't know if that makes sense. Joseph was the closest thing. This is probably why I'm dreading academic week so much. Too close to what I experienced…"

My phone vibrated in my pocket.

Dad: Em casa. Text when you want me to pick you up.

Of course, he had to drive back to pick me up. It wasn't like we had a private driver available for my every need. He would have to brave the open road without a license again and again and again.

"You okay?" James asked.

"Yeah," I said. "Sorry. Didn't mean to cut you off." I waved the phone in the air. "My dad."

The waitress returned with the drinks and told us she'd be back to take our orders in a few.

James held up his drink and said, "Cheers."

"To our sad stories?" I said, the tip of my straw between my teeth as I freed it from its paper wrapping.

"To better days?" His eyebrows arched up.

Our cups clinked, and then I blurted out the first thing that came to my mind. "You owe me a story." Listening to him would be a good distraction.

"I do, don't I?" He folded his arms on the edge of the table. "I traveled a lot when I was a kid. Conferences and stuff like that. My parents would drag me along with them. I wanted to go to my friends' birthday parties or to games on the weekends, but I got to go to my parents' speaking engagements instead. Playing with kids at those isn't as fun."

"And what do they talk about? Your parents?" I sipped from my drink.

"Stuff that some people care about more than they should," he replied, clearly measuring his words in his head.

"Did you always live in Framingham?" I asked.

"Always had a house here," he said. "But I only got to stick around more often after I became a teenager. Parents got to keep on traveling and I got to fly solo at the house most of the time." He drank from his cup. "And you? Now you owe me a story."

I sucked air through my teeth. "Born in Brazil. Moved to the States when I was seven. Been in Framingham ever since."

"Do you miss home?" he asked.

There was a concept I hadn't thought about that often. I was usually so consumed with my undocumented reality that

I'd forget about the years I called Brazil home. The memories were vague, but the feelings I experienced from that time were suddenly alive in my head.

"I miss feeling so free," I said. "Brazil was a home for the kid in me. The US is a home for the teenager now."

"I can relate," he said.

"*You* can relate?"

"Not the whole moving out of the country part, obviously." He chuckled. "The freedom part. The being a kid and feeling like you can be who you are without judgment."

"Until someone actually judges you," I added.

The waiter returned to take our order. We hadn't even looked at the menu and decided on burgers for both, but not before we had agreed on nachos as our appetizer. This was good. What happened with me, Dad, and that cop was just an echo at this point. The conversation grew lighter. Maybe nachos had that superpower. We chatted about music, movies, and shows and art before our main course arrived.

He told me about this artist on DevianArtBook who painted watercolors depicting her nightmares. He talked about this one piece where a man sat under a tree, holding his heart in his hand. According to James, that was one of the hardest things a person could ever do: share their heart with someone who deserved it. Sharing your heart meant sharing your secrets. It was our secrets that made us who we really were.

"So, what's your secret?" he asked after the burgers arrived. "Any you want to share?"

I smiled. "If I remember correctly, I asked *you* that in class first."

"And I'm asking *you* now."

The toothpick holding the burger together suddenly looked like a toy. I pulled it and stuck it back into the buns repeatedly, trying to buy time so I could get an answer out. Yes, I had secrets, and little did he know he was becoming one of them.

"You don't have to answer," he said to my relief. "We earn the right to learn secrets. Maybe I'll have that privilege in the future."

"Of learning mine?" I asked.

"Yes," he answered. "And sharing mine with you."

DevianArtBook became the topic of conversation again, and all the while I kept thinking about how much of my truth he could handle.

"What are you doing after this?" James asked, sipping from the Coke that was now mostly water, since the ice had melted. "Feel like coming over?" he asked before I gave him an actual response. "We could play games and hang out."

"I wish, but I got to head home," I said in a disappointed tone. "Got stuff to do." By stuff I meant checking on my family. Because that was me. I needed to make sure they were all right, especially after the police encounter I caused.

"Mind if I give you a ride home?"

"Sure," I replied, secretly relieved.

I grabbed my wallet when the waitress brought the bill. But by the time I revealed the cash, James had already handed her his card.

"On me," he said with a weird wink. I thought a bug had flown into his eye—until he tried again.

"You should never wink." I held back a laugh. "Like, ever."

"Noted." His cheeks blushed.

"And why did you pay?" I asked as we walked to the exit. "You're already giving me a ride."

"You were great company, Matty," he said. "It's the least I can do."

"So, who's picking us up?" I asked as he rushed a few steps to hold the door open.

"I got the car," he answered as I walked past him.

"But don't you need a parent to drive if you're under eighteen?" I quickly sent Dad a text telling him I was hitching a ride from a friend.

"Who are you, the cops?" He rushed his pace so he could walk next to me.

"Definitely not."

"And yes," he continued. "You do need to be eighteen, but my parents don't need to know our little secret." He glanced over his shoulder. "See? Sharing mine already."

The sky was this beautiful shade of orange and red. Fall sunsets were my favorite. James had one hand in his pocket. He twirled his car keys with the other. He glanced behind me as we approached a gray Nissan. I guess he wanted to make sure I hadn't run off after he confessed we were about to break the law. Ha, little did he know every breath I took in this place was illegal.

The car was spotless. It smelled like pine and expensive cologne. If not for the half-full Dunkin' Donuts coffee cup, I would've assumed the car had come straight from the dealer.

He turned the keys, connected his phone, and said, "Want to play DJ?"

"That's a huge responsibility for our first car ride," I said.

"Scared?" He put a hand on the headrest behind me and looked back while reversing the car. His dimpled chin had never been so close.

"Of your driving? Yes," I said. "Of being the DJ, absolutely not. I have perfect taste in music." I scrolled down his library and found Maroon 5. "Moves Like Jagger" blasted at full volume. The song earned a crooked smile and a wobbling headshake from him.

"I don't get that reaction," I said. "You approve?"

"I would've turned it off by now if I hadn't!" he shouted once the lyrics came on. "This is my shower song."

"Shower song?" I asked.

"Yeah," he said. "Everyone has one. It's the song you play when you hold your shampoo bottle like a microphone and pretend you're performing for a crowd."

"I've never done that."

"You're missing out on so much."

I tapped his shoulder with his phone. "You want this back, shower boy?"

"No," he said. "You're in charge of the music until I drop you off. DJ duties."

I knew a lot of the artists he liked, but it wasn't the familiar or the unknown artists that called my attention. It was the playlist named "Paradise." I tapped on the first song immediately. The first notes of Claude Debussy's "Clair de Lune" replaced Christina Aguilera's bridge.

"Oh, I forgot—I made…"

"Paradise?"

"Pretty dramatic name, huh?" He curled his hand into a fist and pressed it hard against his dimpled chin. I wanted to be that hand.

"Very, but why did you name it that?"

"A story for when you come over," he replied with a smirk.

"Deal?"

"Deal."

6

DISSOLVED

September 2011

The Forbidden Fortress was meeting at the Crusty Pie for breakfast, our go-to spot whenever we had juicy stuff to share or just craved a caffeine high with loads of dairy and sugar. I didn't mind the thirty-minute walk—especially after yesterday's incident with the cop. There would be no driving requests from me for a while. The brief possibility of my dad ending up in jail and then deported was traumatizing enough.

Everybody was already there when I arrived. They were at our usual table by the window, next to an old bookshelf that got redecorated whenever the seasons changed. There were already a few fall leaves scattered over and around the books. Fa's hoodie was its own statement: "Biblical Whore" was printed in bold beige letters. The color of Diana's jacket matched the letters on her sweetheart's chest. Pedro was in full black. His white Converses were a canvas for anime sketches and cuss words in Portuguese. My friends, aka the most impatient humans on the planet, already had their coffees with them.

But the girl at the counter, Gabriella, was the big surprise. I hadn't expected to see her, since she usually didn't work on Sundays. Freshman year, she had stuck a letter inside my locker. It had a drawing of a couple of stick figures that I assumed were supposed to be us running through a field. There was a question at the end: "Coffee?" and two circles under the word, one saying "yes" and the other "no." I never gave her an answer. I also never brought up the letter. I obviously knew she had a thing for me, but I didn't have it in me to tell her I didn't feel—and would never feel—the same way. I thought about what would hurt her less. Radio silence or her finding the letter back in her locker with an X on the circle next to "no."

I had told the Forbidden Fortress about the letter at the time. Pedro thought I was crazy for not going after her. "How can you resist such a beautiful morena, Mateus?" were his exact words.

I could've faked it. I could've pretended her long black hair and big brown eyes made me feel the things you're supposed to feel when you have a crush on someone. I could've sent a letter back with an X on "yes" or talked to her in school. But I could never hurt another by being in a relationship with someone I wasn't really attracted to. Being alone was the safer choice. I would only hurt myself in the end.

Gabriella switched schools a few months after the letter thing. I had always wondered if I was the reason for her leaving Joseph. She never talked about it. Whenever I was hanging out at the Crusty Pie by myself, I'd sometimes think she'd randomly walk up to me one day and question my silence, but she never did.

"Thank you for waiting, guys." I unrolled my scarf.

"Café com leite waits for no one, Matt," Pedro said with a hint of whipped cream on his upper lip. "But I *did* tell Gabriella to bring your chocolate cake the moment you walked in."

"For the record," Diana raised a finger, "Fa and I were totally against it."

"What the hell, Pedro?" I pulled up a chair, almost smashing the back against the bookshelf.

"You'll thank me later," Pedro said, cocking his head toward the counter. Gabriella was already on her way over, holding a plate with a slice of red velvet.

"Hey, Matt." She set the cake on the table. "Awesome seeing you here today." She had the hint of an accent. If I were straight, that alone would've made my knees shake.

"Hey, Gabriella." I couldn't say the same thing she said. She'd assume I was flirting. "Having a good day at work? I know you don't usually work on Sundays."

"Didn't mind the extra shift," she said. "Helping mi mamá at the house with the bills, you know."

Pedro could've drooled all over the table as she talked.

"Everything okay at home?" Pedro asked.

"Sí," she said. "Just want to help out more. Dad hurt his back last week. He has to rest for some time."

"At least we'll get to see you more often around here," Pedro said, doing this weird thing with his face. His expression fell somewhere between flirtatious and just plain stupid.

"I have to get back to work." Gabriella wiped her hands on her apron and looked at me. "Enjoy the cake."

"Listen," Pedro whispered. "If you aren't going to do anything, then do you mind—"

"By all means," I replied. "I mean, you'll clearly get tons of cake."

We all laughed.

"We need to find you someone, Matty," Diana said.

"What's the point?" I shrugged. "I definitely don't think my family and I are staying after what happened yesterday."

I told them the whole cop-pulled-us-over story. Not a single interruption—which was pretty unusual. Usually, we'd talk about four different things at once.

"Holy shit, dude," Fa chewed on her bagel.

"Listen," Diana said. "I'm glad nothing happened to you or your dad. I mean, after that raid…"

"It was nuts," I continued. "And don't bring this up in front of anyone. But if my calculations are correct, 2012 will see the end of the Forbidden Fortress as we know it. The Moreiras getting arrested by ICE was already the cherry on the cake. Yesterday was the same thing as putting a bomb inside that cake and exploding it on everyone's faces."

"So much can still change." Fa grabbed my hand. "We shouldn't mourn you leaving yet."

"She's right," Pedro agreed. "Remember how my dad kept saying we were also bouncing two years ago? Still here. He even went on a date with that woman. I think his marriage might actually end up being legit."

"We should have an award ceremony for our guardians." Diana facepalmed. "Like, seriously. There should be a college for parents. You have a kid. You go to parent college."

"And for extra credit, they should take classes on how to properly tell your kids they have no papers," Pedro said.

"Now, there's a lucrative business," Fa said.

"So messed up," Diana said with a tiny smile.

"*Fucked* up, Diana." Pedro sipped from his coffee. "Fucked. Up. You can cuss when shit gets messy. Listen, I love my dad, but this situation is fucked up. Not messed up."

"Kind of liberating, babe," Fa said. "Shit. Merda. Fuck. Puta que pariu…"

"I may be a lesbian, but my mouth still belongs to the Lord," Diana said.

The laugh we shared briefly shook off the impending doom.

"Where was your dad driving you, anyway?" Fa sipped from her yellow mug.

I flinched. Why the fuck did I do that? Having lunch with

James wasn't a crime. I scurried to find a good answer. Groceries? The library? The dollar store? The adult store could sound believable.

"Hello!" Pedro waved a hand on my face. "Anyone there?"

"Jesus." I flinched. "Patience. I had a few errands to run. They don't trust me with either of their cars just yet." I hoped they wouldn't see past my lie. "I don't think they'll let me drive either of them anytime soon after yesterday. I kind of get it, you know," I continued, hoping to switch subjects. "My parents wanting to up and leave. I don't think they had any idea how fucked up this entire situation could get. And at the same time we have no papers, we are also privileged to live in a good house and drive okay cars. Undocumented aside, we have it pretty good. God, this is fucked."

"You only know something is fucked up when you live it," Fa added. "That's also the only way to fix it."

"You need to frame the things you say and sell them on eBay," Pedro said. "I swear." He slapped the edge of the table and glanced at me. "Listen, you're not the only with a juicy story today."

"Pedro." Fa pressed her fingers on her forehead. "Learn how to read the room. Matt is pouring his heart out, which is a rare thing for him."

"I was pretty much done, and him reading the room won't give me a green card, so…" I waved my hand as a sign that Pedro could start his juicy tale.

"I went out with this girl from Framingham High last night," Pedro revealed. "It was amazing. She had—"

"Get to the point." Diana held up a hand when he gestured two boobs on his chest. "We don't need to hear your erotic tale again."

"Again?" I asked.

"He shared it before you got here," Diana said with a shrug. "We were bored waiting."

"Worry not," Pedro exclaimed in a horrible British accent and lifted a finger. "I promise to send details via text."

"You want my sweater?" Fa asked. "Biblical Whore suits you. You went out last night with this girl and now you're flirting with sweet Gabriella."

"Ha-ha," Pedro said. "Funny. Anyway, so she tells me she knows James; had class with him. He was beat up at school for kissing a guy in the gym's locker room. The dude he kissed was some hotshot football player and said James jumped him out of nowhere."

"Holy. Fucking. Shit," I said. "Wait, you think that's true?"

"There's always two sides of a story." Fa puckered her lips, her face revealing she had theories bopping around in her head.

"Lesbians One and Two had a few things to say," Pedro said.

"Of course we did." Diana played with her braid.

"We're not saying stories like this don't happen," Fa said. "But what if the football dude actually *wanted* James and came up with some lame excuse *after* they were caught by his team? Think, people. Think." She repeatedly tapped a finger on her temple. "The girl from Rio can definitely think for all of you."

"Whether the story is true or not, James should be the one to say something first," Diana added in a calm voice. "I know from experience, being forced to come out is like a baby being born before its time. You can live, but it's a struggle until you start to. The people around act like hospital machines. They think they can keep you alive by giving you their opinions all the time. You must be mentally ready for that. Mom and Tia Jo did the best they could, but, God, it was exhausting."

Fa and Diana shared an intimate stare. The kind that showed the entire room they were the only ones who mattered for a few seconds. Shy smiles appeared on their faces.

"I can attest to that," Fa mentioned. "It wasn't even the fact that my mom wasn't accepting. It just felt like the story I was meant to tell the world was stolen from me by some lame freshmen kids last year. Sure, they caught me and Diana kissing in the library, but why out us to our families?"

"Exactly." Diana banged a fist on a table as if passing a sentence. It was the first time I had ever seen her do that. "When Tia Jo showed me the picture those kids had sent her, I couldn't help but grieve over the fact that I had lost my chance to share this part of me the way I wanted."

"Mom went on and on about how I didn't trust them," Fa said. "And how I should've felt comfortable telling them and this and that. I was just embarrassed that my life was exposed without my consent."

"We were talking about telling our families," Diana said. "We had thought about a dinner or writing a letter…"

My mind drifted. I wished for a coming-out accident—something that removed the responsibility from my shoulders. Not that coming out was a responsibility for every queer person out there. Some didn't feel the need to tell anyone. And that was fine. But out of my two secret identities, this was the one I was documented for. I just didn't have the guts to wave my gay ID around.

"Wasn't it sort of a relief as well?" I asked.

"What do you mean, Elder Wizard?" Diana asked.

"Well, you didn't have to chew over the countless ways you would tell people around you," I said. "It was sort of done for you."

"Temporary relief doesn't solve anything." Fa shrugged. "Look at us. The only reason why we aren't called 'illegal aliens,'" she said, using air quotes while referring to our people, "is because of our age. Temporary protection. Once we hit eighteen, baby, it's everyone for themselves. Then our sentence will be made official. See? Temporary relief." Fa took a determined sip from her hot chocolate. "We didn't share our story. We explained it. Don't you remember? You heard it from your mom, Matt." She wiped her lips with the sleeve of her sweater. "I mean, what was that? I know Brazilians love a good gossip, but boy did news of Diana and me travel fast."

"We would've told you," Diana added, undoing her red braid over her shoulder. "But in our way. Our time. We knew it was going to be a surprise for you and Pedro. We met in middle school, became inseparable, then boom, your two friends who are also girls get together freshman year."

Would it be a surprise? Did they suspect?

"I was surprised, but not really," Pedro mentioned with a grin. "I noticed the two of you checking out chicks from time to time."

"There's a lot of talk about coming out lately," Fa continued. "And I think it's amazing. But there's one thing that should also be talked about: the price you pay for moving *out* of the closet."

"It takes guts," I said. "That's for sure."

Guts I don't have, I thought.

"So, if this is James's truth," Diana said, "then we need to give him space to share that truth if he wants to. He doesn't know we've got no papers, either. We all have secrets. Some hurt more than others. I'm sure he didn't ask to be beat up. We didn't ask to be undocumented."

"So we pretend we don't know?" Pedro asked.

"No," Diana replied. "Being quiet isn't pretending. We wait for the right moment to say something."

Okay, so I was waiting. That was it. I was waiting for the right time. It may never come. But hey.

"What if there's never a right time?" I asked. "What if sometimes the only thing you can do is hold on to your silence because it's the anchor that keeps you safe?"

The three of them stared as if I was Fa's second reincarnation.

"Maybe James will never tell that story because it'll always hurt too much," I continued. "Just like we don't go around telling other kids we aren't going to college like they are or getting our permits like they are because we're breaking the law by simply being here."

"We're more than all those things, Matty," Fa said.

"But we are still those things." My hands curled into fists. "I'm tired of hoping and waiting for the right moment to speak up or to get papers or, you know, to do… whatever. I feel like I'm literally an ice cube under the sun just waiting to melt away."

The Elder Wizard had cast a gloomy spell over the Forbidden Fortress. Things got really quiet really fast.

"Sorry, but ever thought about what life would be like if any of you went back?" I tried to break the tension. "Like, where would we even start or fit in? Fa, you were, what, four, five? And Pedro was six, and Diana was eight. I was nine. I don't know. I guess I'm in over my head today after what happened."

"We ignore that reality for so long," Fa said. "We fool ourselves into thinking we actually belong here, right?"

"But how long can we keep on ignoring it?" Diana asked.

"I guess we'll wait and see," Pedro said.

Mom was at the dinner table when I got home from the Crusty Pie. She sniffled when she noticed me standing by the doorway. She quickly wiped her eyes with a wrist and rushed to the sink, dumping whatever was left of her coffee down the drain.

"Que foi, Mãe?" I paused my music.

"Got a call." Her voice was shaky. "They verified my social at work."

7

FALL

October 2011

Mom got fired. They had requested a new social security number by the first week of October. Though my friends called me the Elder Wizard, I lacked the ability to conjure one. She was on the phone every time I got home from school, calling people, hoping to find work under the table.

Her unemployment led Dad to spiral back to an old habit—one he had left behind since we moved here, at least to my knowledge. Beer bottles were in our fridge almost every day. They were there in the evening and would be gone the next day. Every single one of them. Dad bought them after he left work, drank them before he slept until dinner, and left the empty bottles for us to throw away.

Dad reeking of alcohol brought back memories I had spent years tucking away. Back in Fogo Dourado, in the days when my age lacked the word "teen" at the end, if he wasn't home past eleven, I stayed awake because I knew there was a possibility of violence. I never had the guts to ask Laila if she remembered the sounds of breaking glass or slamming doors. Alcohol did something to my dad, something to his mind. Some people were criers when they drank. Others got too clingy. Not Dad. He was an angry drunk.

Back then, when Dad was out too late, Mom would stroll around the house, waiting for him. I wondered if she paced from anxiety or just because she was pissed her husband was out that late without a phone call. I was always ready to storm out of my room in case things got too loud.

Lately, I felt like I was back there; I was that little boy again, drowning in the one million scenarios of how things could fail if we went back. Dad would have the store and his drinking buddies around again. If he was getting shit-faced here, he'd get ten times worse there. The screaming would return and the yelling and the violence. He didn't pull that shit here, because of deportation. It would be a different story back home. Funny how I was suddenly glad for our undocumented truth.

School would be a dread, that's for sure. I'd be finishing up senior year while trying to re-learn Portuguese. God, failure would be imminent.

Then there was dating. I'd probably end up like one of those pastors you read about in the news. You claim you've turned straight and then you marry a girl and somehow manage to have kids, but you live this quiet life where you secretly meet up with all these men from your church or from some obscure bar.

I decided to reprise my childhood role of staying up late, listening for any noise that served as a sign that Dad was spiraling out of control. If my room was a retreat before, now it had become a fortress. Pen, paper, and pencil had always been my escape, but suddenly they were weapons, keeping me protected while my thoughts spiraled. Eyes. I had been drawing them more often now that I was on night guard duty. Every single one ended up looking like James's. We were voracious texters. We shared playlists, art, and movie suggestions almost every day. He wasn't a big fan of social media. He told me he'd had Facebook a while back but deleted it.

My talks with James never got too deep since lunch at Dos Slices. I assumed the fear I had of being too vulnerable was mutual. And the story Pedro had shared didn't make it easier to strike up a more meaningful conversation. I didn't want to trip over my own thoughts and blurt out something that showed him I had heard the rumors. That's all it was for now. Rumors. I needed confirmation to know it was true.

The four of us acted as if we hadn't heard anything. In theory, things were normal. Well, nothing was normal for me after James arrived, but normal enough that no one suspected anything.

He hadn't joined the Forbidden Fortress chat yet, but he was close. The five of us were going to the movies tonight, the first time we were all doing something with James outside of school—a much-needed escape from the new reality that had settled in my house.

Tonight was about *Shadow of a Tree*. Diana had picked the movie. It was about some girl that gets kidnapped by a spirit and is trapped in a forest. It sounded like a predictable horror movie where you know someone will be left behind so they can be killed off, but at least my mind would be entertained.

James offered to drive. Not that the four undocumented humans complained.

I was the first stop. He lowered the windows as I strolled to the car, turning up the volume to an instrumental most likely composed for a battle scene in a movie. The closer I got, the louder the song. He lowered the music when I sat in the passenger seat.

"Glad to know you understand that I require epic themes whenever I make an entrance." I buckled my seatbelt. His gelled hair and leather jacket were a welcome sight. The smell of his cologne alone got the wand in my pants all riled up. It was too dark for him to notice anything.

"Couldn't help it." He smirked, driving away. "You walked like a hero going on a journey. You deserved the song."

Of course I noticed the Dunkin' Donuts coffee in the cup holder.

"You didn't have to!" I grabbed it out of its cozy enclosure.

"Wait, no, no—" He shouted as I took a sip.

"All right." I forced the lukewarm coffee down my throat. "This tastes like dirt water."

"It's been sitting in the car all day, Matty." He looked at the left mirror while making a turn. "I was going to suggest we stop at Dunkin' *on the way* to the movies."

"That's a solid idea," I agreed, with the bitter taste in my mouth.

"You good with DJ duty?" He handed me his phone.

"Do you even have to ask?" I typed his passcode. One. One. One. One. Creative.

"That last playlist you sent was pretty good," he said. "Those Lady Gaga bootleg remixes you found were nice, but I was wondering about something."

"What?"

"What's your favorite Brazilian song?" he asked.

I laughed, thinking he was joking, but he looked confused at my reaction.

"I'm serious," he said. "You have to have one. I know you moved here when you were a kid, but your parents lived there for much longer."

"I don't listen to Brazilian music that much," I said. "But one comes to mind."

There was one Mom had played a few times at the house when she was cleaning. It was about a dude who got rich overnight and bought a yellow Camaro. I looked for the song and turned up the volume as soon as I found it. James bopped his head to the beat. When the singer started singing the lyrics, he smiled, bopping his head even harder. He was all in when the chorus hit, tapping the steering wheel while trying to mouth the words. He asked me what the guy was singing about. I gave him the basic idea behind the song.

"Screenshot the name," he said. "I need to save that to a playlist."

I did as he asked. "So," I started. "Before we pick up the others, I want you to name a song you secretly like."

"Wait, wait, wait," he said. "So we're sharing secret stuff like this now?"

My cheeks blushed. I coiled in my seat. "It's just a song…"

"Sharing a secret song is like showering after the gym. You're butt-naked in front of an entire crowd," he said. "If I tell you that one, then that means we're ready to share deep stuff."

Deep stuff. As in, the stuff we usually kept locked away. The stuff we needed to wait for the right time. Like there was ever a right time for the good and the bad things. I stared at his face for a few seconds before the silence got too awkward.

"Tell me the song," I said.

"You already found it."

"I did?"

"'Clair de Lune,'" he said. "I actually blast it in the car when I'm alone."

"So I discovered your secret song on our first car ride."

"You're a good detective, Matty," he said.

I searched for the song and pressed play. "I like it," I said as the intro played. "It'll always remind me of you now."

"I'm honored," he said.

Neither of us said anything. But the silence wasn't weird. It felt right to be next to him, listening to the song, driving somewhere, and knowing we both enjoyed the company, the music, the destination. I didn't want to go deeper than this. I was leaving next year. What was the point of getting too close? I'd have to say goodbye and it'd hurt too much.

The song ended a few minutes before we arrived at Fa's house. The others were there. Things got a bit gloomy when they got in the car. Fa started rambling on about this book she read on the Granary Burying Ground in Boston. Diana added to the story, saying that paranormal experts claimed the spot was one of the most haunted places in America. Then she shared a picture that had been circulating around Facebook of a spirit standing on one of the graves.

"You know what I don't understand?" Diana said as we pulled up to the drive-thru at Dunkin'. "How come every ghost has to have these medieval clothes, chains, and all that crap? Why can't we get a ghost dressed up like, I don't know, Michael Jackson or Britney Spears?"

"Oh, God." Fa cackled. "Imagine! It's thriller, bitch."

A loud laugh blasted from the drive-thru's speaker. It took a few seconds for the girl to compose herself before she took our orders. Once we drove up, she wanted to meet the genius behind the thriller bitch joke.

We chugged down our coffees. Literally. Dunkin' was about a five-minute drive from the theater, and we weren't allowed to bring in any outside drinks. We grabbed our tickets and were lucky enough to get—in my opinion—the best seats. The last row was paradise. The screen was in full view, the audio could be fully appreciated, and little kids would never sit this far back. Not that I expected them at a PG-13 horror flick.

Pedro sat on the far left beside Diana. Fa ended up in the middle. James was to her right and I next to him. The trailers started rolling and our entire row was still empty.

Perfect. No interruptions from strangers.

The creepy soundtrack began, paving the way for a few jump scares as the movie went on. But it wasn't the adrenaline of watching the girl being chased in the woods that had me hot and my heart beating faster.

James and I had been sharing the left armrest of my seat since the trailers. I expected him to move, but if anything, he'd softly nudge me in the dark, making sure I was aware that his arm touched mine. There was no need to remind me. I *was* fully aware, even though we both wore long sleeves.

He removed his leather jacket halfway through the movie. His arm landed on the exact same spot. I removed my coat and put my arm next to his. Our skins touched and sent tingles all over my body. I was glad my coat was on my lap. Just in case.

James's pinky touched mine. It had to be an accident. But his stubborn pinky stayed put. Then my pinky wrapped around his. He didn't pull away. I leaned back a bit to get a better view of the others. Diana had her arms around Fa, who had her entire face hidden underneath her hoodie. Guess the movie was too much for the biblical whore.

I took things a little further. I pulled his hand under my own. He smirked without flinching, keeping his eyes on the screen.

I didn't want the movie to end. Not because it was great, because honestly, some things were corny and predictable. But leaving James right now felt like a crime—one I wasn't willing to commit.

My fingers stroked his knuckles. My heart pounded the entire time. I started breathing weird. The rest of the movie was just background noise. Our hands were the main act until the credits rolled up on screen.

"Thought it was okay," Pedro mentioned as we headed out of the theater. "I had no one to hold me like Lesbians One and Two here, but the experience was still decent."

"So, Fa," James started, "were you all coiled up because you were cold or scared or…"

"Excuse me." Fa raised a finger. "I was both cold and scared. Don't judge me for having feelings. Sorry I didn't take off my jacket to look all tough inside that refrigerator people call a theater. Vá te fuder."

"Classy!" I yelled.

"What does that mean?" James asked as we braced the cold outside. "What she said?"

"Fuck you," I translated.

"He's lying." Diana nudged James with an elbow. "It means 'I love you.'"

"In your no-cussing-allowed world," Pedro said snidely.

The drive back consisted of music, laughter, and an in-depth session dissecting the movie. I deserved a medal. I acted like nothing happened. Well, nothing happened. But then, it sort of did. I could play along regardless.

The jokes and the laughing were gone after Lesbians One and Two and Pedro were dropped off. James and I were the only ones in the car. Who was going to say something first? Were we going to say anything at all, or was this a secret we now both shared?

8
ONE STEP AT A TIME

October 2011

Some song played in the car. I had no idea what it was. Maybe I knew it, but my mind was too busy being haunted by the pinky war I had survived at the movie theater. Were we never going to talk about it? Because I wanted to. But I didn't. What if things had changed between James and me? I couldn't bear the idea of adding what had happened to my pile of secrets. I wasn't ready to talk about it. I wasn't ready not to talk about it—proof that no one was ever ready for any curveballs life tossed our way.

I saw him from the corner of my eyes. He had one hand on the steering wheel and another on his chin, looking like a philosopher who was deep in thought. Did he want to talk about what happened? He had acted like nothing happened when we walked out. Was that a thing one did in this situation?

I didn't have all the time in the world. He was going to drop me off at some point tonight. We were literally heading to my house.

"Can I see your phone?" I said.

"Missing DJ duties?" He handed it to me.

"Maybe." I pressed play on "Clair de Lune."

"That song is ours now," he said with a smile.

"Another secret we get to share," I said, struggling so I wouldn't stumble over my own words.

"It's no secret I won that pinky war," James casually mentioned. "No question there."

All right, I was in the clear to talk about it.

"I pulled your hand under mine." I pretended to look at something outside the window. "I think victory is mine?" Fuck pretending. I shifted my eyes so I was looking right at him. "Wouldn't you say?"

"A tie, then?" He proudly raised his head, probably not noticing that the act seemed like an invitation for me to gaze at his dimpled chin that made me think of his ass.

"No, no," I said. "I won for sure. I made the bolder move."

"The bolder move," he said behind a laugh. "All right, points to Matty."

"Thank you for being a fair judge."

"Is that what we're doing?" he asked. "Judging?"

"No. Not me, at least. I am analyzing facts and I won."

"All right, you did." He ran his hand over my hair.

"Thank you," I said, bowing my head. He was about to pull his hand away but I held it.

"Rematch?" he asked.

"No." My cheeks burned as if someone was barbecuing over them. "I just want to hold your hand."

"More points to Matty," he said. "I'll add in a bonus victory," he continued. "Remember how I told you I was going to tell you the story behind the Paradise playlist when you came over?"

"Absolutely."

He sucked in a breath. "What if I tell you now?"

"I'm all ears."

There was joy and relief in his eyes, like he had been waiting for someone to be worthy of this moment. "Something happened to me. And the way I coped with the situation for some reason was curating playlists. I spent hours looking up obscure and famous composers and carefully put their songs together so they told a story. 'Clair de Lune' was the first song I added to my very first playlist. Paradise. So those songs are pretty much a map of my emotions during that strange time. I curated about fifty playlists after, but honestly, none compare to Paradise."

I glanced at his phone in my hand. For a moment, I assumed the story Pedro shared was real. I imagined him locked up in his room, looking for songs while suffering in silence.

"What happened to you?" I chanced the question.

He blew out a puff of air. "One step at a time." His words were close to a whisper. "We just started our pinky war today."

My body trembled. Judging by the secrecy, one could only assume the story Pedro shared was true. Or some of it, at least. But I didn't want to push him. There was something else I wanted to do regardless of whatever truth he carried inside of him.

I kissed the top of his hand.

"What are you doing?" he asked.

"Starting another war."

"And what is this war called?" His grip around my hand grew tighter.

"Fear."

"What are you afraid of?" he asked.

"Of going one step at a time," I said. "Of going too slow. Not going at all. Or going too fast."

"We'll go at your pace," he said.

I held his hand for the rest of the drive. He'd do this thing where he'd open my hand with his fingers and he'd trail his nails over my palm. I had never felt this way before. It felt right and wrong and confusing and clear. But the big departure popped into my head as I felt his touch. Why spend time on this? This story wouldn't have a happy ending. I'd break his heart with my truth and he'd break my heart by saying goodbye.

But my desire to enjoy the moment was louder than anything else. I paid attention to his hand and how it moved. Then I looked at his face and the way he watched the road. "Clair de Lune" was on repeat the whole time. But at one point, the song turned into background noise.

He let my hand go when he parked in front of my house. Both cars were parked next to each other on the driveway. Mom and Dad. What would they think if they ever found out what I had done? All the lights in the house were off.

"Hope you enjoyed the night, Matty," James said with both of his hands on the steering wheel.

"You, too."

"Do we do this again soon?" he asked.

"That would be cool," I said. "And if you ever want to—"

My words were stolen with a kiss. And not the gentle kind. His hand grabbed the nape of my neck. I gripped his arm and tugged him closer. His lips moved. I followed. His breath brushed my face, throwing a party in my pants. This, this was how a first kiss should feel. Time ran fast and slow and somewhere in between. Then I lost track of time until he gently nibbled on my bottom lip and said, "Now I win."

I quickly opened the car door and walked to my house. I didn't know what to do. He slowly drove away once I got to the door. I didn't turn a single light on as I walked through the house. I knew it well enough to navigate the darkness. My mind was still in James's car and in the theater, and on his mouth, all at the same time.

I slowly walked up the stairs and went into my room. I

turned on the light and plopped on the bed. The ceiling was like a television replaying everything. I grabbed my phone after I replayed our kiss in my head about a hundred times. It was almost midnight. James was home by now.

Me: That was incredible.

I grabbed my headphones from my backpack and opened the link to the Paradise playlist he had sent me. I didn't get past "Clair de Lune." I let it play a few times while reminiscing on tonight, until I realized James had never replied to my text.

Me: You there?

I searched for the sketchpad under my bed. My conté pencil was tucked inside it. I opened it on the page with ten versions of James's eyes. I resumed working on one of them. I started a new one and by the time I finished it, James still hadn't replied.
Shit.

9
YING YANG

October 2011

"I think I'm going to be able to work again," Mom said with her coffee in one hand and a slice of French bread with butter on the other. In the middle of the table was a plate of cheesebread. She had made them from scratch this morning. They had been my favorite thing to eat since I was a kid. No matter how long I lived here, I'd never be able to depart from them. "There's this couple moving out of state," she continued. "And they have a cleaning schedule with a few houses. I'd be cleaning about five of them a day. Heavy work, but better than nothing. I guess going back to basics it is."

I struggled to stay present in the conversation. Laila looked interested. I was happy for Mom, but all I could think about was last night. James, the kiss, and his silence. My last message had finally gone through this morning, but he still hadn't replied.

"When do you start?" I asked, hoping she wouldn't notice how out of it I was.

"End of the month," she answered, tilting her head to the side. "Tudo bem, Mateus?"

Mom and her superpowers.

"All good, Mom."

"Had fun yesterday?"

"I did," I said. "The movie was terrible, though. Like, really bad."

"What's with Dad drinking again?" Laila asked out of the blue. "I was small, but I have memories. So, what's with the alcoholism?"

I was suddenly aware of my mother's every move on her chair. The disappointment on her face was too noticeable. For a moment, her eyes were a movie screen replaying all the drunk-Dad episodes we had all starred in.

"God, who knows?" Mom's finger circled the brim of her mug. "But I don't. I'm just glad I'm going back to work. Maybe that will help him—"

Help? Help?! The way she implied that he was the victim spurred me on. "He's a grown man," I said. "He knows what he's doing. He can't keep blaming the whole world for his mistakes. So, what, because you lost your job, he can now drink his life away? So, it's your fault?"

Mom usually tried to protect Dad's image whenever I spewed things like that. I expected her to finish what she was saying before; tell me that she felt sorry for my dad or something to that extent. Not today.

Laila and I shared a worried glance.

"Mom," Laila continued. "Are you okay?"

"Está tudo bem," Mom replied. "Now finish your breakfast so you can get ready. Isn't your friend picking you up to go to the mall this morning? Dad left fifty dollars."

Laila took one last bite from her bread, chugged down her coffee, grabbed three cheese-breads, and rushed upstairs.

"Mom," I said. "Aside from this whole we-are-leaving-America thing, are you okay?"

She measured her words in her head. The way she looked at nothing, but her eyes were filled with worry, denoted as much.

"Things will be all right, Mateus," she answered. "What do you have going on today?"

"Nothing big planned yet," I replied, pretending to believe her. "I might just stay in my room. Draw stuff."

Her arms folded over the table. "I thought drawing was going to be just a phase," she said. "Since you were a kid, you always preferred the company of your mind over everything and everyone. You became more social, but you still love it. It's your true passion."

"Why are you saying this?"

"Good things should not change," she said. "We should nurture them instead. Now, the things damaging us, those need to disappear."

"I'm going to go upstairs." Those were the only words I managed to get out. "Knock if you need me, Mom."

I locked my bedroom door, grabbed my sketchbook, and sat on my bed, only to have my plans defeated.

James: You know that park on Arlington and Gordon?
Me: Yes.
James: Can you meet me there in thirty?
Me: That fast, huh?
James: Can you?
Me: Sure.

All right, something was definitely off. I grabbed the first pair of jeans in my closet, threw on a beanie and a long-sleeve shirt, put on a jacket, and marched down the stairs.

"What happened to drawing?" Mom asked while washing the dishes.

"Meeting a friend at the park," I said. "I'll be back in a few."

"Want me to drive you? It's cold."

"No, thank you," I replied. The tension of being in the car

with an undocumented family member was something I wasn't willing to risk today of all days.

The park was about a twenty-minute walk from my place. I naturally walked faster than others. I had the habit of walking next to someone, but then I always ended up ahead of them. Thank God I had no company today, because I was sprinting. I didn't even bother with music.

The rusty swings and green slides were finally in view. He was there when I arrived, back against the crisscross metal fence separating the park from the sidewalk. He saw me from afar. There was a hint of a smile until a frown erased it.

"Hey," he said with a lazy wave.

"Hi," I said, heart racing. "Everything okay?"

"You walked all the way here?" He scratched the back of his head.

"I certainly didn't fly…"

"I could've picked you up if I knew—"

"It's fine," I said. "Came as fast as I could. You all right?"

He raised his shoulders and let out a breath between his teeth. "I need to… apologize."

"Apolo—what? For what?"

His thumb scraped his dimpled chin. He ran his hand across his hair, messing it up even more. "I feel…" He kicked his foot on the ground, burying the tip of his boots under the orange leaves. "I think I went too far yesterday. Couldn't stop thinking about it. I wasn't even sure if you were… I had a feeling… but…" He cracked every single knuckle on his hands. "And at the movies, I was really holding back. Knowing that our arms were touching was enough, but then you… and the kiss. But you never told me if you're—"

A shaky breath replaced his words when I grabbed his hand.

"Yes," I said, not giving a fuck if we were in a public place.

"Yes, I am." I let out this weird mixture of a chuckle, a snort, and a laugh. "Ha, it's the first time I'm saying it out loud. I'm glad you're the one who gets to hear it. It's better than having you pull away. You had me thinking all sorts of things. Your silence and the message not going through."

"I shut off my phone. I don't know. I was scared that I had done something out of line. Didn't I overstep? Maybe you weren't ready to come out or, I don't know, do what we did. You aren't even out, are you?"

For the first time in my life, I'd have to speak about an identity I never revealed to anyone. And to my surprise, I wasn't scared or hesitant. I was relieved.

"I won't lie," I said. "That's a part of me I hid for a long time. I still do. Maybe because I don't want to be so different. So many other things already make me different. When I was a kid, being gay meant that you were weak and less than other boys. And when I realized the possibility that I'd be bullied or just ignored, I decided to pretend to be someone I was not. But then you came along."

"You had to pretend to Fa, Diana, and Pedro as well?"

"I think so," I said. "I hide it well, though. I think I do. They've never brought it up. I know Fa and Diana would be excited, but then Pedro… He may be nothing like the other boys that called me all those things, but I don't know. It's weird to be something knowing that whatever you are can cost you the people you love the most."

"Those people that told you being gay makes you less of a man know nothing." He squeezed my hand. "Wouldn't you say it takes more strength to be your true self than to be what everybody expects you to be?"

"That's the problem," I said. "It does take more strength. And the load is a lot heavier. I've been different from everyone in so many ways already. I guess I wanted some part of me to be normal."

James scrunched his face. "That word is so boring." He let go of my hand and strolled toward one of the swings. I followed. "Normal is what people call the things that don't make them think. It's an excuse for people to stay where they are. Be normal. That's not normal. Normal. Fuck normal."

"Look at you making progress and cussing," I said.

He smiled and sat on the rubber seat.

"Maybe I don't want to make people think so much," I continued.

"That's not an option." He flailed his legs back and forth. "Your truth is. What others do with it, now that's on them."

He swung like a kid. It was comforting to watch him, the innocence suddenly displayed on his face.

"So this is how we're going to talk?" I asked. The creaking of the swing's chain sounded like a high-pitched meow. "We're going to swing as if we're five?"

"You could join me!" he shouted, soaring above my head.

"There's an empty one next to me."

"Aren't we too old for this?"

"Says who?" he yelled back. "Who set all these rules?"

I glanced around the park. It was pretty dead. And it wasn't like I'd remember anyone strolling by. They might remember seeing two teenagers swinging like a couple of preschoolers. And what if they did?

I caved in. Ass on the rubber seat; hand on the cold chains; legs swaying back and forth. I swung as high as he did. There was a cold chill in my stomach. Maybe from swinging. Or maybe because I had just sort of come out to James, the first person to ever hear me admit that I was as gay as a rainbow.

My lungs could suddenly take in a lot more oxygen. My

shoulders were light, and being here beside him didn't feel like a crime or something I had to hide.

To announce the end of our swinging adventure, James shot his body out of his seat when the swing was at its highest, jumping up and landing perfectly on his two feet. I tried to do the same and landed like a drunk ostrich.

"Why did you pick this place?" I sat on one of the benches under a tree. He sat next to me.

"This park means something to me." He rested his arms over the backrest of the bench. "My parents would bring me here when I was a kid. Life was simple back then. At least in my head. My priority was my Game Boy Advance and Pokémon FireRed and drawing heroes and villains and cars and trucks." He smirked. "This park always felt like a safe place. So it felt right to talk to you here. I didn't know what you were going to say."

"The last feeling is definitely mutual." His finger gently stroked the back of my shoulder. "I've always known in some way who I was." I buried my eyes in his. "And you were the first one that made me want to open it."

"Look," he squeezed my hand, "you let that part of you be public whenever you're ready. Just make sure you do it in your own terms and at your own time." I noticed tension in his words.

"Did something happen to you?"

He let out a long breath. "Mind if we talk about that some other day? This kind of feels perfect, and I don't want to spoil the mood."

The conversation shifted to more ordinary things. And the whole time, I thought about my uncertain future. My family was still set on leaving—or so they said. But apparently this time it was for real. What was the point of taking a risk with James? If we did, we would be sailing like the Titanic, doomed to strike an iceberg and sink.

He offered to drive me home. He had one hand on the steering wheel and the other laced with mine. This was strange, yet it felt right, like a prize I had worked so hard for.

I was glad for his tinted windows when I spotted Dad's car on the driveway, because I desperately wanted his lips on mine. I leaned in. It was my turn to steal one after all. The warmth of his breath brushed my face as our lips pressed hard. I followed his lead. He gently bit my bottom lip before I pulled away.

I didn't even remember walking to my front door. My heart kept on racing once I was inside. Mom sat at the kitchen table, surrounded by a whole bunch of grocery bags on the floor. But it was the three empty bottles of wine by the sink that held her sad eyes.

"Mom?" I quickly looked around the house.

"He's upstairs sleeping," she said with a shudder.

"Did something happen?" I asked, the brief silence between my question and her answer feeling like a century.

"He came home from work," she replied, avoiding my gaze. "He said these were a gift from his boss. I went to the grocery store and then came home to this. All three of them empty."

"Where's Laila?"

"Still at the mall."

"You okay?" I asked. "Need anything?"

"I'll be fine," she replied with a deadpan face.

I grabbed the three empty bottles and threw them in the trash can under the sink while Mom remained still.

My mind brought to light memories I had long buried. Dad screaming after coming home from the bar; Dad breaking a whole bunch of drinking glasses; Dad putting his hand on her.

I slowly marched up the stairs and locked my bedroom door.

I was six when the worst evening of my life happened. Mom was crying at an empty pantry, Laila was in her bedroom playing with her dolls, and I paced from the kitchen to Laila's bedroom, thinking of a thousand possibilities for how Dad was going to behave when he got home.

It was around one a.m. when the sound of breaking glass forced me to jump out of my bed. I didn't follow the shouting and the screaming. My sister's bedroom was my destination. She was awake, sitting on her bed with bulging eyes. I locked the door from the inside and told her to stay there until I came back.

Dad held Mom by the throat. He shouted slurs and one sentence. "Isso tudo é sua culpa." He stank of booze and sweat. The white linen shirt was unbuttoned down to his chest, revealing the flaming color of his skin. I begged him to stop. But he was too drunk. Eventually his knees buckled, and he plopped on a chair.

Mom grabbed me and Laila and ran out of the house. I knew where she was taking us. Grandma wouldn't mind hosting us so late. The entire time, I had one single thought in my head.

Why?

10

THE NEB EFFECT

October 2011

James was MIA from the bus this morning. His parents were in town, and dropping him off at school was their thing when they weren't traveling for work. He dreaded this. I dreaded this. I wanted to see him more than ever, especially after the park yesterday. And it was a Monday on academic week. Fuck, this day was going to drag.

The Forbidden Fortress chatted away over bagels, muffins, and chocolate milk. I nodded and smiled at everyone's comments, since my mind was extremely busy. I wished James was the only one taking up space in my brain this morning. That was definitely not the case. He and my dad competed for mental real estate. Mom sitting at that table. The empty bottles. My dad's alcoholic resurrection made me feel nervous and sometimes even afraid. I never knew what was going to happen.

I was afraid of a lot of things at the moment. Even though what happened with James was exciting, there was still fear in the back of my mind. The future was just a big question mark.

I wanted to tell the Forbidden Fortress everything, but they were so into their own conversation that it felt wrong to interrupt them. The bell finally rang and we went our separate ways.

The library was going to host my English class during first period. We had a book report due and my teacher, Mr. Redland, said that studying at different locations helped our brains retain information better. I didn't care if what he said was real or not. I liked change. The thing was that whenever the library was the designated spot for this change, Mr. Redland would leave us to fend for ourselves as he surfed the web on one of the public computers.

The smell of books and coffee welcomed me when I pulled the door open. Mrs. Crass was at her desk. Her hair was always held up by very eccentric hair pins. Today's were shaped like roses. She greeted me with waving fingers and pointed to the corner separated for my class.

The big windows of the library gave way for a view of the football field and the tree line. Staring at the red and orange leaves outside gave me a sense of peace.

There were three long wooden tables lined up on the far back wall. I grabbed my phone out of my pocket and headed to the last one, sitting on the chair by the window.

James: Awake or already asleep? I just got here. Wish we would've seen each other.

Me: Trying to stay awake is more like it. And same. I missed you this morning.

James: Algebra hasn't even started and I already want to fall asleep.

Me: Just don't drool all over your desk and you should be okay.

"Morning, Matt." The sound of Neb's morning voice set my phone off on a juggle between my hands. He pulled a chair in front of me.

"Hey… hey, Neb."

"Someone's on edge this morning," he said.

"I'm just sleepy." I set the phone on the table. "That's all."

"Long night?" he asked.

Neb was making small talk. That was a rare thing.

"My mind kept me awake," I said. "But all is good."

"I didn't sleep much either," he said. I noticed a hint of sadness on his face.

"You okay?"

We both knew how awkward it was for me to ask him if he was okay. We hadn't had an actual conversation since freshman year. He looked surprised-slash-confused.

"I think so," he said. "Struggles help you become a better person, right?"

"I guess," I said.

"We don't ask for crap, but we have to deal with it," he said. "Sometimes I wish I could just forget them…"

His voice trailed off when my phone's screen lit up. A text from James.

Is it crazy that I miss swinging with you? We need a second swing date.

I smiled when I read the message.

Me: Name the date and time!

"Who was that?" he asked.

"Just James." I regretted my answer as soon as I heard the words come out of my mouth.

"You like trouble? Is that it?" The sadness on his face made way for anger.

"What do you mean?"

Air puffed out of his mouth as his eyes rolled around. "I told you to be careful. You're still talking to him. This can mess things up for many people. Trust me, James is not as innocent as he seems."

"I like giving people a chance, Neb," I said. "You know, sometimes having good manners pays off. You make friends and stuff. And that's how you get people to listen to you."

Was he about to lecture me this early in the morning? I was relieved when he turned his chair around, but he quickly faced me again. "There's a lot you don't know about that kid, Matt. Keep your distance."

Was I wearing a neon sign that said, "Looking for Advice?" Maybe people at his church enjoyed this crap. I didn't fuck with it one bit.

"Listen, I get that you're having a tough day. We all have those sometimes. But why do you keep saying these things about James? Ever considered talking to him if he bothers you so much?"

"People at my church know exactly why he left that school. The story isn't pretty. He's no good company to keep. What he did with—"

"Shut the fuck up," I said. "You need to stop. This isn't your church. You don't get to talk shit like that. Jesus, you sound like a fucking preacher sometimes. And not the kind that tells you God will give you money, but the kind that tells people they are always going to hell. You don't get to force me to tell you stuff like you forced that kid at your church that day."

"Force him? I gave him strength to confess. The Bible tells us to confess our sins in front of—"

"Do you hear yourself when you talk?" My blood was boiling. "How did it go again? 'Confess your sins in public so you can be strong.' And then you forced this kid to come out in front of a hundred people. Hearing him talk about how disgusted he felt with himself made me want to vomit. And then you finished your message by telling people that your church could help boys and girls 'struggling' with homosexuality." Neb nodded his head the entire time as if he knew better than me. "You said you had the cure to set them straight," I continued. "You really think I'm going to listen—or trust you—after all that crap?"

He remained unbothered, behaving like my words were just random echoes. "There's a lot you—"

"How's any of this your business, Nebu-fucking-chadnezzar?"

He hated when people called him by his first full name. I added a nice little "fuck" to make a point.

"You have no idea where this guy has been," Neb said with an edge. "You met him, what, last month? You said you're willing to give people a chance. Then listen to me. Have coffee with me and I'll explain."

What gave Neb guts to pull shit like this today?

"Wait, wait, you're inviting me out for coffee?"

"That's how serious this situation is," he said.

"So, hold on. Let me get this straight. On his first day, you're all chatty with him and he even ends up sitting at your table. Then as soon as I invite him over to mine, you start acting as if he's your business. And now you're inviting me for coffee?"

"You should've never invited him to your corner," he said. "Things would've been fixed by now if he'd stayed with me."

I waved a finger in the air. "Why don't you turn around—"

"Dad heard it from someone at church about James," he continued as if I was interested in what he had to say. "The plus side of being a pastor's kid."

I laid my hands on my lap as they curled into fists. "Where's this coming from? This whole James lecture?"

"I didn't want to tell you," he said. "I know you were with him yesterday. So does my dad. People at the park saw you swinging."

"And?"

"You don't think you two are getting way too close?" he asked.

"Shut the fuck up!" I snapped as the other students settled down, suddenly noticing how loud I was. I glanced at Mr. Redland. He was getting coffee in the corner, too busy to notice. "What, you have people spying on us? Is that it?"

"Be careful, Matt," he said, using the tip of his foot to turn his chair around.

Mr. Red got everyone to settle down and start writing their reports. I quietly worked on mine, wishing headphones were allowed so I could sink into oblivion and forget Neb was in front of me. He sneered over his shoulder a few times.

I tried to recollect the few faces of the people at the park yesterday. I didn't remember seeing anyone I recognized.

My phone vibrated.

A text message from Neb.

He was literally in front of me.

What.

The.

Fuck.

A screenshot of a text message.

Brian: This is how he talked to me all the time. He seduced me, dude. He really did. I didn't mean for it to happen.

Under the message were a few more screenshots.

James: Hey, stud. Meet me in the locker room?
James: You liked that little trick?
James: You want me to go harder next time?

I wanted to throw my phone at Neb's head. He wasn't that far from me after all. Mr. Redland was busy on a computer. I was safe to reply.

Me: Why did you send me these?
Neb: In case he never brings up Brian. I don't know how close you two are. I'm doing the right thing. You need to know the truth.

His text got no reply from me. I tried to stay focused on my report while counting down the seconds for the bell to ring. Neb didn't text again but kept looking over his shoulder. I ignored him.

The bell. Finally. He strolled out of the class as I tucked my things inside my backpack.

Neb: Ask him about this.

Another screenshot.

James: I see how wrong I was. I need to be straight. I want to stick it out.

I jetted out of that class, rushing my pace more than usual so I could catch up with Neb.

"What the fuck do you think you're doing?" The sleeve of his jacket served as a handle for me to pull him to a halt.

"Hey, hey, Matt. We're going to end up at the principal's office like this."

I hated how condescending this kid was. He walked and talked as if the entire world belonged to him.

"What are you doing, Neb? You think sending messages like this is the right thing to do? Is that how fucked up you are in your head?"

"Listen." His bushy eyebrows arched up. "You should be thanking me, buddy. Ask James about Brian. He is hiding something important."

"Don't be a sore loser." I tightened my grasp. "Not everyone wants to be around you and your holier-than-thou attitude. You have a problem with James hanging out with me? Mad he ditched your table for mine? Jealous? Are you sure you aren't in the closet?"

He jerked his arm free. "The gays are like a virus. You get one of them around you and then you have a whole bunch of people infected. First Fa and Diana. Then James comes in. Who knows what'll happen next?"

I wanted to punch someone in the face for the first time in my life.

"And how's that your business?" I asked.

"James is my business." He stabbed a finger to my shoulder. "See you in biology."

He paraded in the middle of the ocean of students like he owned them. My hands trembled. In my head, I did punch him. But then *he* appeared from the crowd. James. My heart turned into a malfunctioning metronome when I saw him. Neb's eyes followed him. James didn't look at Neb as he walked past him. Neb halted, making sure I saw him staring.

"Surprise," James said with a quick shrug, one hand on the strap of his backpack, the other in his pocket.

"A very nice surprise," I said as Neb held up a finger in the air, waving it as a sign that talking to James was forbidden.

"What are you staring at?" James followed my gaze.

Neb waved and went on his way.

"Such a mood-killer," James said. "That kid hovers too much."

"Yeah." I cleared my throat.

"You all right?" he asked. "You're flushed."

"You bring it out of me," I said. If only that were the case. It was probably the aftermath of the Neb-effect. "To what do I owe this surprise?"

He tucked his hands in his pockets. His smile was one of the most beautiful things in the world, but the most beautiful was south of it. The dimple. I couldn't stop staring. But even the dimple wasn't enough to calm me down. "Just thought I could manage being a few seconds late so I could see you," he said.

"Your class is on the other side," I said, struggling to hide my rage from my voice. "You'll be more than a few seconds late."

His teeth grazing his bottom lip. "Are you sure you're okay? Was it Neb?"

I hated Neb even more. His accusations whirled in my head. How could I ask James about those texts? Maybe my fear wasn't so much asking. It was coming to terms with a truth that would make me look at him differently. "I'm all right. Just very happy to see you."

"I couldn't wait until the bus," he said. "I keep thinking about yesterday. You're making me feel all sorts of things, Matty."

"So are you." *Now* he was the culprit behind my burning cheeks. "What do you have next?"

"English," he replied, excited. "You?"

"Biology. With Neb. Again." I cringed. "Wish me luck?"

He leaned in for a hug but squeezed in a quick peck on my cheek without anyone noticing. "See you later, you."

"See you later, you…"

I headed to biology. The other students were still settling in when I arrived. Neb watched me like I was a criminal who had just broken out of jail. He sat on the opposite end of the class.

I thought about deleting the texts. But then I thought that I might need them at some point. I hated this. Who was this Brian? Did he have anything to do with the story Pedro heard about James?

Something *had* happened. James *had* mentioned it. But rumors are watered-down versions of the truth. I wasn't going to force the truth out of James.

Class started, and Neb's attention was finally on something other than my face. I pretended to listen to Mrs. Kram's explanation of cellular chemistry.

My phone vibrated. I waited until Mrs. Kram had her back to the class to see what the notification was.

A text from Neb.

Brian: Thank you for helping me find the truth, Neb. I owe you big.

11
TRUTH

October 2011

It was a rare event. One of those things that scientists claimed happened once in a thousand years. My family and I were going out to dinner on a Tuesday night.

Dad drove the three of us to the restaurant in his van. It was uncomfortable to watch him and Mom struggle to find topics of conversation. Laila and I exchanged a few eyerolls and smirks while listening to their awkwardness. I wondered at what point after they met, they thought they were right for each other.

Mom had probably orchestrated this event, hoping to bring us closer to reconnect or whatever she named her secret family mission in her head. I also knew Dad too well. There were one thousand excuses as to why we shouldn't be doing this. From putting us all at risk of being pulled over to spending money when we had food at the house, he was skilled at dumping a bucket of water over high expectations. Maybe he had agreed to this because of the drinking. Maybe he was going to apologize. Maybe he was going to bring up the subject and make it super awkward and promise he'd stop.

Since we moved here, Dad always claimed that we shouldn't be spending so much on traveling and stuff. We had to save.

Save. Save. Save. Well, we were still saving. It was the whole reason we hadn't left yet.

Gossip and rumors spread like wildfire when you lived in a small town like Fogo Dourado. Mom had told one of her friends about the debt. Two days later and the entire town knew.

Maybe that's why he was obsessed with saving every single dime. He wanted to go back to redeem his pride and show everyone else that he had turned things around. I could relate to that part of him.

We finally arrived at Sabor Mineiro, the Brazilian restaurant. After we grabbed our table, someone came over to take our drink order. We headed to the buffet station, stuffed our plates, and returned to our seats to a basket of pão de queijo.

"This is nice, huh?" Mom said after we had our drinks.

"Very," Laila said, popping her soda can and stuffing two cheese-breads in her mouth.

"The food isn't going to run away, Laila," I said.

"I'm just hungry," she said.

"What's the special occasion?" I snagged a cheesy ball before Laila vacuumed up the rest of them.

"Us being together?" Mom's tone implied that I had just asked the obvious. "It's been a while since we've done this. I thought we could all use a night out."

"We have *never* done this." Laila frowned. "That's why it's so awkward."

"That's not true," Dad said, cutting the picanha on his plate. "We went to Chuck E. Cheese for your birthday, remember?"

"I was eight, Dad," Laila said. "That's, like, an eternity ago."

What did Dad have to gain by always acting so distant? I had no memory of him ever showing any interest in my life or Laila's. Sometimes I wondered if he regretted the decision to have a family.

"The food here is expensive," Dad said with his mouth full. "Então aproveitem."

"Maybe we're out here to celebrate my new job," Mom suggested. "It's not all about bad things."

Mom commented on the food and how great the steak was and how the salad dressing wasn't too salty. Dad agreed with everything she said, his mind off somewhere else. But there was more than just casual conversation in store tonight. I could feel it. They both had something to share but were reluctant to do so.

There were a few TVs scattered across the restaurant. One was right in front of us. Some of them were tuned to Brazilian channels, but ours was on CNN. Thankfully they had subtitles, since everybody talked louder than the TV.

Latinos were planning on protesting Obama's decision to support a program designed to go after undocumented people with a criminal record. They were afraid the program wanted to use their information to deport all of them. Feds raved about the program and said that it would let them catch criminals who would've otherwise slipped through the cracks. A few of the tables ignored the broadcast. Others changed their conversation to match the tone of the subject.

"See?" Dad pointed his fork at the TV. "This is why I'm tired of this place. All this immigration talk. This whole back-and-forth. This place makes people like us look so small. We're second-class citizens here. We have no rights."

"Claudio," Mom said. "Perhaps we should show more gratitude to this place. You learned English."

"Yeah, because my kids forgot their language." He shrugged.

"You also paid off your debt." I grabbed a cheese-bread. "You couldn't have done that back home." I popped it in my mouth. Laila ate her food without saying a word.

I saw remorse in his eyes. I expected him to erupt, to raise his voice and cause a scene. He folded his hands on the table and started, "Eu falhei. I did. I want to make things better, but I can't do that here. *We* can't do that here." He stared into the distance. "I wish I had made better decisions, but I can't go back in the past."

Silence lingered, longer than I expected.

"Your father and I did the math," Mom said. "We're pretty good. We can go back and even enjoy some time off before opening the store again." I didn't miss the trembling in her voice when she said the last two words.

"June," Dad said. "We're set on leaving in June. You kids will be done with school. I am already in talks to buy a place for the store. Think of this as a clean slate."

"We?" I folded my arms. "*We* are set on leaving?"

My parents were confused.

"You said 'we,' right?" I insisted.

"Sim," Dad said.

When they told me we were moving to America, I never protested, because I didn't care that much about the life I was leaving behind. Sure, I'd miss my grandma and uncles and aunts, and, like, two friends, but none of them could live my life for me. Leaving this time meant leaving my entire life behind. The Forbidden Fortress. Joseph. Visual arts. James. All these things were far from perfect, but they were all I had.

"Funny." I turned to Laila. "You remember them asking your opinion about this whole thing, sister?"

"No," she said, surprised.

"Me neither," I said. "Did I miss the parent-son talk we never had?"

"Rapaz." Dad's face was red. "You're sixteen."

"And because I'm a teenager, I don't have an opinion? I

definitely have one about all your drinking and your money issues. And we're going back to the place that started it all."

Laila tried to hide the smirk on her face. Mom looked shocked.

"I don't care about your opinion, Mateus Franco," Dad said. "I'm your father and you will show some respect."

"And I'm the son." I pointed at Laila. "And she's the daughter. The fact I stayed quiet all this time is your sign of respect. But hey, you decided to drag us across an ocean and now you're dragging us back. I'm pretty sure your drinking friends in Fogo Dourado will be happy to see you again."

I dragged my chair from under the table and jumped to my feet, ready to go wait for them in the car.

"You sit down!" Mom said. "Senta agora, Mateus."

A few people in the restaurant tried to hide their curiosity and failed miserably. I did as she asked. We tried to eat as if nothing had happened. I was tired of being tossed around in this decision as if my opinion didn't matter or as if I didn't have anything to lose.

"Mistakes were made." Mom eventually broke the uncomfortable silence. "Coming to America was us trying to start fixing them. Filhos, I have to live with the fear that our entire lives could be uprooted every single day. And we no longer need that. If something happens to your Dad and me while we're here…" She couldn't finish the sentence. "Just try to see things from our end."

"I feel like a tennis ball," Laila said. "And you're throwing me around like this is a game. You want to leave? Then let's leave. Just don't keep going back on your word, because then I don't know what to think. Like, do I make new friends? Do I plan on which high school I'm going to go to? Do I just stop in time and wait for this big day to get here? Should I start watching Brazilian novelas so I can learn Portuguese?"

"I'll make it really simple," Dad said. "June. We're going back. Now plan for it."

*

"How can it only be Wednesday?" Fa slouched over a pile of books besides her empty coffee mug. The neon "open" sign of the Crusty Pie cast a blueish hue on her face. "And these are not even novels. Just random books that I have to use for research. Ugh, ever heard of the internet? But no, I have to use the books Ms. Romena told us to use. I swear, it's because of people like her that our generation is repressed. What happened to embracing the future?"

"Ever heard of SparkNotes?" Pedro asked. "You can find a summary of all these books there."

"I don't cheat, sweetheart." She blew him a kiss. "I excel."

"I wish we had a class on academic week that taught us how to deal with the bullshit of the world," Diana added. "We need to be ready to live life, after all. How's me adding letters and numbers supposed to help me in the future?"

My book was on the table, a fictional biography I had to read for English about a pianist born with half a heart. I looked at the creases on the spine of the book, observing the slight bends on the pages that had been dog-eared by past readers. Being around the Forbidden Fortress at the Crusty Pie allowed me to forget—even if briefly—how confusing last night had been.

"Matt!" Pedro punched my shoulder.

My hands slammed the side of the table. "Can you not do that when you don't get attention?" I grabbed the book and beat it on his arm. "Holy shit, Pedro."

"I just asked if you want to go to the movies this weekend," he said, defeated. "Jeez, so violent."

"And you couldn't wait for an answer?" My arm throbbed. "Jesus."

"He did ask you three times," Diana mentioned.

"You okay, Matt?" Fa drilled her gaze into mine. God, I hated when she did that. Suddenly she was a magical creature with the ability to read people's deepest thoughts.

"Everything is fine," I said.

"Just spill it." Diana frowned.

"It's us, dude," Pedro said. "We know something is off. You can tell us."

I started to miss them even though they were literally next to me. I missed the Crusty Pie, the coffee, and the food and everything else.

"I'm about to set off a time bomb." The heels of my feet rested on the edge of my seat as I wrapped my arms around my legs. "We only have eight more months together."

"Dude, you breaking up with us?" Pedro blurted out but quickly picked up on what I meant. "Oh, you mean…"

"They set *another* date for doomsday?" Diana asked.

"A month, actually," I revealed. "June." I turned to Pedro. "For those of us who aren't that good at math," I said snidely.

"Not a time for jokes," he said. "But I *am* sorry I hit you."

"They're for real this time, I think." I forced a smile. "I'm kind of relieved, you know. Mad and scared but also relieved."

"Relieved?" Fa sneered. "Holy shit, Matt. Relieved to be leaving? Relieved that the Forbidden Fortress will end? You're relieved your entire life will be taken from you like that?"

"A life built on sand, Fa. At least I won't live in uncertainty every fucking day. At least now I know what to expect. I hate playing this let's-stay-then-let's-leave-then-let's-stay game. I'm so done. I feel as if I'm sick and I finally found standing still is the right treatment."

"Think about this," she said with a fist on the table. "What happens when you go back? Do you have this beautiful plan of what life will look like after you get there? I mean, you never really talked in detail about your life back then, but from the little I know, it wasn't the greatest thing in the world. You lost the store and all your money…"

I prickled at the spine of the book in my hand as if the old cover could answer her question.

"Exactly," she said.

"What do you want me to do?" I shrugged. "What can I do? It's not like they're giving me and my sister a choice. After I left the restaurant yesterday, I kept thinking about this thing I watched on the news when we were at dinner."

"What thing?" Diana asked.

"They were talking about Latinos and a plan to protest all these immigration issues," I said. "And for a moment I was like, 'Damn, I'd be down to join a protest and fight.' But what would that solve? At least in our case? Kids like us? Dad fucked up many times, but he's right about one thing. Leaving also means going back to a life where I don't have to keep searching Google for immigration fixes. I don't have to worry about any of that crap."

"You'll just have new shit to worry about," Diana said.

We were all quiet. She never cussed. Ever.

"Okay, potty mouth," Pedro said.

"There's no other word to use." Diana shrugged.

"Matt, you were six when you moved here," Pedro said. "Man, I can't even think…"

"You think I can?" I said. "Jesus, they took us to that expensive Brazilian restaurant on Route Nine just to break the news. 'Oh, here's the best food in the world. By the way, your entire world is about to collapse.' And Dad has been drinking again. I thought we were going out so he could apologize or, I don't know, give us a whole speech on how he'll try to do better or whatever."

"Well, people drink," Pedro said.

"No, no." I held up a finger. "Dad inhales an entire case of beer almost every day now. Ever since Mom lost her job. But she found one already. I don't get it."

"You can live with me and my dad," Pedro suggested.

"With you?" I chuckled. "Come on, Pedro. Your dad likes me and I like him a lot. But living with you guys, I could never do that."

"Why not?" he insisted. "We're going to be juniors next year. If you and I get a job in visual arts, we can work full time during shop week and part time on academic. School rules, remember? We can even find a place to live after we graduate."

"We have no papers, Pedro," I said. "How are we going to find jobs in visual arts? Know any agencies hiring illegals?"

"We'll figure it out," Pedro said. "We'll take it one step at a time. But if it comes to it and your family does end up jumping ship next summer, you can live with me."

"I don't know..."

"Stop being so stubborn." Diana pinched my arm. "Listen to him. God, Matt, stop being so uptight about this."

"Uptight?" I repeated. "I would have to leave my family—"

"We'll all have to do that at some point," Fa said. "There's nothing wrong with you being the first."

I slouched back on my chair, my feet hanging. I looked at the awkward spinning fan on the ceiling. "Whatever decision I make will fucking hurt."

"Just make sure the *pain* you feel is the consequence of your decision," Fa said.

"You should get *that* on a sweater," I said.

12

JAMIE

October 2011

Friday. Finally.

I went straight to my locker and tucked the extra backpack inside before heading to the cafeteria for breakfast. I didn't want the Forbidden Fortress conducting a Q&A—especially after the past couple of days. James had invited me for a sleepover tonight. After my week, I'd gladly welcome any distraction from all the bullshit. And maybe he'd say something that would confirm or deny those messages Neb had sent me.

Thankfully, none of the members of the Forbidden Fortress let anything slip during breakfast. We were good at keeping each other's secrets. I acted as if everything was normal. Well, my normal, at least. James revealed this trick with his tongue where he could fold it in the shape of an "S"; Fa said that *Zodiac Weekly* predicted a great week for Aquarius; Diana suggested we go to Salem for Halloween; and Pedro went on and on about this new anime series where the hero could turn into an amoeba.

And that was the most exciting part of my day. Academic week sucked. Period. I counted down the minutes, seconds, and milliseconds for the last bell to ring—especially today, since James's house was my destination after school. Neb kept his distance. He stared here and there. We hadn't spoken since the screenshots. Not that I cared, honestly.

James and I finally reunited on the bus after my sluggish day.

"So what'd you tell your parents?" James asked as the bus drove out of the school's lot, his hands over the backpack on his lap.

"About?" I grabbed a pack of gum from my pocket.

"Tonight?" His right eyebrow arched up. "You told them you were sleeping at Pedro's or Fatima's?"

"My parents may be many things—" I pulled out a piece of gum and handed it to him, "—but they trust me. I told them I was sleeping at your place. No need to lie."

"Oh?" He unwrapped the gum and tossed it in his mouth. "But how did you talk about me? Your friend James? Your acquaintance? Sir James?"

"Sir James," I said with an obvious shrug. "Good enough?"

"Absolutely," he replied.

I wondered if this bothered him. The secrecy. I thought about asking him on the ride, but instead, we heavily debated on the possibility of Jurassic Park ever happening for real. We settled on a "maybe" shortly before the bus pulled up to his stop, which until then had been uncharted territory for me.

He lived in the north side of town, where big homes had been built on top of carefully manicured hills. His house blended right in. Two tall columns were next to the brown door set in a wall of stone bricks. The windows were as tall as I was. The Halloween-Christmas décor in the front yard was cinematic. Jack Skellington and Sally held hands. They were surrounded by Christmas trees covered in spiderwebs and lights.

"I call this smart decorating," he said, unlocking the door. "Half Christmas, half Halloween. After pumpkin season, we just get rid of the demons and leave up all the pagan Christmas stuff."

"You guys definitely take decorating very seriously," I observed.

"Well, I'm the one who gets to enjoy most of it," he revealed. "They're never home, especially around Christmas. They have all these engagements and conferences…"

Dark wood floors and a crystal chandelier greeted me after he took me inside. The house was spotless—the kind of clean that made it seem like no one lived there. It was decorated in tones of brown and white, making everything look super expensive.

"Guest bathroom." He pointed at the door to my left. "Kitchen is right there." He clapped his hands as I followed. "But the best part is the living room."

He wasn't kidding. They had an LED-based flat screen TV that probably cost as much as my mom's car. There was also a home theater system and one of those L-shaped leather couches where every seat reclined. A PS3 sat snugly between the TV and a sculpture depicting Jesus carrying the cross.

"And we have this all to ourselves?" I asked.

"Of course not. Don't dismiss the ghost in the basement like that." He cackled and cleared the hair off his face. "Let's go upstairs."

"How long are your parents gone this time?" I followed him up.

"Two weeks," he replied. "Story of my life. I'm the angsty teenager who spends most of his time solo."

"You must enjoy having this entire place to yourself," I said.

He halted halfway up. "I like having you around better."

"I know." I winked. "I'm great company."

"Teach me how to do that," he said.

"You're a lost cause when it comes to the art of winking, sir," I said.

We went into his room. It was neat enough. James had his own bathroom. The bed was made, but the sheets were slightly crumpled and wrinkly. The window by the bed had a view of the fall vegetation in his backyard. There was a bookshelf next to the television. I scanned the spines of the books on display. He was a fan of classics. He also had an impressive vinyl collection. I must've been a celebrity to him as I wandered around. He never took his eyes off me.

"No TV up here?" I asked.

"Not in my room," he said. "I'd rather use the living room for gaming and stuff. Which brings me to something you might find really cool. There's this game I bought. You have to build your empire with someone. You want to play it?"

"Open world?" I asked.

"Oh, yeah," he replied. "We can wage war on a whole bunch of people." He took off his jacket and tossed it on his bed.

"Then fuck yeah!" I dropped my backpack on the floor and repeated his gesture. "I'm down to pour all my anger and frustration on virtual strangers."

We rushed downstairs to the fully equipped living room. He turned on the PS3 and sat next to me, legs folded on the couch, eyes on the screen. The intro screen popped up, displaying a half-naked Zeus and an even more naked Athena. He looked like a kid in a candy store while talking about how the graphics were amazing and how we could choose any historical society to play.

He wanted me to choose one, but I noticed how his eyes lit up when the little golden box highlighted the Romans. We had to find ways to build our city, invite people to live in it, collect taxes, and whatnot.

I didn't have the heart to tell him that I thought the game was all right. That was it. Graphics were decent. I noticed how invested he was in building and fixing and destroying. He guided me during missions but would give me space to also make a few decisions. After a while, we had a town with temples, buildings, and citizens. We also had growling stomachs.

We ordered a pizza without pausing the game and played until our attack on a village was interrupted by the delivery guy. James answered the door and stopped by the kitchen to grab some napkins before returning to the living room.

"Your parents know about me?" I asked after we had turned the center coffee table into a pizza station.

"They do," he said with the flicker of a smile.

"And who am I to them?" I asked.

"Someone very special to me." He grabbed a slice, his smile untainted.

"So they know about you?" I asked.

"They do." He nibbled on the tip of the pizza. "Ah, it's hot."

"Does it bother you that mine don't?" I asked. "They don't know about you or about me…"

"No," he replied. "It would bother me if they knew about you or me without you wanting them to know. You tell them whenever you're ready. I wish I had been given that chance."

"Oh?"

"Let's just say my truth was exposed rather than shared," he said. "Definitely not the way I wanted it."

"You weren't the one to tell them?"

"I wish." Other people beat me to the punch. But hey, at least my parents heard about you from me first. They heard about other things from… other people."

"Was there really that much to share about me?"

"Absolutely," he answered. "But I simply told them I had met someone incredible. That's all."

My cheeks burned. He definitely noticed. He set his slice of pizza back on the box and dragged himself closer. "You're like this mysterious treasure that I want to find again and again." He enjoyed doing this to me. "I don't know. When I saw you the first time I walked in class, I knew I wanted you around. And we had never even talked to each other."

"All right, Mr. Treasure Hunter." I held up two fingers, waving them between us. "What are we now?"

"What are you ready for us to be?" he asked.

I set my pizza back on the box and leaned closer, our faces so close, I felt his breath on my cheeks. "Together."

"I want to go at your pace, Matty," he said, his lips grazing mine. "My chance to tell the truth about me was stolen." He pecked me on the lips. "I won't do that to you. Whenever you're ready to tell the Forbidden Fortress and anyone else, I'll be ready with you. And I would love to keep kissing you." He slid away with a smile. "But I'm starving."

"Is it okay if I ask you about your truth stealer?" I asked as he reached for his slice of pizza.

He took a bite and remained quiet.

"Did I earn the right to learn that secret yet?" I asked.

"He was the reason I switched schools." His gaze shifted to the ground. "We got caught kissing in the gym's locker room. Lucky me that the boys who spotted us disliked me already and were a part of his church crew or whatever. They snapped a picture of me kissing him and emailed it to my parents using an anonymous email address. The same was done to him."

"How did you find out who it was?" I asked.

"Those church boys told me." He bit his lips. "According to them, they did it so I could be saved. I needed to learn a lesson or whatever. I needed a taste of the pain of hell."

Suddenly, I didn't know if I was in hell, because every bone in my body burned in anger.

"I need to have the 'gay prayed away' and be confronted for my sin. The picture got out there and the entire school found out. It was the most embarrassing thing that ever happened to me. But it didn't stop there. They also leaked messages I shared with this other guy. Intimate things…"

I wanted to ask him about his parents' reaction. I wanted to tell him that Neb had sent me those screenshots, but his face was already too sad. He never mentioned the name Brian. Now I really wondered if those messages were authentic.

We played until another kingdom's army snuck up and destroyed everything we built. The destruction was so bad, we gave up on restarting the mission and decided to return to the game in the morning.

"Those pricks," James said once we walked inside his room. "Fuck, after all that time we spent." He opened one of the drawers on his dresser and grabbed a lighter.

"It happens," I said as he lit the candle by his bed. "I'm sad they attacked that temple. That statue of Athena looked pretty great at the entrance."

"They only did that for the coins." He removed his shirt. I wasn't ready for the chest and slightly visible abs. I had fantasized about them—jerked off a few times. I wished he had given me a heads up so I could've prepared myself. He unbuckled his belt and took off his pants, revealing his thick thighs. "Let me grab you a towel," he said, unaware of the rising wood in my pants.

The red underwear with polka dots held my eyes hostage until he walked out of the room. Then the buckled dots from his bulging silhouette in front grabbed my attention as he returned with a gray towel around his neck and a black one in his hand. I leaned forward and put my elbows on my knees as the party downstairs became too noticeable. He tossed the gray towel on the bed next to me and continued on to the bathroom.

"You want to shower first by any chance?" he said. I quickly followed the soft trail of hair under his belly button.

"You can go first, Jamie," I said.

"Jamie?" He frowned.

"You call me Matty. Only fair."

He turned around with a smile and took off his underwear. What the fuck was breathing? His ass was round and smooth. Fuck the dimpled chin and all its glory. I wanted those cheeks.

The water started running, but the bathroom door was still open. I fell back on the bed, searching the ceiling for a clue about what to do next. "Clair de Lune" joined the trickling water. Of course he had a speaker in the shower. He did say he was the type to grab a shampoo bottle and throw a concert in the bathroom.

I hesitated so much in my life because I couldn't do much. I couldn't drive without a sense of danger. I couldn't plan for the future without thinking that the future I wanted now might never happen. But being here with James, in this moment, this was something I had decided for myself. And what was to happen next was also up to me.

I threw my legs in the air, jumped on my feet, and took off my clothes. I wrapped the towel around my waist and followed the rising steam.

He scrubbed his fingers through his soapy hair. I took in a breath and approached the glass shower door.

He glanced over his shoulders and smiled as I opened the door.

"I want them to know," I said, lying naked next to him on the bed.

"Them who?" he asked, twirling my damp hair between his fingers.

"The Forbidden Fortress," I replied.

"That's all it took?" His raised his eyebrows. "Damn, Matty."

"That was my first time… with a guy… with everything," I revealed. "And honestly, something that good shouldn't be kept a secret, right? I don't want us to be a secret. I've kept so much of my life hidden. If we're going to start something, then I want them to know."

"When did you start keeping yourself a secret?" he asked.

"When I was a kid, the boys in school called me names because I was artsy," I started. "I liked books and drawing more than soccer games. They brought *Playboy*s to school one time. They all hid in the bathroom to look at them. I didn't last five seconds."

"Sorry," he said.

"They related anything I liked to being gay, which would've been okay if being gay to them didn't mean your worth was less than everyone else. And then you pretend. You have different faces for different moments."

"But then you get tired of creating these faces," he said. "You just want to have one. Your own."

"Until now, I thought I was sparing people," I continued. "Saving them the burden of having a gay guy around. But then it hit me. What about me? Don't I deserve to be spared of their expectations?"

"What's your final conclusion?" He laid his head on my chest.

"That I deserve to breathe," I whispered into his hair. "And not think that every part of me is too much for people to handle."

"Something I learned," he said. "We shouldn't lie. We should live out our truth. How people handle that truth reflects who they are. Not who we are."

"Can we do this by steps?" I asked. "First the Forbidden Fortress. My parents after."

"Sure," he agreed. "I have to ask, though. Since we're planning all these steps, we first have to make things official between us, no?"

I sucked in the air through my teeth and lay on top of him, pinning him down.

"What? Holding me hostage now?" he asked with a chuckle. "Afraid I'm going to run away?"

"Just being safe," I said. "Jamie, you want to be my boyfriend?"

"Since the first time I saw you."

13

THE CAFFEINATED TRUTH

October 2011

I texted the Forbidden Fortress as soon as we were up the next morning. We all agreed to meet at the Crusty Pie for brunch.

We hopped in the Nissan, him being the driver. We held hands the entire time. There was music playing, but I wasn't really listening. I was thinking about the best way to tell them.

Fa and Diana were going to be psyched. I hoped Pedro would be okay and wouldn't be weirded out. He never acted like those straight boys who treated the gays like a virus, but one could never know. I hoped he wouldn't give up on the idea of us living together if I stayed.

If.

The big "if" in my life.

Now *there* was something I hadn't considered. I'll blame my brief amnesia on the sight of James's perfect ass. I was getting really close when I should've been pushing away. Not because of his secrets, but my illegal ones.

I wanted to do this, be with him. But at what cost? I'd be a selfish little brat if I didn't weigh out the consequences. On one side of the scale was my forced departure and on the other my chance at romance. "Hey," I said, my hands sweaty. "There's something I have to tell you first before we tell them."

"Are you breaking up with me already?" he said dryly, keeping his eyes on the road. "What's up?"

The words traveled to my lips. My heart rushed as I geared up to finally spill the other half of my truth. As selfish as it was, I just couldn't reveal two identities in less than twenty-four hours. "I... um... own a whole bunch of dinosaur toys. I brought them with me when I moved to the States."

His brows were a warped bridge. "And why are you telling me this now?" he asked, confused.

"Just making sure you're prepared for the baggage," I said.

"I can live with that." He kissed the top of my hand. "My little Dr. Grant."

Dr. Grant. The paleontologist from the *Jurassic Park* movies. Sounded appropriate. Because, just like him, I was taking a walk through a very dangerous park.

James and I were the first ones to arrive. I was so ready to spill my guts that I forgot one tiny detail. Gabri-fucking-ella. Today was Saturday. She always worked Saturday mornings. Her big smile greeted me when I walked in. The smile turned into a frown when she eyed James.

"Morning, Gabriella." I walked up to the counter with a shrug.

"Hey, Matt," she said. "New friend?"

"Morning," James said with a look that hinted he had picked up on the awkwardness. "James."

"He doesn't have many new faces around him often," she said.

"Good to know I'm the first one in a while," James said.

"And let me guess." She pointed a finger at me. "Coffee with milk and sugar, right?"

"You got it," I said.

"Oh." James smirked. "You *do* come here often."

"He always orders the same thing," Gabriella said. "Been doing so since I started working here."

"You know what," James said. "I'll have the same."

She tried to be discreet about staring while making our coffees. She wasn't that great at it. James smirked every time he noticed her looking.

"Known her long?" James asked while we stood by the counter, waiting on our drinks.

"She used to go to Joseph," I said. "Hid a love letter in my locker one time. I never replied to the letter and then she left."

"Matty, the heartbreaker," he said with a deadpan face.

Ouch. Suddenly he was predicting the future. Maybe this was all a bad idea. Maybe it was just better to tell him. I could do it. Rip the band-aid right off.

The rest of the Forbidden Fortress walked inside as soon as we sat down at our usual table with our drinks.

"Excuse me!" Fa put her hands around her waist and marched our way the moment she spotted us from the entrance. "You already have your coffees?" The people sitting at the coffee shop had turned into Fa's private audience.

"Um, hello to you as well." I raised the cup as if cheering her, the audience still watching. "We literally just got these and we literally just sat down."

"If it helps," James clicked his tongue, "we haven't grabbed food yet."

"Now that's very considerate," Diana said. "At least someone is."

"Very funny," I said.

"Ladies." Pedro pulled a chair next to me. "Mind grabbing me a hot chocolate? Thanks. Oh, and a bagel."

"What do we look like?" Diana frowned.

"Two friends who love me." Pedro folded his arms behind his head.

Fa stretched out a hand to him. Pedro high-fived her.

"Excuse me," Fa said. "The cash, please?"

"Shouldn't my friendship be enough?" Pedro smiled. "Kidding." He reached into his pocket, grabbed his beat-up Pokémon wallet, and handed her the cash.

"Aren't we all grabbing something to eat?" Diana asked, expecting us to follow them to the register.

"Oh, yeah." I grabbed the cash out of my wallet. "Just a bagel for me as well. Cream cheese, please."

"You're lucky we like you," Fa said.

"Oh, in that case," James jumped in. "Muffin for me."

Fa silently grabbed his money and walked away.

"I love you," I shouted, gesturing a megaphone with a hand. They ignored me. "So, what did you do last night, Pedro?" I asked.

"Finally went on a second date with that girl from Framingham High," Pedro said. "Man, she can talk."

James sucked in air through his teeth. "Framingham High, huh?" He was nervous. "How was the date?"

Pedro paused for a second after he noticed his reaction. "It sucked," he continued. "She kept reaching onto my plate and grabbing my food. I was ready to head out after that. I'll buy you food. Don't take mine. It's a date, not a family meal."

"Wow." James tried to keep a straight face. "Romantic."

"Tell me you didn't leave her at the restaurant?" I asked.

"I'm a gentleman, Matt." He spread out his arms. "And Dad let me drive his car. I wouldn't just leave her there. Even if things go south, I still have a reputation to keep."

"I'm inspired," I said, "Really."

"What about you?" Pedro folded his arms. "Texted you yesterday before agreeing to go on this horrible second date. Still waiting for an answer."

"James and I were hanging out," I revealed.

"And no invitation?" Pedro's cheeks bloated like a blowfish.

"Guy's night? Burgers? An R-rated movie?"

"All right." Diana sat beside me, sliding a cup to Pedro. "Just waiting on the food. Drinks are served." She took a sip from her own.

"And yes," Fa said. "One of you boys will pick up the food."

"I like the choice of statement today." James pointed at her sweater. "'Just a Heathen in Love.' I can relate."

"Well, after Matt's radio silence yesterday, I should've worn the sweater I made that says, 'Worried as Fuck,'" she said.

"Guys…" I shrugged.

"I'm glad you're alive, Mateus Franco," Diana said. "I was relieved when you answered the chat today. I thought you had been abducted last night."

"No, no." Fa held up a finger. "He technically still hasn't answered the chat. He simply invited us here and ignored everything else we said. I'm still waiting for him to acknowledge the quote I sent. I spent five minutes on Facebook scrolling through baby photos before finding it. Do you know how dark things can get there? So, if I find something and share, I expect a beautiful reaction."

"Wow." James scratched the back of his head. "This chat you guys are in sounds very high maintenance."

I reached into my pocket and grabbed my phone. "'I'm like a murderous teddy bear. Cute to look at. Dangerous to play with,'" I read out loud after finding the quote in the middle of the thirteen messages. "Wow. What a find."

"Can we cheer to that?" James raised his coffee cup. "I'm inspired beyond belief."

"We will cheer to that *after* you pick up our food." Diana pointed at the counter. "You need to be baptized, James. It's your first time here with us."

"With pleasure," he said.

"So why did you go MIA on us yesterday?" Diana asked as James headed to the counter.

"Smooth, guys," I said.

"He was hanging out with James," Pedro said.

"No invitation?" Diana's eyes were like golf balls. "Wow."

"Inclusion, man." Fa scowled. "Keep up with the times. Meu Deus do céu."

"We're all here now." I shrugged. "Inclusion is happening."

"Unbelievable," Diana said.

"What is?" James set the tray of food on the table. "Don't tell me Fa has managed to come up with something more legendary than the quote on her sweater?"

"You'd be surprised," Fa said, claiming her slice of chocolate cake.

"Oh. Oh. Oh." Pedro grabbed his bagel. "We should go see that horror movie about the little girl—"

"I'm gay," I said.

Everyone was quiet. The kind of quiet where you're waiting for someone to be brave enough to say something so it doesn't get too awkward. I didn't get words, but I did get weird gestures. Pedro literally had his mouth half-opened, holding the bagel a few inches from his lips. Diana and Fa high-fived each other and giggled.

"What?" I asked. "What's that reaction?"

"So happy you decided to finally tell us," Diana said with a sigh. "God, I was worried you were going to be a forty-year-old gay virgin and never come out."

James squeezed my shoulder with the hint of a smile on his face.

"What, you knew?" I asked.

"I won't say we knew, since you never told us until now," Fa affirmed. "We suspected it, though. Gaydar is a real thing."

"So you and James…" Pedro put his bagel back on the tray.

"We made it official last night," I said.

"Yeah," Pedro mumbled, distant in thought. "I guess I wouldn't have enjoyed the night as much you as you guys did."

"I wanted you guys to be the first to know," I said.

"Wow." Diana's eyes welled up. "Oh, wow. I can't… Wow… Can I hug you two?"

"Yeah," I said.

"I'm down for a hug," James agreed.

She waved her hands at her teary eyes while coming to us. The hug was a bit longer than I had anticipated. To be honest, I wasn't expecting any tears at all. Our audience, of course, got way more invested in us.

Once Diana decided to release us, I noticed Fa struggling to hide her twinkling eyes by tossing her hoodie over her head.

"Wow." I squinted. "Lesbian One is crying?"

"Excuse me," she said. "I have a heart."

"You better take good care of him," Pedro said. "I mean it. You seem like a chill guy, but don't break his heart. This is my best friend, and I don't care if he's gay or if people think that we're gay together now or whatever. You be good to him."

James shot me a stare full of words. I was surprised I understood every single of them. It was a stare of joy and relief. I had been so concerned about Pedro. I was glad to have given him the chance to know.

"I wouldn't dream of hurting him, Pedro," James said.

"I think it's amazing that you finally said something, Matt." Diana's voice trembled. "You did it on your own terms, you know. You weren't caught or discovered or outed."

Fa fixed Diana's hair behind her ears and dragged her chair closer so they could hold hands.

"I definitely know that feeling," James said behind a breath.

"Exposing parts of you that you aren't ready to show is fucking traumatizing."

"I'm assuming this isn't your official coming-out moment?" Pedro asked.

James's eyes shifted to the food display case, scanning a haunted house of memories. "Definitely not," he said. "I wish it had been like this—surrounded by friends and good coffee... and a few people around us staring." He chuckled to lighten the moment and come back.

"So where do you go from here?" Fa asked.

"I wanted to start with you three," I said. "We've always been there for one another. Out of everyone I know, I figured you three would understand. And if you didn't, you would at least make an effort." I turned to Pedro. "I was scared I was going to... lose you..."

"What?" His "what" was so high pitched, he sounded like a Mariah Carey whistle tone.

"I know you're okay with Fa and Diana," I said. "But me, I don't know. I didn't know how you were going to react."

"I'll always be here for you, Matt," he said. "No matter what. Come to think of it, the Elder Wizard had to be gay. Ian McKellen played Gandalf. He is gay. Whatever we have planned, none of it changes. I need you to know that."

"Thank you," I said.

We hung out for a little longer. I had to go to the bathroom before we headed out. The four of them waited for me by the entrance of the Crusty Pie. On my way to them, I noticed Gabriella staring. It didn't take a genius to know she probably wondered about the letter she left me. And I wondered why she had left Joseph.

14

A CHRISTMAS TO REMEMBER

December 2011

The smell of the cooked ham took over my room as I fixed my hair in the mirror. I had a cowlick right on top of my head that sometimes decided to be extremely stubborn. Tonight was one of those times. Not even a messy look could hide it.

A music battle was happening beyond my walls. In the room next to mine, Laila listened to her playlist consisting of Brazilian and American music—the most prominent being Michel Teló and some obscure Adele remixes. Downstairs, Mom played Sinatra's Christmas songs. My bedroom was the filter. I wasn't mad about it, though.

In the event of my parents still set on leaving and me still weighing if I should leave with them, live with Pedro, and finally tell James the truth, I enjoyed the simple fact we were hosting Christmas this year.

For Brazilians, Christmas happened on the twenty-fourth with a fancy dinner, friends, and drinks. We got dressed in our best to hang out in our living rooms and take pictures.

The Forbidden Fortress and I had an entire plan for tonight. We were holiday-party hopping. We were going to start at my place, then head to Fa's, and then we'd spend the night at

Pedro's, our final stop. It was the first time James was going to be around my parents. And no, not as my boyfriend. Not yet, at least. My friends knew, and that was enough for now.

My personal post-new year plan was also drafted. I was set on breaking the news that I was a) considering staying and living with Pedro and b) that I was super gay and had a boyfriend.

Telling James was next. For a brief moment, I wanted to freeze time like Adam Sandler in *Click* and never go into the new year. But we don't get to control, bribe, or cheat time. We only get to enjoy it.

Lesbian Two: Merry Christmas, humans! Question, do we want brigadeiros tonight?

Manga Boy: Are you baking them? Your last batch was a disaster.

Lesbian One: I am!!!! And wow, attacking someone on Christmas Eve.

Donut Boy: Wait, aren't brigadeiros those chocolate balls you can get at the Brazilian market?

Elder Wizard: I'm so happy that you are acquainted with such a Brazilian delicacy.

Lesbian Two: I will bypass the personal attack and revel on the fact that we will have chocolate and Christmas music tonight.

Manga Boy: If All I Want for Christmas is on the playlist, I swear to dear baby Jesus that I will burst.

Lesbian One: We know what we're playing on repeat!

I'd still get goosebumps when Donut Boy popped up in our chat. James, of course. We had all agreed it was going to be a tribute to him winning that box of donuts his first week at Joseph. Getting a nickname like that meant he had officially been knighted as a member of the Forbidden Fortress.

At one point, I had thought the original members of the Forbidden Fortress were going to be upset I kept my gayness a secret from them. You see it in movies. You read it in books. Friends get pissed off. Then the main character wallows in sorrow and pain, thinking about a thousand reasons they didn't share the truth with their friends in the first place. Then something dramatic happens and the bond between them is either made stronger or they go their separate ways and never speak to each other again.

Yes, our friendship was as strong as the foundations of Shopper's World on Route Nine, but not because they had asked me why I had hidden the truth from them. They respected my time to share it. Pedro even promised to go to a Pride parade with me.

I was still struggling with my cowlick when I spotted a car parking on the driveway from my window. One of the perks of having a room on the second floor was that I got to spy on all the guests before they walked into my house. It was the couple my parents had invited tonight, Helton and Maria Silva. Dad had met Helton at the bakery a few years back and invited him and his wife for dinner one time. They became one of the very few family friends who actually visited us here and there. Helton had even offered his name to register my car in the future since they all had papers. He was way more ahead of the game than I was. At least I'd have that covered when and if the time came.

The Silvas were okay when they weren't trying to set me up with their daughter, Tania. I was about to return to the mirror after Helton and Maria walked out of the car, but seeing Tania pop out of the passenger seat held me in my spot. What was she doing here? My parents hadn't told me she was coming. Wasn't she supposed to be in Florida with her friends? That's what Mom had told me, at least. She was dressed in a very fancy beige coat. She glanced up at the window. I jumped up, hoping she hadn't spotted me, but the quick wave and the half-hearted smile proved otherwise.

Shit. Shit. Shit. Shit. This was going to be awkward.

I mean, maybe it wouldn't be that bad. The Silvas would probably make a few comments about my girlfriendlessness and then mention for the one thousandth time how Tania was amazing and how Democrats were destroying America and blah blah blah. Then they'd talk about immigration, obviously. Because to them, having green cards meant having the right to criticize every single immigrant in America as if they had been born here. Maybe Tania would like Pedro. Yes, Pedro! I could introduce them, and if they liked each other, I'd be off the hook. Okay, a perfect plan.

A knock on my bedroom door.

"Come—"

"You like this?" Laila spread out her arms, showing me her leather jacket.

"Wait for me to actually tell you to come in next time," I said.

"Sure." She rolled her eyes. "Come on, you like this?"

"I do," I replied. "But you're thirteen. Shouldn't you be wearing, I don't know, an innocent dress with teddy bears or something?"

"Very funny," she said, definitely noticing the tortured look on my face. "Tudo bem?"

"I just hate when they invite random people over and don't tell us," I said.

"Who are the randoms?" she asked.

"Tania," I replied.

"Oh, I didn't know she was coming." She shrugged. "Maybe you'll smooch her tonight." She pouted her lips and made kissing noises.

"Stop," I said. "She can be so fucking annoying."

"Ah, ah." She held up a finger. "You're cussing again."

"Ha, just know that I'll be doing that a lot in my head tonight," I said.

I heard Mom greeting them downstairs. Dad stepped out of the bedroom, looking half decent with his combed hair and light blue shirt. He gave Laila and me a lazy smile before going downstairs.

"It's like everything for him is torture," Laila said. "I swear. It's not like he was any different back in FG."

"FG?" I asked.

"Come on, Matty," she said. "Fogo Dourado. Keep up."

"I'll remember that," I said. I actually preferred FG. Fogo Dourado could be too wordy sometimes.

"All right." Laila slapped my arm. "I need to finish getting ready. Italo Dantas is coming. He is so dreamy."

"Wow." I shrugged. "And no one told me? Are we expecting anyone else? Lady Gaga, maybe?"

"You think the world revolves around you, Mateus," she said and went into her room.

I never liked surprises. Surprise birthday parties were a painful event where I spent half the time trying to act surprised and the other half pretending to have a good time.

I fixed the collar of my shirt in the mirror and took a long breath. "Let the holidays begin," I said and left my room.

The Silvas were in the kitchen with my parents, holding their red plastic cups. I scanned the dinner table and noticed a case of beer. When did those get here? This was definitely not the Silvas' doing. Had Dad gone out to buy them while I was in the shower? I opened the fridge to grab a water and noticed the case of beer from earlier today was gone.

Dad seemed okay, though. His speech was coherent. He was

wobbling. He was fine.

They commented on how I had grown and how I looked more like my dad as I got older. The comment made my stomach churn. Did I look like an alcoholic, too? Tania looked at me side-eyed, waving her cup around as if I owed her an explanation as to why I stood in my own kitchen. Maybe she was pissed I hadn't said hello to her first. Technically I had, from my bedroom window. She tended to be pretty entitled. Whenever she spoke Portuguese, she pretended to have this accent as if she was an American girl trying to speak it. I knew she could speak it without a problem. But she liked it when people wondered.

"Bem vinda, Tania," I said.

"Obrigada." She sipped from her drink and looked at me like I was too late to talk to her already.

A car parked in the driveway. I would've recognized the sound of the rattling muffler anywhere. Pedro driving his dad's car. I rushed to the front door and waited like a butler before he knocked. He spotted me through the glass and smirked. He probably read the expression on my face and knew how uncomfortable I was.

"Welcome," I said.

"Okay," he said. "You're never this nice to me at school."

"Don't get used to it," I said as he followed me into the kitchen.

"Pedro!" Mom threw her hands in the air and gave him a hug. "Good to see you."

"Thank you, Tia," he said. "Hey, Mr. Franco." He shook Dad's hand.

"Welcome, Pedro," Dad said and introduced him to the Silvas.

Laila joined us in the kitchen and fist-bumped Pedro the moment she saw him. Tania went to the living room without saying a single word and sat alone on the couch next to the

Christmas tree.

"Pedro, I have to show you something in my room," I said. "Come up real quick?"

"Sure," he agreed.

Laila watched us dart out of the kitchen with eyes that convicted me for leaving her alone with the Silvas. It was now her turn to make small talk.

"Who's the chick in the living room?" Pedro asked after I closed my bedroom door.

"Tania. She goes to Framingham High," I said.

"Maybe she'll recognize your boyfriend." He sat on the edge of my bed.

Fuck, I hadn't thought about that. If she did, not only would she know him, but she would most likely know the locker-room story.

"Oh, man," I said. "This could be bad."

"Or just really awkward," he said.

"You don't say." I plopped beside him. "Should I just tell him not to come?"

"That would make it even more awkward." He hooked one arm around my shoulder. "I mean, you're already bringing your secret boyfriend to Christmas with your family and they don't know you're gay, so…"

"Way to calm me down, asshole." I shrugged him off and stood up. "Fa and Diana need to get here soon." I walked to the window.

A familiar car pulled into the driveway. God, he was here and he looked fucking amazing. The black leather jacket and the gelled hair. This was going to be harder than I'd thought.

"Our *friend* is here," Pedro said.

The two of us rushed down and bolted to the front door, almost tripping over each other.

"Is the Pope coming to this?" Dad asked.

I opened the door before he knocked. He held up a fist in the air, confused as fuck.

"Okay..." James smiled. "Have a magic ball somewhere?"

I have two and you've seen both of them. That's what I wanted to say. His dimpled chin still made me weak in the knees.

"Hi," I said, welcoming him with an awkward fist bump. "Come in. Let me introduce you around. The girls should be here soon."

It felt incredible to walk into my house with a secret as deep as ours. We had our own little world, and no matter who was around us, they couldn't destroy it, because they didn't know it even existed. I wanted to hold his hand and take him around the room and introduce him for who he really was. But there was something, this excitement, about being just the two of us for now.

My parents greeted him like any of my other friends. The Silvas immediately commented on his hazel eyes. Awkward, but better than I anticipated. Laila high-fived him, most likely an attempt to look cool. It worked.

"James?" Tania joined us in the kitchen. "This is a surprise."

His face was as white as a blank canvas. She was suddenly a ghost, and not the Casper kind.

"Ta...Tania. Hi."

Fuck. Fuck. Fuck.

"Been a while." She folded her arms. "September, right?"

"Yeah, yeah."

"Didn't know you two were friends." She waved her red cup like it was an expensive piece of jewelry. "I heard you went to Joseph. Didn't know if the rumors were true. No Facebook update?"

"Been there for a few months now," he said. "And no, I've been staying away from posting stuff on social media."

"So how's life?" She grabbed him by the wrist and pulled him into the living room. "Tell me everything. Anything interesting since B—"

"Actually." He yanked his arm free. "I need to use the bathroom."

"I'll show you where it is." I rushed up the stairs. He followed me.

"Nice place," he said, clearly trying to hide the tremble in his voice.

"Thanks," I said, standing on top of the stairs. "Bathroom is here." I pointed to the door facing my bedroom.

"Thanks. So how do you know Tania?"

"Through her parents," I said. "We don't hang out or anything. I honestly didn't know she was even going to be here. I found out when they got here, and then I remembered how I don't like random people showing up to things I am at and I didn't know they're going to be there, and then…" He looked uncomfortable while I talked, like someone walking with a very sharp pebble in their shoes. "You okay?"

"Yeah, yeah." He sucked air through his teeth. "Just wasn't expecting to see her here."

"That makes two of us." I held his hand. "Hey." Our eyes locked. "Did something happen between you and…"

He tilted his head to the side. "No, nothing happened between us, but she knows the story. I just wasn't ready to see her here tonight. I've avoided a lot of the people from there."

"I would have warned you if I could," I said. "Apparently inviting randoms into your own home is a thing Brazilian parents do more often than I thought."

He smiled. It was forced. I could tell. I gave him a quick peck on the lips to help him return to his former self from before the Tania disaster.

"Dangerous, no?" He smirked.

"We were safe," I said. "Everyone is downstairs."

Fa and Diana arrived with a bouquet of flowers for Mom and a Tupperware of brigadeiros for Dad. They greeted the Silvas and Mr. Dantas, who arrived with Italo, aka Laila's crush, a few minutes before Lesbians One and Two. To my knowledge—and I sincerely hoped—those were all the guests for tonight.

Tania never tried to make conversation with the Forbidden Fortress once we were all together. We chose the front room as our hangout spot for the night. The adults were in the kitchen and lonely Tania enjoyed the company of my Christmas tree. Perfect.

Our conversation was entertaining, but not enough for me to miss the fact that the case of beer was now being shared by my dad and Mr. Silva. Mom and Mrs. Silva chatted away. Mom struggled to keep a straight face when Dad reached his sixth beer can before we had even eaten dinner. Yes, I was counting them.

And yes, people drank at parties. To an outsider, Dad sipping from his can was probably an innocent thing. He was drinking with his buddy. That was all. No big deal. It wasn't major news. But Dad didn't know when to stop. Or if he did, he lacked some serious self-control.

"I think revealing your dinosaur collection to Tania will send her away," Fa whispered, looking at the girl as she scrolled through her phone. "I mean, none of us would mind if she was gone, right?"

"If your sweater didn't frighten her, then I don't think the dinos will," I said. "Christmas is a Political Affair" was her statement of choice tonight.

"Wait, wait," James said. "You did mention that you had your dinosaur toys. I need to see them."

"No, no," Diana said. "*We* must all see this."

"You've seen them," I said. "Remember when we thought it was a great idea to take pictures of them in middle school for that class project?"

"And where are these pictures?" James insisted.

"Probably lost in my computer somewhere." Diana slapped my arm with the back of her hand. "But why settle for pics when we can see them live? Come on, Dino Boy."

"I may actually call you that from now on," James said. "Can we change his name on the group chat?"

"That'll be a big no and an ever bigger thank-you," I said.

They insisted on seeing those dino toys. I hadn't looked at them in years. I led them all into my room. Suddenly the space felt like a tiny box, crowded with people who used my bed as a chair.

James was in my room. On my bed. Okay. And he was about to look at my dino toy collection. One thing was for sure. I'd never thought the next time I grabbed those toys would be to show them to my boyfriend.

"Bed bouncy enough for you, James?" Fa asked as I searched my closet.

James chuckled. "It's a fine bed."

"Of course it is," Diana said. "I don't think it'd break with the two of you—"

"Ah!" I retrieved the clear plastic container from my closet. "Here it is."

"Oh, my God," James said. "And here I thought I was going to see, like, five dinosaurs. But you have a whole bunch."

"Didn't pack much when I was nine." I sat next to him.

"Just the essentials," Diana added.

I proudly named every dinosaur, explaining the reason behind every scratch, paint peel, and missing limb. James listened, never interrupting me. There was a sense of poetic justice as I showed them around. Last time I put these away, I had been oblivious to the true meaning of being undocumented. I had also been hell of confused about my sexuality. And now they were all coming out of the closet with me.

"Bored yet, James?" Pedro asked. "He's like Ross from *Friends* when he talks about this shit."

"I think it's cute as fuck," James said. "Dino Boy. Come on. Let's change it on the chat."

"No, no," I said. "Elder Wizard remains. The Elder Wizard could just make Jurassic Park real with the wave of his wand."

"That sounded wrong on so many levels," Pedro said, earning a loud laugh from everyone.

"I have to say," James started after recovering his ability to breathe. "I think I like you even more after meeting your toys."

It was pure impulse. The comment begged me to. He was in my room, after all. And I never thought someone would be so welcoming of the real me. Not just the gay part. But all these things about me that I thought were so weird for so long. I wanted to kiss him. Having him here now made it super hard not to. Just a quick peck. I went in. But maybe it was the sound of the laughter and chatter mixed with the music coming from downstairs that drowned the footsteps coming up the stairs. I was so caught up in the moment that I forgot the door of my room was still open, and to my fucking luck, Dad was right outside.

I'd never forget the look on his face: a mixture of disgust and surprise. He was flat-out drunk. I could tell from the redness of his skin and the way his body slowly rocked back and forth.

"You all need to leave," Dad slurred. "Now. Out of my house."

"Wait, what?" I protested.

"Mateus Franco." Dad's voice grew louder. "Todos fora daqui agora."

The four of them looked at me, not really sure what to do.

"Out!" Dad shouted.

They ran out of my bedroom. James shot me a worried stare before he disappeared downstairs.

"Dad, I don't think now is the best time to have this conversation," I said.

"Why?" He had a really hard time getting the word out.

"Dad…"

"There's a girl downstairs and you're up here kissing boys." Dad wobbled forward. "What's wrong with you, Mateus? É bicha agora? Not enough being an artist? You have to be gay?"

Bicha. The word I had heard many times when I was a kid. Faggot. Dad called me a faggot. In a split second, I could hear all those kids from my time in Brazil calling me the same. In my head, they had joined a church choir and decided to perform a song that repeated the word over and over again.

"Thank God we're leaving this country," he continued. "It has fucked you up."

I slammed the door in his face and locked it with a trembling hand. He banged on it three times before going downstairs.

I grabbed my iPod, headphones on, and plopped on my bed like a limp fish. My white ceiling served as a screen, replaying what had just happened.

Crying didn't come easy to me. I could count on both hands the number of times I cried in the past decade. Suddenly my strength to hold back tears was gone. I grabbed a pillow, buried my face in it and wept until my eyelids got the best of me.

15
A CHRISTMAS GHOST

December 2011

7:30 a.m.

Christmas morning.

I sat with my back against the headboard, my sketchbook on my lap. Music still blasted in my headphones. I didn't know the artist. I had fallen asleep with them on the night before and never took them off when I woke up in the middle of the night. I still had the same clothes on. I had slept in jeans and didn't even feel like changing out of them.

The pads of my fingers were smudged with conté. Eraser shavings were over my sheets and pillow. My bed was crowded with pieces of paper I had crumbled up and ripped out of my sketchbook once I was done sketching on them. Sketches of people dying. People screaming. A boy falling down a black hole. People. Person. Someone. Anyone. Me.

The Forbidden Fortress chat was on fire. Diana had tried to liven things up by sending a picture of Sailor Moon dressed as Santa Claus. Even Fa ignored her text. She sent an entire paragraph just to ask me how I was doing. The text opened the floodgates. Pedro sent a whole bunch of exclamation points and then a photo of him worried. Diana sent me a YouTube link to the "My Immortal" video by Evanescence with a text that said, "I will wipe away your tears." They all sent messages. Everyone but James. No text on the chat. No private message. Not a single word.

As much as I wanted to stay cooped up in here and think about last night and the one thousand reasons why James had been MIA, it was Christmas morning, and I had to face my family at some point.

I headed to the bathroom for a shower. The image of Dad calling me a "bicha" haunted me the whole time. My mind swayed between two thoughts: the whole faggot thing and his comment about America fucking me up. What if that was true? What if this whole illegal shit messed up the way I looked at life?

But today wasn't the day to have a debate about staying or going or getting deported. There was a 99.9% chance Dad had told Mom he saw me kiss James. Then there was another 99.9% chance she would beat around the bush before drilling me with questions.

I got out of the shower, the house too quiet for a Christmas morning. We always did these get-togethers on Christmas Eve and managed to wake up super early the next day. I guess everyone decided to sleep in a bit today. Mom was usually up at six a.m. on Christmas morning, and it was sacred that we joined her. If we didn't, she would blast Christmas music until we all got out of bed to help make breakfast. Even Dad joined us sometimes.

I locked my bedroom door and went into my closet to pick out an outfit for my Christmas Q&A. I picked a red long-sleeve tee and these green pajama pants I wore every holiday because they were too hot to sleep in. I glanced in the mirror before heading into the kitchen. Life had already changed last night, but today those changes would be made official even if I wasn't ready for them.

So much for doing things in my own time.

I finally stepped out of my room and walked down the stairs.

Laila and Mom were in the kitchen, fresh out of bed, looking like Christmas was something you put up with and not something you celebrated.

"Has someone died?" I headed to the cabinet for a bowl. "No Christmas music?"

"You didn't hear them last night?" Laila asked with an edge.

Her question made me change course. The bowl of cereal could wait. I sat with them at the table. Mom had a fist pressed to her cheek.

"What happened?" My heart was competing in a marathon at this point.

Mom slowly shifted her gaze to me, revealing the bruise on her face.

"Mom?" My body was numb.

Her chin trembled as she reached for my hand and Laila's, holding them tight.

"Is he still upstairs?" I asked as I tried to control my breathing.

"He left this morning," Laila replied. "He slept down here on the couch."

"Why didn't anyone knock?" I pushed the chair away from the table and jumped to my feet. "What the hell? You guys just left me in the bedroom while all this shit happened?"

"Matt." Laila gave me a look that demanded I sit back down.

"Sorry, sorry…" I took a seat again.

Was I the reason for the bruise on my mother's face? While I threw a pity party for myself last night, I failed to protect her. Failed to protect them. He could've come for my sister as well. Did he? He was drinking at the party and was drunk when he saw his son smooching a boy. I should've known. I probably didn't hear them because of the damn headphones. My thoughts couldn't have been that loud.

"It's Christmas." Mom wiped the tears off her face. "Let's make pancakes and open presents. Pode ser?"

Laila and I helped her in the kitchen. She forced a few smiles and tried a few jokes. No matter what she did, nothing sent my guilt away. If Dad blamed this place for how fucked up I had become, staying here meant things could get worse. Much worse. Telling them I wanted to stay could have serious consequences. He could get angrier. He could drink more. My decision could lead to another fight.

We opened gifts by the tree, drank hot cocoa, and then watched a Christmas movie. Everyone tried their best to pretend last night hadn't happened. My curiosity burned like a wildfire. Had he mentioned the kiss? I wanted to know why he had gotten violent. I wanted to call the cops. That was always my first thought when I heard stories of men beating up women, but now that the nightmare had returned, I knew if we did, Dad would get deported, leaving our family in an even more difficult situation. Mom's money wasn't enough to pay the bills, especially now that she was a housekeeper. According to them, we had enough to go back, but if I called the cops on Dad, would Mom still have a husband if we did leave?

The day went on. Dad never came home. James never texted. The Forbidden Fortress chat fell quiet.

My room and my sketchbook—or whatever was left of it—were my escape.

A knock on my door announced Laila's entry early in the evening. Thankfully the obscure art I had worked on was tucked under my mattress when she did.

"Can we talk?" she asked.

"Of course," I said, legs folded over my bed, the sketchbook on my lap.

"You really didn't hear them?" She sat next to me.

"I fell asleep with my headphones on," I said. "I woke up around—"

"Did you really kiss that guy?" she blurted out while prickling at the corner of her thumb. I guess we had that in common. We both blurted out things before we thought about them. And there it was. The confirmation I needed. So he *did* bring it up.

"I did," I replied.

"So, you're gay," she said.

"Yep."

"Is he, like, your boyfriend?" she asked.

"Yeah," I replied, running my hand across the back of my neck. "He is. Well, at least I think he still is. Last night was a nightmare. The way Dad looked at my friends. The things he said to me."

"You're pretty brave," she said. "Finding a boyfriend when you know we're leaving for real this time." We are leaving. *We*. Her eyes glistened—proof that I couldn't stay here if they left. How could I leave her alone with him?

"So…" My chest tightened. "My kiss—was that the reason they fought yesterday?"

"I don't know if that's what started it." She fixed her hair behind her ears. "I tried to hear them through the wall. Dad mentioned it, though. I heard that much. They went at it when people left around one. I burst inside their room when I heard a loud thud. Mom was on the floor with a hand on her face."

"Why didn't you knock, Laila?" My eyes welled up. "Pounded on my door until I woke up? I could've protected you both. I could've done something."

She sighed. "When Dad caught you and James, did he say something nice? Like 'Oh, I'm so proud of my gay son?'"

"No," I replied through gritted teeth, wanting to tell her what he actually said. I just didn't find it in me to repeat the word.

"You were angry at him, right?" she asked.

"Yes."

"What would have happened if I had called you? Maybe Dad wouldn't be at his friend's now. Maybe he'd be in jail. You might've done something you'd regret for the rest of your life."

"This is all so fucked up, isn't it?" I let out a long sigh. "You know what I wish sometimes?"

"What's that?" she asked.

"That he would leave for good." I was fully aware of how twisted my affirmation was. "That he'd disappear, you know. But then I think that if he did, there would still be this… this ghost in our lives. We'd still be haunted regardless."

"Why do you say that?"

"The store closed its doors because of his financial decisions. We live this illegal life because he hid from us all the money he borrowed from people. It was his screw-up that brought us here. And it's not like we were told what being illegal meant. And no matter where we end up in the future, we'll always carry that with us. We're the illegal kids, and even if we go back to where we came from, we no longer belong. We're too American for Brazil and too foreign for America to welcome us. We don't belong anywhere."

My phone buzzed on the bed. James's name was on the screen.

"I'll be in my room if you need me," she said.

James: Are you all right?
James: I'm okay. Can we talk?

I tried calling him on video, but he declined the call.

James: In person? Too tricky?
Me: When?

James: Tomorrow at the Crusty Pie? 10?
Me: I'll see you there.

My nose was about to fall off my face when I walked in. He was in the far-left corner. There were two mugs on the table. He didn't see me walking in. He was paying attention to something outside the window.

"Hey," I whispered, pulling a chair.

"That seat is taken." The thin smile on his face was a relief.

"Too bad." I grabbed one of the mugs. "I assume this also belongs to this person you speak of?"

"Yes," he said. "I don't think he'll mind you having it."

"Glad to hear," I said, taking a sip. He watched me drink my coffee, crack my knuckles, fix the collar of my jacket about ten thousand times, and still remained silent.

"Glad you texted," I finally managed to say.

"Didn't know if that was going to be well-received."

"Why?" I asked.

"I wanted to respect your space," he said. "I didn't want to pry."

"Pry? Your silence made me feel like you never wanted to see me again."

Disappointment was suddenly a neon sign on his face. "That was the first thing that crossed your mind?" he asked.

"Yes," I said sharply.

"Then I must be doing a fucked-up job of showing you how important you are to me."

"How else should I have taken it?" I asked.

"Truth needs space to breathe," he said. "Especially when it's not shared the way we want to. I wanted to stay. I wanted to text you the moment I got home. God, I wanted to show up at your house."

"We can't have what we want all the time," I said, eyes distant. "My entire life has proven that."

"What's that supposed to mean?" he asked.

"Things got really fucked up last night," I confessed. "I woke up to find out Dad put his hands on my mom after the party. Obviously, he had to drink like a teenager at a basement party. Anyway, I woke up and he was gone. Do you think I asked life to give me that beautiful moment? Hell to the no."

"I'm sorry." He grabbed my hand. "I'm so sorry. Did he do that because… of… us?"

"I don't know." His face blurred behind my tears. "I don't know. I want to call the cops, but then I think about seeing my dad in cuffs. When I set foot in the States, I wanted many things. Expected a lot of them to change for the better. Some things did. There was finally some money in my house, even if in those first years, even if all we could afford were clothes from the Salvation Army and unbranded cereal boxes. But there was one thing I lost after I crossed an ocean. My sense of belonging. I don't belong here. I don't belong back there. And if my dad put his hands on my mom because of me, then the idea of me not belonging with my own family—"

"Dino Boy." He squeezed my hand. "What your father did is about who he is, not who you are."

"But what if what I did—kissing you—triggered his actions…"

"That still doesn't put the blame on you," he affirmed. "As terrible as all of this is, never think that you don't belong just because of who you are."

"It's not just about being gay, James." I let go of his hand. "That's more of an inconvenience if you compare it to what I'm about to tell you."

He clutched his coffee mug.

"My entire family is undocumented." The ground disappeared from under me. "I can't get a license. I can't get a job at a McDonald's or at a local market or something. Right now, under the law, I'm somewhat protected because I'm not eighteen yet. But once I am, then things will be very different."

He searched my eyes as I told him about our family's debt back in Brazil.

"There are so many people living here undocumented," he said. "They still manage to get by—"

"Get by," I repeated. "Get by…. Exactly. They don't live, James. They get by. They're afraid all the time. Earlier this year, a dude my parents knew got deported. Up until then, my parents had talked about leaving but always changed their minds. But when the story happened at our doorstep, things got more serious. And then that day we had lunch for the first time, remember?"

"Yes."

"Dad got pulled over while driving me," I said. "That whole theory that you see your entire life flash before your eyes when something bad is happening is true. I can tell you that much. So, if I don't leave—"

"Leave?"

This was it. The moment I had dreaded. I was about to break his heart. "My family and I are leaving in June." I searched for something to hold my gaze. Anything but his face. "They're just waiting for the school year to finish. I was planning on rooming with Pedro after they left. I was planning on staying. But I can't. Not after last night."

"Ah." He tucked his hands inside the pockets of his sweatshirt. "Got it. Now you're suddenly leaving—"

"Not suddenly," I revealed. "They decided a few months ago. Last night had nothing to do with it." His eyes begged for a deeper explanation. "I knew I liked you," I continued. "The day you walked into class, you made me feel all sorts of things—the stuff people write about. The stuff you see in some cheesy romantic movie with a white cover and red letters for the title. The day I told the Forbidden Fortress about us, I almost didn't. I knew that I would end up breaking your heart. I chose to ignore my truth to tell them ours. I wanted to take a chance at the one person who made me feel like I belonged. And that's why I can't hurt you any further or put you in these situations anymore. I have an expiration date, Jamie."

"And there's nothing you can do to stay?" he asked.

"Nothing legal as of right now." I folded my arms on the table as if I was in a wrestling match against myself.

"You know what would really hurt me, Matty?" His chin trembled. "If I didn't get to spend the next few months with you."

"I don't think you get it—"

"I do," he affirmed. "But did you seriously think that story was going to be enough for us to be apart?" He forced my arms out of their lock and grabbed my hand like I was about to flee. The table next to ours glanced at the gesture. Like I could afford to care about them right now. "If six months is what we have," he continued. "Then I'll take it. At least we have something many don't."

"What?"

"Time." He slouched forward. "Don't think about leaving just yet. Think about the now. We're here now. We can look in each other's eyes and hold each other's hands. Fuck the future. Praise the present and its countless opportunities."

"Won't it feel like we're a time bomb?" I asked.

"Life is a time bomb. We just don't know when it'll explode. But in waiting for our demise, there are these in-betweens worth sticking around for—even if they have an expiration date."

"And you're willing to wait even if you know when this bomb will explode?" I asked.

"Absolutely," he replied. "Some people wait a lifetime to find someone like you… Dino Boy."

He insisted on driving me. We were silent for most of the drive. Not because things got awkward and we had nothing to say. We were simply enjoying each other's company. He dropped me off right around the corner from my house so my parents wouldn't see us. We parted ways with a kiss. What a gem James was. He was so brave, not even my time bomb was enough scare him away.

The Christmas lights in the neighborhood could've fooled me into forgetting my impending doom, but the sight of my dad's car on the driveway reminded me of my nightmare. My body went numb for a second. My hands clutched hard. I had to face him sooner or later.

There was a random bouquet of flowers on the dining table. Random because I had no recollection of anyone ever buying flowers in this house.

Laila was in the living room watching TV, the Christmas tree lit up in the corner.

"Everything all right?" I asked, my pulse pounding in my ear.

"He's home," she said. "Got here not too long ago. Been quiet since then. I think he's taking a shower."

"And Mom?"

"Upstairs in their room," she said.

I sat beside her, my back never touching the couch. My leg bounced up and down until a door opened upstairs. I froze. Muffled footsteps. Mom joined us in the living room, the bruise on her face setting me on edge.

"What are you guys watching?" she asked, her voice cold.

"Just some show on MTV," Laila said. "Nada demais."

"Is it good?" Mom's posture was too stiff and her face too serious.

"It's all right," Laila answered with a skeptical stare.

Footsteps rushed down.

"Claudio," Mom said as Dad made his way into the kitchen. "Vem aqui, por favor."

Was I suddenly caught in a setup to talk about the kiss? Was this the plan behind Mom joining us? I needed a speech prepared in my head.

He grabbed a bottle of water from the fridge and sat next to Laila. He couldn't look at our faces—especially mine. He scanned the room but skipped me.

Laila lowered the volume of the TV and sat up straight, eyes on me.

"I want a divorce," Mom pierced the silence. "And I want to ask for it in front of our kids, since they can see my face and what you did to it."

If there was such a thing as an elastic jaw, Dad's would've plunged to the floor.

"Yesterday was just another confirmation that this is no longer working," Mom said. "It's been too long."

"A divorce?" Dad's face turned as red as when he was drunk. "Really?"

"Are you surprised?" Mom asked. "What, you thought those flowers were going to make it all okay? Don't play that card in front of our children. I won't call the cops on you because I don't want our children to see you arrested. I don't want you to be deported. But this is it for us."

Dad set the water bottle on the living room table.

"I know what this is." He jumped on his feet. "An excuse

for the three of you to stay here without me. I get the message. You'll ditch me, Ana, so you can find an American to marry and give you papers. Vão tudo tomar no cú…"

His voice trailed off as he stomped up the stairs. The three of us didn't move. I heard him talk on the phone with someone. He returned with a bag minutes later. He went into the kitchen, grabbed the bouquet, and tossed it in the backyard before he screeched tires on the driveway.

16

GABRIELLA

January 2012

Dad called me a few times. He had been living with a buddy from work in Natick. Since Christmas, I didn't know how to talk to him. I didn't really want to. He tried calling Laila, but she never answered. He thought her radio silence was an invitation for him to ask me about her. What was there to say? It wasn't my place to give him any intel on her.

Mom had given me and my sister the choice of living with him if we wanted to. Like any of us would do it. She probably thought I hadn't heard her on the phone with him the other day. He refused to help out with money. He definitely said something about leaving, since Mom told him she'd never ask him for anything once he was gone.

That was when I thought about the future. I didn't know if we—as in me, Laila, and Mom—were still leaving. What I did know was that money was going to be short until they sorted out what to do with the money they had. We weren't leaving tomorrow. We still had rent to pay and groceries to buy. Without Dad's help, it would be too much of a burden for Mom.

Though Dad was still living a few minutes away, it already felt as if he had left. Not an ounce of my body wanted to see him. I'd answer his calls out of the need to not be an asshole, not because I wanted to.

But in the middle of all the things I didn't want to do, I decided to try something. Mom didn't know. Neither did Laila. I was going to walk inside the Crusty Pie to apply for a part-time job. Fingers crossed Mr. Oliver, the owner, would be one of those people willing to find a loophole in their company to hire people like me. I had never seen a "Now Hiring" sign anywhere, but one could hope. I already hung out at the place all the time. Making money there was a very logical idea. And if they weren't hiring, maybe he'd point me somewhere where people hired others like me.

I had an ITIN number instead of a social security number. Anyone could get an ITIN from the government. It worked like a social when it came to paying taxes. It even had the same amount of digits. Undocumented people were allowed to get one because that way, the government could still get its money. For people like me, having an ITIN meant you either ended up extremely lucky and your number was never verified by your employer, or they checked it and asked you to double-check your social. And if they did, then you knew you were out of there.

If we still ended up leaving in June, I'd have a few months ahead of me to save up for my grand arrival at FG. Yes, I was sticking to FG. as well. It made the town sound like a brand-new place. I'd much rather think of it that way.

I grabbed my thickest jacket, put on my headphones, and walked out ready to face the winter cold. Mom was working today, and there was no way in heaven or hell I was asking Dad to drive me to the Crusty Pie.

The Forbidden Fortress group text was flooded with good-luck messages. I took a selfie and captioned it: Frozen and unemployed. James sent me a private message right after.

Jamie: Proud of you. Good luck today! Your looks alone will get you the job. :)
   Me: Thank you, love.

Love. I called him love. We hadn't said "I love you" to each other yet, and I had just called him "love." I didn't need this today of all days. What if he didn't say it back? I mean, it wasn't an official "I love you."

   Jamie: Love, huh??? ;)
   Me: :P
   amie: Beijos pra você.
   Me: You definitely Googled that one!

James was being sweet and supportive. It wasn't his fault that his text set a different kind of time bomb in my head. Mom never mentioned our kiss. She definitely knew about it. She also knew James and I spent a lot of time together. There were no questions asked. I'd tell her I was going out with him, and she'd simply tell me to have fun. I thought about bringing up the subject, but considering the whole my-husband-left-me-with-two-kids situation, I figured I would spare her the conversation.

I had always spared them, though. It always seemed like a burden to spill my guts out and tell them I liked guys. There never seemed to be a right time. Something or someone was always in the way. I also hadn't had the heart to ask her if Dad put his hands on her *because* of the kiss. So we had that in common. We didn't ask each other the tough questions.

Surprisingly, I was able to tuck all these thoughts in a drawer when I saw the Crusty Pie. The place was packed. It was Saturday morning, after all. They had two baristas today. Gabriella was working the register. Great. I'd order coffee and casually ask her if they were hiring. Pretty solid plan. If Mr. Oliver was here, she'd go out back and call him and then I'd talk to him. Easy. Okay.

She smiled when I got in line. There were two people ahead of me. I sent the Forbidden Fortress a selfie of me making a peace sign.

"Hey, Matt," Gabriella said. The two people were already at the end of the counter waiting for their drinks, and I was about six feet away from the register.

"Hey." I tucked my phone in my pocket. "Sorry. Got distracted."

She laughed. "The usual?"

"I'll actually have a hot chocolate," I said.

"Oh." She started typing things on the screen of the register. "I don't think you ever ordered that one with me."

"Trying new things today," I said. "Are you, um, hiring by any chance?"

"Is you trying to get a job here part of this new plan?" She smirked.

"Definitely."

"Actually." She glanced over my shoulder to make sure there was no one else behind me. "I'm leaving next week. Talk about perfect timing."

"Oh. Got another job?" I asked.

"No, no," she said. "Moving back… to Colombia." Her eyes were sad when she was done speaking.

"Really?" I tucked my hands inside my pockets. "Why?"

Why? Why? I really needed to learn to think before I said things.

"Sorry, I didn't mean to be so…"

"You're okay." She chuckled as a woman and two kids walked in and stood behind me.

"Listen," she said. "I'm going to take my break in ten. We can chat for a bit, if you want."

"Sounds good," I said. "I'll grab a table."

"Cool. I'll bring your drink and we can talk."

I recognized her sadness. I knew it too well. She didn't want to go. I picked a table in the middle. The only one available. I put my jacket on the chair, sat down, and waited. She took less than the ten minutes. She set my mug on the table and sat in front of me, holding her own.

"Sorry if I came on too strong when I asked 'why,'" I said. "It's something I do. I say things before thinking about them."

"No worries," she said. "I guess you come on too strong with your words and your silence, too."

I knew what she meant. The. Fucking. Letter.

"So. Leaving," she continued. "Yeah. Mi mama is staying here to help me pay for college back in Bogotá. I can't afford to go to college here. Too expensive and I can't apply for anything. The perks of being an illegal kid, right?"

"Wait, you're a…"

"Dreamer as well," she said. "We're on the same boat. I overheard you guys in freshman year talking about it," she said and looked down. "I had a big crush on you, as you probably know, and there was this time in the cafeteria when I heard the four of you talking about immigration stuff."

I wasn't that surprised when she revealed her undocumented identity. I was, though, a little scared of the fact that people could overhear our conversations in the cafeteria.

"And how did you end up here?" I asked.

"The border," she said. "I was too small, so I don't remember much. Mama avoids talking about it. I don't ask either."

"How old were you?" I asked.

"I want to say two…" She shrugged. "Yeah, too small. Can't

speak Spanish. I only know a few words. But at least I won't have any illegal presence, because I am leaving before I turn eighteen." She prickled at the side of her thumb. "This will be good."

She was trying to find happiness in returning, but I could tell she was struggling.

"And you want to go?" I asked.

"Not much of a choice," she said. "I *have* to be okay with leaving. You know how it is. You feel American. You think American. But you don't have the papers to prove it. I am not down to marry someone just for papers. Too risky." She looked out the window. The light of the sun made her brown eyes lighter. "I've always wanted to be a doctor," she continued. "Make my mom proud. And I can't be that here. I can't keep delaying this anymore. I'm delaying the inevitable."

"Sorry I never brought up the letter, Gabriella," I said. "I didn't know what to say."

"It's okay."

"Was that why you left the school?"

"No," she said behind a laugh. "I liked you, Brazileño, but no. We moved to Natick, and I ended up going to high school there. I had a big crush on you, but honestly, my biggest crush was on how you had friends who understood. I never had a group like yours. When you didn't reply, I just figured you weren't interested, and then I never bothered asking, because why would I?"

"I never sent a letter back because I didn't want to hurt you," I said. "I'm gay. I knew I was back then but just didn't have it in me to tell people. It took some time to get here. But hey, I'm also leaving. I think. In June. I don't know. It's a weird situation—"

"I'll talk to Mr. Oliver for you," she said, cutting the conversation short. "Put in a good word."

"And he knew you were…"

"Yeah. He pays me cash. Not a big deal. Every Friday he comes to me at the end of the day and hands me an envelope with the money."

"Thank you," I said. "And sorry. Again."

"I was honest about how I felt. You were also honest about how you felt. Now we're even."

"Yeah…"

"He's here," she said. "Mr. Oliver. I'm going to go talk to him. Wait here?"

"Sounds good."

She walked toward the counter and went through the door on the far left. She didn't take long to return with him. He always wore hats. Sometimes they were black, but other times he picked bold colors like yellow or bright blue. Today's was yellow. His glasses were big and arched above his bushy brows. He had a job application on his hand.

"Mr. O!" she said. "This is Mateus, the perfect person to take my place."

"You'll be a hard one to replace, Gabby," he said, sliding his glasses to the tip of his nose. "We've chatted before, right, son?"

"Yes," I said. "I'm always here with my friends."

"Oh, yes," he said. "I've seen you around. Better to hire someone who knows the place already. So, you two friends?"

"We went to the same school for a while," she said. "But I always see him here. Honestly, I think he could even make his own coffee already."

We shared a laugh.

"All right," Gabriella said. "I have to get back to my shift. You good, Mateus?" She held up a thumb.

"All good here," I said.

"Talk later," she said and walked to the counter, tying the back of her apron.

"All right, son." Mr. Oliver handed me the application and grabbed a pen from his pocket. "Fill this out and bring it to me. My office is through that door behind the counter."

The table I always sat at with the Forbidden Fortress was empty now. I sat there and filled out the form, trusting that Gabriella had really told Mr. Oliver about my situation. His office was to my left, and there was a kitchenette break room to the right and a staff bathroom in the back. The door was slightly open. He sat in front of his computer, looking over his glasses while reading something on the screen. There was a Crusty Pie mug on his desk.

"Mr. Oliver," I said, knocking on the door. "All done."

"Ah, good." He stretched his hand.

I handed him my application. He scanned it and took a sip from his drink. "Oh, you don't live that far. Good."

"It's a quick drive," I said. "Even a short walk."

"Excited to have you join the Crusty Pie, Mateus," he said. "You seem like a good kid."

"Excited to join you guys."

"When can you start, son?"

"Oh… like… so I'm hired?"

He chuckled. "That's why I'm asking you when you can start."

"Monday after school okay?"

"Sounds good to me," he said. "It's flatbread night this coming Monday. It'll be pretty busy."

"Sounds great," I said.

"Payment is every Friday," he said. "I'll leave yours on this desk inside an envelope with your name. You may come in here and get it when you're done with your shift."

Gabriella was busy with customers when I walked out of his office. I gave her a quick wave. She waved back but kept her focus on the guy in front of her.

I got a call from a strange number while walking home. It was Mr. Oliver.

"Mateus," he said. "Sorry to be calling out of the blue, son."

"It's all right. Everything okay?" Shit, he probably regretted hiring me.

"No, everything is fine," he said. "Listen, and you don't have to, but think you could start tomorrow? Gabriella told me she'd rather not come in, so she can have everything ready for when she leaves on Monday."

"Monday?"

"Yes," he said. "That's when she's leaving."

I stopped on the walkway and fell quiet.

"Are you there?" he asked.

"No, I'm… I'm here," I said. "I—wow. Is it okay if I start on Monday? I wasn't expecting to get the job on the spot and I have some homework to catch up on…"

"Absolutely," he said. "Don't worry, Matt. I'll see you Monday."

17

A GHOST IN THE ATTIC

February 2012

I was trained by Patrice. She was nice. Sometimes she'd talk about makeup and clothes too much, but I could live with that. Once I told her I was gay, she assumed I wanted to talk about my skin-care routine or the shampoo I used or if I had some super-secret product to keep my skin blemish free. I never had an answer to those things. At least she wasn't a bitch to the new kid.

Gabriella always popped up in my head. I had sent her a friend request on Facebook, but she never accepted. I had my reasons for never replying to that letter freshman year. She had her reasons for helping me and not wanting to stay in touch or even lying about the day she was going to leave. She respected my silence back then. It was only fair I did the same now.

I was pretty familiar with horror stories about people hiring undocumented immigrants and exploiting them in exchange for silence. My family had been pretty lucky. So was I. Mr. Oliver never asked me about my papers. I felt like everyone else—except on Fridays when I had to grab an envelope full of cash. Sometimes, if he was feeling chatty, he'd ask me about my day and James. When I told him about James, he laughed and said he appreciated how times were changing and how people got to be more themselves. He even confessed that he had kissed a boy in his twenties.

The fifteen-percent-off discount was also a big bonus. Mr. Oliver had allowed me to extend the discount to all members of the Forbidden Fortress. They'd visit almost every day after school and on the weekends. When I was scheduled to work, we'd all hang out for a while before it was time for me to clock in.

I'd always tell James my schedule and break hours in case he wanted to visit. No pressure on him if he couldn't. But today was one of the days he was coming by. And he was right on time. God, I loved when he wore beanies. He had chosen a green one today. He smiled when he saw me at our usual table by the window, waiting for him with his coffee and a grilled chicken sandwich.

"My working man," he said and kissed me on the forehead. Most of the regulars at the Crusty Pie didn't stare at us anymore when we showed PDA. A few of the newbies on the other hand were either a) amazed at how cute we were or b) shocked that we had the guts to do what we did. I didn't care about either one.

"My housewife," I said.

"Are you telling me I need to get a job as well?" he asked.

"No," I said. "I like that you come visit me at work. It's sexy."

"Behave, boyfriend," he said with a smirk.

I got jitters whenever he said the word "boyfriend."

"I want to take you on a date tonight," he continued. "It's Saturday. I think we deserve a night just the two of us. You've been working, and then there's school, and I know we're together in school, but I want to be with you tonight, especially after an academic week."

"Isn't there, like, a game night thing happening at Pedro's?" I asked.

"Yeah," he said with a shrug. "I was wondering if we could skip that."

"Fa is going to flip," I said. But in my mind, I had already agreed to his request.

"She always does," he said. "She'll probably wear a hoodie on Monday that says 'Fuck James Alberte for Stealing my BFF.'"

"Sounds like her," I said.

"I just want to spend time with my sexy working man."

"You think I look sexy in this apron?" I held out the embroidered logo on my chest: a slice of pie with googly eyes and a smile.

"I think you look sexy. Period," he said with a smile. But then his eyes went distant and followed something outside the window. Neb and some random guy. He wasn't uncomfortable in a Neb-is-coming sort of way. His chest was racing and his face was pale.

"Hey," I said. "You okay?"

"Um, yes." He scratched the side of his head. "All good."

"It's just Neb," I said. "We can handle Neb."

"Yeah." His finger traced the rim of his mug. "Sure, we can handle…"

Neb and the other guy approached our table the moment they walked in. The dude next to him was well built, his hair was buzzed on the side, and his eyes were so green, they looked like a lit-up cone of matcha ice cream.

"Matt!" Neb spread out his arms. "Man in the Crusty uniform now. Didn't know you worked here." He pointed at the logo on my chest. "I mean, I don't come here that often. I go to the other coffee shop on the other side of town."

"Hey, Neb." I waved.

"Wow, this is actually kind of perfect," Neb continued. "This is my friend Brian."

Brian. The text messages. So they weren't a product of the Neb-effect. The dude was real.

"Nice to meet you," the guy said in a voice perfect to narrate trailers. He never looked me in the eye. He kept his attention on James, who winced like a scared kid on Halloween.

"Going to say hello, James?" Brian insisted.

"Hey… Brian." He reached for his mug and chugged down his coffee, most likely burning his tongue. James was always so confident. Seeing him so vulnerable was strange.

"What brings you here?" I asked, trying to get over the awkward tension.

"Um, coffee, food," Neb replied. "We're definitely not grocery shopping." He and Brian laughed. James and I just stared. "Well, actually, I'm looking for a place for our next Bible study series."

"Oh," I said.

"The way we do it is we bring a few people in," Neb continued. "We buy food, we spend a few hours here talking about Jesus. It's great for bringing in new customers. Maybe we could have it here? Is the manager around?"

"He's out right now." I deserved an award for flat-out lying. Mr. Oliver was in his office having lunch. I just hoped he wouldn't walk out right now. "I can pass the message along. Mind if I give him your number?"

"Sure," he said. "So can I place my order with you, or…"

"I'm on my break," I replied. "Employees don't usually sit around chatting when they're working, in case you're ever confused in the future, but you're more than welcome to place your order. Patrice will help you."

"Sounds good," he said, slapping my shoulder. Little fucker.

He and Brian talked as they headed to the counter, glancing at James and me a few more times than I would've liked them to.

"I have to run," James said. "See you tonight?"

"Absolutely," I said.

"I'll pick you up," he said and rushed out.

Neb's and Brian's gazes followed James out as they walked to a table next to the shelf with all the mugs and coffee bags for sale. To my disappointment and annoyance, Brian took a seat and Neb walked my way. I still had a few minutes on my break. God, was I going to have to spend those with him?

"What, Neb?" I folded my arms. "I have to get back to work in, like, five minutes."

"Things good with you and James?" he asked. "You two seem pretty solid."

"Why do you care?" I said. "Honestly? You know, I thought you had gotten over your James-is-with-Matt obsession, but apparently it's still there. You don't think you care too much about him? I mean, you were quiet for some time, and I was proud of you because I thought your obsession had died out, but—"

"I think it's hilarious when you think that this isn't my business." Neb scoffed. "You really don't know much about your boyfriend's past." He pointed at Brian, who had his face buried in his phone. "See him? He started doing counseling with one of the ministers at my church. Dude is now as straight as a surfboard. Our community offers resources to the afflicted."

"Afflicted?" My hand turned into a fist. "What are you trying to say? That just because I'm gay, I'm sick? Or because James is gay with me that we're both, like, going to hell on a one-way ticket? I know I don't parade around the school wearing a rainbow shirt or sporting heels with glitter and shit, but I'm not ashamed. I spent too long feeling that way."

"James was doing fine until you came along, buddy." He stabbed a finger on my chest. "Changing schools was supposed to be a good thing for him, you know. He was supposed to get away from all the temptation and distraction and be around people that believed the truth. The real truth. I'd always ask Dad about him. James's counselor would always report to him saying James was making progress."

"What the fu…" I scrunched my face.

"Brian and James were both in counseling together. As a believer, I can't let him live a life of shame. That also benefits you, in a way."

"Benefits me how?"

"Think about it. If James starts counseling again, he'll be like Brian. The confusion and the temptation will be gone from his life." I jumped up and stood inches away from his face. "Things… things…" He fumbled back a step. "Things may look great now, but things may not look so good after you die. Who knows where you'll end up?"

"Ever met someone who died and came back to tell the tale, Neb?" I asked. People in the coffee shop were beginning to stare.

"No," he said.

"Until you do, you don't get to talk to me that way," I said. "And I can't speak for James's life, but I can speak for our relationship. You don't get to come between us. You don't get to tell us how to live. I get that your Christian privilege makes you think that someone's truth is an excuse for you to tell them how to live, but that's not how this works."

"You know what his parents do?" he asked. "You know who they are? James ever showed you pictures?"

"I have to get back work." I tightened my apron behind my back and walked to the counter.

"Be careful," he said.

*

James usually blasted music in his car. Not tonight. Something haunted his mind, and I don't think he knew the ghost reflected in his eyes. We were supposed to go to the movies, but James decided to stay in his house on our way there. Shocker. Parents were gone again.

I hated Neb even more tonight. His words were like a bad song spinning in my head. It was like he was here, sitting on the back seat, whispering them again and again. And the way he talked about counseling. I knew what he truly meant. Conversion therapy. I had looked into it. For a time, I had thought I could change who I was, but after reading stories on how miserable people were when they went through these so-called counseling sessions, I decided that it was better to hide everything than to experience what they did.

The silence in the car wasn't the kind of silence you enjoy because you're with someone special. It was the shitty type of silence, the one where you know something is bothering someone.

I wanted to flat-out ask him about Brian. The anxiety was killing me. But he had respected every single step I had taken when it was my turn to share my truth. He never pried or forced anything out of me. Judging by the sadness in his eyes, I knew I had to do the same.

He parked on his driveway and I followed him inside his house.

"What do you feel like eating tonight?" he asked, his eyes far away.

"Chinese," I said. "What do you think?"

"I'm fine with whatever." He dialed the number on his phone.

I sat on the reclining couch in the living room. He joined me after placing the order, but instead of sitting next to me, he sat on the edge of the other couch.

"Hey." I tapped the empty seat beside me. "What, you're scared of me or something?"

He rubbed his hands really fast. I sat next to him and held his hand. "Hey." We locked eyes. "Listen, I can tell you have something on your mind. You can talk to me when you're ready. Or if you're ever ready. I just want you to know that I'm here, okay?"

He squeezed my hand like I was about to leave him.

"I know you noticed how awkward it got when Brian talked to me," he said. "I never thought I fooled you into thinking there was nothing there. I just… I don't know how to talk about it without going into this place in my heart where things still hurt. And I keep trying to heal, but if I talk about them, they'll hurt again."

There's a kind of sadness that make the eyes empty. Even if they are glistening, life is taken from them for a while. This was one of those cases.

"We don't need to—"

"But I want to," he said. "I'm tired of hurting alone."

"I'll hurt with you."

"My parents…" He took in a breath like he had been racing for a long time. "They're religious speakers. That's why they aren't around that often. They're always at conferences and services and all those events. They used to drag me along until I decided I no longer wanted to go to those because of how… different I felt from everyone around me. I'd hear the way they talked about some things and just knew I'd never be able to think that way."

His hand was sweating.

"I knew I liked boys since I was a kid," he continued. "I knew I was gay. Honestly, it was kind of cool having a secret identity at first—like a superhero-- but then I realized I couldn't share it with just anyone, because my secret identity would attract villains if it was ever out in the open. I bottled everything up. To be safe. To stay safe. How could I not? The things the people in their circle would say. I imagined those people talking shit about them behind their backs if they found out they had a gay son. Our livelihood depended on their purity, and in their eyes, their son was an abomination." His breaths grew heavier. "So, you do things. You program your mind to hide. You create this character in your head. The one they'll actually like. You erase your browser history, and you pretend that Britney Spears and Lady Gaga were accidents in your playlist. And when you realize it, you're buried ten thousand feet deep and you don't know which parts of you are authentic and which ones you created to protect yourself."

I squeezed his hand so tight.

"Then Brian happened," he whispered in regret. "He was a freshman at Framingham High like me. He had moved from upstate New York because his parents got a job at a church here."

"Neb's church," I mentioned.

"Yes," he replied. "We started hanging out after school. We'd go out and stuff. Then he told me he struggled with liking boys." He chuckled. "Struggled…" He still couldn't look me in the eye. "People say that as if who you truly are is such a weight. Anyway, I felt comfortable telling him that he wasn't alone. Friendship turned to something more. And we went with it until…" He bit down on his lips.

"Until Neb caught us kissing in the church's library on a Sunday after service," he continued. "He obviously knew my parents, because his dad was a pastor and Brian's parents were working at his congregation. My parents had spoken at his church before. What I didn't know was how long Neb stuck around to catch the live show." He winced. "Long enough to snap pictures and videos. Those ended up in my dad's inbox." His shoulders rose with a breath. "Now, that was an interesting night. Brian and I started attending these sessions with Neb's dad. We weren't allowed to attend them together, though. We had to be in separate rooms so we wouldn't be tempted or whatever. No social media for us. Nothing. Brian stuck it out. I couldn't handle it. 'Let's pray you straight.' 'You aren't made this way.' 'It's a sin.' 'Read the Bible.' 'If you can't get over it, just don't ever have sex or never be in a relationship.' It was all too much…"

Our hands sweated while holding on to each other.

"Then one day, after gym class, I was changing in the locker room, and Brian walked in. I remember his face was really red. I thought he had been crying or maybe he was just angry. He grabbed me by the shoulder and flipped me around so his back was pressed to the wall and I stood in front of him." A heavy sigh. "Then he kissed me. I let him do it. I wanted it. I was also confused. Until I heard their footsteps. Brian punched me in the stomach and accused me of forcing the kiss. He punched me in the face after and then called me a fag over and over. He kicked me. The other boys joined in. He had orchestrated it. He knew those guys were about to swarm in. He just wanted to make sure they knew he wasn't…" His chin quivered. "He wasn't *the* fag. I was."

A tear streaked down his cheek.

"I told my parents the truth that night," he continued. "They didn't believe me. I needed to be fixed. My condition had to go away. I tried. I decided to attend a few more meetings again, but when I was told I had demons hovering in my head, that was when I begged them not to make me go back." He clenched his teeth. "They agreed, but I'd have to leave Framingham High. The only other option was Joseph. The funny part is that Joseph had been my first choice anyway because of visual arts, but they kept telling me that I was called for ministry school."

The memory of him strolling into class with so much confidence that day flashed in my head. I would've never guessed that Mr. Dimpled Chin carried so much weight.

"I stopped trying to prove myself," he said. "I decided to be myself. People will project what they want on us. No matter how much I tried, my parents just wouldn't listen."

"You're so brave." I kissed the top of his hand. "So brave, Jamie…"

He finally found his way back to us. His eyes lit up. "We're all illegal at some point, Matty." He pulled me closer. "When your dad stood at the door, that just brought me back to the conversation I had with my parents the day they got the email. Mom was neutral so Dad wouldn't be upset. I could tell she had so much to say, but Dad's words defeated any will she had to say something."

"My dad wasn't as willing as yours," I said.

"I'm going to say something really twisted," he said. "I wish my dad was leaving, too. Mom, I can deal with her. But Dad…. Yes, we'd probably struggle or whatever. I think it sucks that they built their entire lives around living for people who will destroy them the moment they don't agree with something. I know if they ever stand up for me, they'll lose everything they built. So as of right now, I'm destined to live as an outcast. A very illegal outcast."

"I have to ask you something," I said. "You went to a different school to be away from Brian, but then you met me. Did I not ruin the plan? Would things have been easier?"

He put his hand on my face, his thumb following the edge of my lips. "You don't get it, do you?" he spoke as if stating the obvious. "My plan was successful *because* of you. Meeting you made everything clear. Brian was my hell. You were my paradise. You didn't make things easier, Matty. You made everything worth it."

My hand grabbed the back of his neck. Our lips pressed hard. He wrapped his arms around me, threw me on the couch, and sat on top of me.

"The food delivery guy will get quite a show." I unbuckled his belt.

"I hope they enjoy it." He took off his shirt with a heavy breath. I did the same. His chest was against mine. Skin to skin. Lip to lip. Hand to waist.

The driver arrived before we got any further. We did keep the shirts off while we ate. The conservation wasn't as heavy once our chicken-fried rice and wings arrived. We ate and watched trashy reality TV.

"I feel it's only fair to show them to you." He struggled to hold his chopsticks.

"Show me you having a hard time with those? Yeah, it's very entertaining. I think you need a fork."

"I got this." He focused on his awkward fingers.

"Like this, Jamie." I held up my chopsticks. "You have to hold them more toward the upper part."

"Ah." He followed my gesture. "Okay, I think I got this."

"And what do you want to show me?"

"My parents," he said, picking up a chunk of rice with his trembling chopsticks. "I've met yours. I've seen yours." He managed to eat his food without dropping a single grain. He then grabbed his phone, scrolled for a few seconds, and handed it to me. "Here you go."

His eyes were his mom's. The dimpled chin belonged to his dad. They were both very good-looking people.

"Meet Mr. and Mrs. Alberte," he said, resuming his struggle between chopstick and rice. "They still act like they don't know or don't want to know the truth between us, but the romantic in me hopes I get to introduce you some day. Like, formally."

"Really?"

"Cheesy, I know. I'd love to do it, though. Bring you home and have you sit at the table." He shrugged, dismissing the thought. "Who am I kidding? That'll never happen."

18

FOUR WHEELS

March 2012

"This is definitely something," Fa said, her dirty boots on the dashboard. "Your car. You bought it with your money. And you bought it cash. You're such an adult."

"It may not be the newest, but it's still mine," I said. "And it was only two grand."

"It's not going to break with us, right?" Fa asked.

"You're good, Ms. Rio," I said.

Fa had refused to ride in the back. She claimed we had been in need of some bonding time, and it wasn't enough to be in the same car together on our way to school. She had to be next to me to feel my vibe and help me refocus my energy.

"Glad Helton kept his promise and allowed me to use his name to buy the car," I said.

"What a gentle soul," Diana said. "If only his daughter was as kind."

"I know," Fa said. "She gave me such bad vibes at Christmas."

"Can we get our feet off the dash? Thanks."

"An adult and a grumpy one." Fa slowly slid her boots off, leaving a few mud stains.

"See?" I said. "Now I have to wipe Paradise's dash again."

"Paradise?" Diana asked, sitting behind me. "That's its name?"

"*Her* name," I corrected. "Respect the lady. And yes. I mean, it's like a private paradise. She takes me places. I get to hide out in here in case some disaster happens. She's perfect."

"And that was the only reason you chose that name?" James toggled at my earlobe from the back seat.

I laughed. "Well, I also named her after the playlist Jamie and I played in his car after our first date."

"Gosh." I caught Diana folding her hands over her chest through the rearview mirror. She pursed her lips and swayed as if dancing to a waltz. "You guys are so cute, I want to barf."

"Please don't," Pedro said. "It already smells back here. And it's not just that old-car stench."

"Come on," I said. "It was a skunk, and the old owner told me it sprayed the back seat, like, two years ago."

"Oh." Fa clapped. "I'm relieved that's what the smell is. I thought someone had forgotten their deodorant today."

"And Matt was offended when I mentioned the stink." Pedro's arms flailed between James and Diana.

"At least the back is spacious," James said. "And Paradise will smell linen fresh after one hundred washes. It's been two years. A few more and boom, she will be a new girl."

"Why are you bringing up space?" Diana scrunched her face. "Did you and Matt have sex in the back seat?"

"No," I said. "Well, not yet. It won't go up with this smell."

"It's like being on the set of some cheap porno movie," Pedro said. "And I don't even get to act on it because I'm not gay."

"You're right, baby." Fa looked over her shoulder and slapped Pedro's leg. "You're in a gay world now."

"Matt." Pedro placed a hand on my shoulder. "I will literally pay for you to wash the inside of this car. Please do it as soon as possible."

"You're welcome for the ride," I said. "And it's obviously been washed since skunkpocalypse. I think that faint smell is here to stay."

I had bought Paradise because I wanted to own a car, no matter how old or cheap. It was also time I learned how to drive. Mom started teaching me years ago, but then she got too busy. Dad never had time for it. Since I couldn't take driver's ed, this was the only way I'd learn. I'd bought her the week before and spent the past few days going around the block and driving through off-road streets so I could get better.

Owning Paradise also distracted me from the future. Mom was happy I got her. She didn't tell me not to get her because we were leaving. I hadn't asked her if we still were after Dad moved out. I just cruised. Having Paradise was a privilege I allowed myself to have. But I knew the risk. One wrong turn or a simple burned-out headlight and a cop would pull me over.

"Do we have time for Dunkin'?" Fa jumped on her seat. "I know it's shop week, but I'm not a big fan of this week's project. Drawing bugs. I mean, what is that?"

"We'd be risking being late." I held up a finger. "But if there's a mutual agreement in the car…"

"You know we're all going to agree, so can we just go?" Pedro said. "Give me that caffeine, caralho."

James repeated the last word in the thickest accent, rolling the "R" like a true American boy.

"You're learning all the right words," I said.

"Thank you." He waved his hand and bowed his head as if he had just finished a play. "What does it mean?"

"Dick," Fa said.

"Oh." James shrugged. "I *am* learning all the good words." He tried that awkward wink of his. It was probably the wink that made the entire car go quiet.

We grabbed our order from the drive-thru, consumed it as

fast as we could, and walked in right when the bell rang. Everyone was in class, including Neb. I avoided him even more since that whole thing at the Crusty Pie. He never talked to me after what happened. He even pretended like I wasn't in class anymore.

If I wasn't careful with my thoughts, I'd drift away into imagining him standing in a corner, watching James kiss that Brian dude, holding up his phone, already planning what he would do with that footage.

The rest of the Forbidden Fortress wasn't aware of the incident at the Crusty Pie with Brian. Neither did they know the backstory behind James's coming to Joseph. Those were James's stories to tell—if he ever felt like sharing them.

Mr. H's electronica playlist was muted as soon as a suited man walked in the shop. He had a leather binder in hand, round glasses resting on the tip of his nose. The light bounced off his bald head.

"Ah!" Mr. H strode to him after lowering the music. "Mr. Vine. Thank you for coming."

"My pleasure." The man shook his hand.

"Hey class," Mr. H said. "I have a surprise for you. This is Mr. Vine. He's from the Art Academy in Boston. He'll be conducting brief interviews with a few of you today. He'll be asking you about your future goals, reviewing some of our portfolio pieces, and telling you a bit more about the school."

"This is awesome," James whispered in my ear.

"Why?" I asked.

"These people usually visit classes when they feel like granting scholarships," he replied.

"Like, full scholarships?" Pedro asked from the far right, jolting his head forward. "Didn't mean to eavesdrop, but we're that close in every single way."

"Sometimes," James answered.

"Keep working on your assignments," Mr. H continued. "Mr. Vine and I will chat a bit in the computer lab."

Since the lab was all glass, there was no way I could have missed the gigantic folder Mr. H handed Mr. Vine after they sat down. Mr. Vine placed it on a table and looked at what I assumed were drawings as they talked.

A few minutes later and my curiosity around the man vanished, since I didn't really know what he was looking at. He nodded and frowned and fixed his glasses over his nose as if he was doing some deep thinking, but that was about it. I returned to my assignment. I covered my head with a hoodie in the hopes of concealing the single headphone in my ear and returned to drawing my moth.

There was some chatter when Mr. H finally exited the computer lab and Mr. Vine called one of the students. Others followed. I kept working on the details of my moth's wing until I heard my name. I quickly slid the headphone out of my ear and jumbled it into my pocket.

"Mr. Franco," Mr. Vine repeated, standing by the door leading into the lab. "Mind bringing that drawing as well?"

The Forbidden Fortress stared proudly as I joined him inside the computer lab, the moth drawing in my hand.

"Please sit." He waved at the empty chair in front of him.

"Thanks," I said.

Two of my art pieces were on the table beside him, both done in conté, drawn on eighteen-by-twenty-four poster paper. One was a portrait of Fa and Diana at the Crusty Pie, drawn from reference, and the other a medieval knight in front of a castle, which was done freehand.

"These are very good, Mr. Franco," he said.

"Thank you."

"If I judge this situation by your skills," he pointed at the drawings, "I can only assume you're serious about a career in the arts?"

"I am," I said. "I mean, it's what I know."

He waved a hand toward the moth drawing on my lap. "Mind if I take a look?"

"Careful with the edges." I handed the paper to him. "It might smudge your hands. I have to spray it after I'm done."

"I gather some people are in this class because they're still figuring out what they want to do in the future." He scanned the drawing. "But judging by the lines and the details, you're not one of them."

The moth joined the other two pieces on the table next to him. He crossed his legs and put his hands over his knees, waiting for me to say something.

"It's what I've always done," I said. "Art. Started when I was three. I got better when I joined visual arts here at Joseph. It's what I see myself doing. I hope I get to live off it."

"Mr. H already submitted some of your work to us, starting your freshman year," he revealed.

"He did?" I asked, surprised.

"The first time you visited Visual Arts, he gave you all an assignment to draw whatever you wanted," he said. "You drew a woman with tears in her eyes. I still remember how detailed those eyes were."

"And he sent you that?" I shrugged. "Definitely not my best work."

"Spoken like a true artist."

"I have a thing with eyes," I said. "Sometimes I spend hours drawing them. It's the quickest way to a person's soul."

"Our school is impressed, Mateus," he said.

"Thanks," I said, cracking every knuckle on my fingers.

"We want you to consider us for your future." A smile slowly popped up on his face. "On a full scholarship."

"Sorry—" I chocked and coughed. "Sorry… a full scholarship…"

"Your tuition will be paid in full," he said. "You clearly have what it takes to succeed as an artist. There are so many fields to explore." He opened his leather suitcase and handed me a brochure. "Here's some more information about the school. We'd love for you to consider us."

"I… I don't know what to say." I scanned the glossy picture of the castle-looking building on the cover.

"No need to say anything," he said. "Your art speaks for itself. Your name will be in our records. You let us know if you decide to discuss this further."

"Absolutely."

"Have any other questions for me?"

"Not right now," I said. "But thank you."

"Of course," he said. "My card is inside that brochure. Feel free to reach out."

I got up from the chair feeling like a hero, but walked out like a soldier who had just lost a battle. It was great that the Art Academy of Boston wanted me, but there was no way in hell I could get that scholarship. It was all part of the undocumented package. Talent didn't matter. Drive didn't matter. Papers mattered.

Mr. Vine followed me out of the room. I returned to my seat and watched him go to Mr. H's desk, whisper something, and walk out.

"So?" James nudged me with his elbow. "How did it go?"

"Good," I said.

"Just good?" Fa asked. "We could see him smiling, and it was just good?"

"He just wanted to tell me how amazing the school was and blah blah blah."

"And is it amazing?" Pedro asked.

"It's all right," I said.

"And he said nothing else?" Diana frowned. "Commented on your art?"

"No," I said. "He just gave me the brochure and asked me to consider them for my future."

The truth would break their hearts. They knew the consequences of our status, and James was just entering this world within his world. I wasn't in the mood to get a pep talk about life's unexpected possibilities. Because that's what would happen.

We returned to our assignments. I wasn't sure if they had bought into my excuses or if they noticed I didn't want to talk about it.

The harsh truth was that until we were eighteen and in school, we were treated like everyone else and told we had the same chances. Then reality slapped you in the face when you aged out and were left to fend for yourself.

I imagined what it would have been like if my situation was different. I could've said yes on the spot. I could've maybe booked a school tour and met a few professors and students. A guy could dream.

We piled into Paradise for the ride home. No questions about Mr. Vine. I dropped off the original members of the Forbidden Fortress first. On my way to James's house, I could see the way he looked at me from the corners of his eyes. He wanted to ask me something, but he also wanted to be okay with my silence.

"Hey." James laced fingers with me when we pulled up in front of his house. "I'm here if you need to talk, okay?"

"What if I just want to sit in silence?" I asked.

"We can do that too," he said, not trying to hide his confusion.

"I wasn't completely honest about my conversation with Mr. Vine."

"Nooooo." He slapped his hands on his cheeks.

I scoffed behind a sad smile. "All right, so you didn't buy into it."

"I don't think anyone did. I just think everyone noticed how much you didn't want to talk about it."

"I was offered a full scholarship."

"Matty!" He grabbed my arm and shook me. "That's amazing, baby. Shouldn't we be celebrating that?"

Yes, we should. In a different universe.

"I won't be able to accept it." My heart hurt after I said the words.

"But that would be crazy."

"As crazy as being illegal, James?"

Regret replaced the excitement in his eyes. "Sorry, I didn't… I was just… Wow, Matt…" He held my hand.

"No need to apologize." I scrunched my face, hoping to drain the tears building up in my eyes. "I wish things were different. That's all. See? A normal reaction would be what you just did. I should've been excited, you know. It's an artist's dream. But I can't even celebrate that accomplishment because I can't even pursue it. And I got it."

"Exactly." His grip grew tighter around my hand. "You got it. All on your own. No one else did. You could've settled. You could've said, 'Since I have no fucking clue where life will take me, I'll just cruise.' But you didn't. It's not like we're going to college tomorrow, Matty."

"I know, but…"

"If the time comes and you can't accept the scholarship,

then you look for something else. For another way. But right now, can we just celebrate the fact that the most prestigious art school in our state offered you a scholarship? That's already an awesome achievement."

"I love you, Jamie," I blurted out. "I do."

"And I love you, Matty."

Mom and Laila were watching a movie in the living room when I got home from school around four. I went to my bedroom after we said hello and plopped on my bed with my headphones on. I had a two-hour window before going to the Crusty Pie for the night shift.

I scrolled through my phone and pressed play on "Clair de Lune." We had said "I love you" to each other. Fuck, I never thought I'd actually get to say that to anyone. And James was right. Even if I couldn't attend the Art Academy, they had offered me a full scholarship. And that wasn't me suffering the consequences of anyone else. That reward came from me and me alone.

I needed to enjoy these temporary achievements. Buying Paradise. Being offered that scholarship. I wasn't sure how long those things would last, but at least they were here now.

I got the brochure Mr. Vine had given me out of my backpack. I stared at the cover for a while: a moss-covered building with a whole bunch of students going up this gigantic staircase. "Maybe one day," I whispered and tucked it under my mattress. I didn't want Mom to know. Her heart would be crushed, since there was nothing she could do to help me. Sure, she would be proud at first, but then she would wallow in sadness.

Chatter leaked through my bedroom window. I looked out. Dad was here? He walked out of a blue car I had never seen before. He said something to the driver as he walked to the front door. He turned around, paced back and forth, looked around the neighborhood, and then continued on his way.

I tossed my headphones and my phone on the bed and rushed downstairs.

"Why's Dad here?" I asked.

"É o que?" Mom asked.

A knock on the door.

"He's here?" Laila was on the couch, her phone in hand.

"Não sei," Mom rushed to the front door.

A knock.

Mom peeked through the peephole.

"Ana," Dad said, standing outside.

"O que você quer, Claudio?" she shouted.

"Posso entrar?" Dad asked with a knock.

Mom unlocked the door. "O que quer aqui, Claudio?" she asked, the door half open.

"I'd like to talk to my kids, Ana," he said. "Pedro from the bakery is waiting outside."

Mom glanced our way, her stare asking us whether we wanted to talk to him or not. Laila and I nodded, giving her permission to let him in.

His steps were slow. His khakis were wrinkled. He looked at the floor while walking to the living room.

"Tudo bem, filhos?" he asked.

"Tudo," I answered. Laila was more entertained by the lamp on the ceiling.

"Good to hear your voices." His gaze met ours as he sat on the couch beside us.

Laila had her eyes on the floor as she tossed the remote back and forth between her hands. Mom stood behind the couch.

"I won't take long." Dad rubbed his hands and looked around the house, struggling to get his words out.

"Claudio," Mom said. "Tudo okay?"

He gazed at her. There was no hate in his eyes. More like regret; eyes that realized that it was too late to fix things.

"I'm leaving tomorrow," he said. "For good."

"Oh." Mom crossed her arms.

"I tried calling you kids, but no one answered."

Laila and I didn't force the conversation. I didn't know what to say or feel. Maybe she felt the same.

"I wanted to say goodbye—"

"Goodbye," Laila said in less than a second after he was done.

He tried to get another word out, but nothing. None of us said anything else. I tried. I did. But I had nothing to say. He kissed my forehead, kissed Laila's cheek, and rushed out.

The world imploded when I heard him drive away. This was it. Dad was going to be on the other side of the ocean, and I didn't know when we would ever see each other again.

19

SURPRISE, SURPRISE

April 2012

My mind was all over the place while I took people's orders at the Crusty Pie. I wasn't even supposed to work today. I was called in because Patrice was lucky enough to catch the flu. James was hosting a movie night later. I was going to be late, but I'd still be able to catch half the movie and some popcorn.

I thought about Dad and the life he had been living back in Brazil in the past few weeks. I somewhat felt bad for him. I even started taking his calls at first. But even from far away, it was hard to forget why I had wanted him to leave. Every phone call ended up with a few jabs at how miserable my sister and I would be if we stayed in America with Mom.

He blamed the divorce on me and my sister during one of these calls. That was when I joined the Laila club and promised myself I would avoid him. I had a whole bunch of arguments as to why he had lost his family the way he did. Dad was far now—too far; farther than that scholarship, than papers, than any legal status I could ever have.

Suddenly, no thought was loud enough to steal my attention away from Neb stepping into the Crusty Pie with Brian. We locked eyes. Neb waved, his chest puffed. Brian smirked when he saw me. They hurried to the table near the bookshelf in the back. A guy followed them. The man wore a black sweater despite the weather being a bit too warm for April. He said something to them and walked up to the counter.

"Three coffees and three bagels, please," he said.

I typed his order on the computer and stared at Neb and Brian chatting at the table.

"Everything okay, kid?" asked the man.

"Yeah, everything is good," I said. "I know them."

"I know," he said. "That's why we came here."

"Because I know who they are?"

"Where do I pick up my order?" He ignored my question.

"At the end of the counter," I said. "That'll be nine fifty-eight."

He handed me twelve. "Keep the change."

I tended to the other customers. The man joined Neb and Brian after he got his order. Customers came in and walked out, and the man kept talking to the two of them. They nodded and said a few things here and there. Sweater man led the conversation. He read from the Bible a few times.

But I didn't miss the way Brian and Neb looked at each other when the man looked down to read. I knew what their eyes said to one another. It couldn't be. Could it? I even saw a smile from Neb at one point.

I was making a latte when I noticed Neb running his hand down Brian's leg while sweater man read from his Bible. I thought I was seeing things until Brian returned the gesture. Neb noticed me staring. His hand quickly recoiled from Brian's thigh. The mug in my hand plunged to the floor; my jaw tried to fall out of my face.

Everyone looked. They looked. Brian stared at Neb, but Neb's eyes were too busy glancing at me.

I cleaned up my mess and went to the bathroom for a leak.

A few seconds after, and Neb walked in.

He didn't do anything. He just stood by the sink, arms folded, waiting for something.

"Can I help you, Neb?" I asked as I zipped up.

"I know what you saw," he said.

"Listen, it's not—"

"It's not like you weren't staring," he said.

"And it's not like you didn't have your hands all over Brian. What, you want me to say 'congratulations'? You want me to throw you a party?"

"I'm not the guy you saw out there. I'm fighting my urges away. I'm working on myself. I just relapsed."

"Why are you here?" I asked. "Why the Crusty Pie? That dude just told me a while ago that it was because of me."

"It was," he said. "He brought me here so I could face the guy who tempted me to give in to my temptations."

"Give in to your temptations? Wait, are you talking about me?"

"You and James. Seeing the two of you made me think about things I've felt since I was a kid. I thought about them so much that I decided to make a move on Brian a few weeks ago. We got caught. Pastor Paul said that I needed to show you that I was working to better myself. I was going to talk to you about it."

Pity. Then empathy. Then anger.

"Listen, you don't owe me jack. You owe some people an apology. Especially James and all the other people you made feel like shit, Neb. What did you expect? That you being gay would make all the shitty things you did go away? The pictures and videos you emailed? Those texts and screenshots…"

"I only started thinking about surrendering to these urges after you and James got together. You two were my stumbling block. Being around you two, seeing the two of you…"

It was hard to digest Neb saying phrases like "surrender" and "stumbling block" when he clearly just wanted to be a normal kid.

"Neb, listen, if you're gay, then that's fine. But are you trying to tell me that you blame James and me for what you're feeling right now?"

His eyes bulged. His face flushed. "I said it before, and I'll say it again. The gays are like a virus. It seems like I was the next victim. I'm not this guy. This is not who I am."

"You don't catch the gay, Neb. You don't pray it away. You just end up being gay."

Neb's hand turned into a fist and smashed the wall. His knuckles cracked. His eyes held mine. The muscles on his face trembled.

My face was next. Eyes never lied. His were shouting that he wanted to punch me. He slammed the door and jolted out of the bathroom instead.

They had already started the movie when I arrived at James's. There was enough pizza and soda to feed an army. I joined them in the living room and told them the story over junk food and Coke.

"So they were all touchy-feely when Bible guy wasn't looking?" Fa had her arms around her knees while her feet pressed on the edge of the coffee table.

"Telling you," I said, head on James's chest while I licked the pizza sauce off my fingers. He had an arm around me, back sunk into the couch. "And then Neb followed me into the bathroom and punched the wall. I thought he was going to break my face after."

James twirled my hair with his finger. It was nice at

first—until I noticed the empty stare in his eyes.

"Anyone home?" I asked, squeezing his ticklish knee.

He jerked up, face rigid. "Just thinking," he said. "I kind of feel bad for Neb."

The original members of the Forbidden Fortress were as quiet as that girl in the kitchen in *Jurassic Park*.

"You feel bad for him?" Pedro shifted positions on the floor. He went from lying on his side to kneeling with a gaping jaw. "How can you say that? Neb is a jerk, dude."

"I relate to him." James sat forward, elbows on his knees. "Religious parents. Public figures. There's so much of you that you have to hide so your parents don't think you're an abomination or whatever. Don't even get me started on how you must make sure their friends aren't suspicious of you. That's a whole 'nother thing. In that circle, at least, when your kids don't follow your faith, it means you failed."

"How's that an excuse for Neb's behavior?" Pedro poured more soda into his cup.

"It's not," James continued. "I'm just saying I get it. In his case, the whole sinful gay speech was actually him rejecting himself this entire time. I never got a vibe from him, though."

"Me neither," Diana said. "He hid it really well."

"And Brian?" I asked, heart beating a bit faster. "You relate to him, too?"

"There's a fine line between inner struggle and plain evil, my Matty," James said.

The rest of the Forbidden Fortress were confused.

"Brian?" Pedro asked. "Wait, you know this Brian? Are we missing something here?"

"They don't know?" James looked at me when he asked the question.

"Your thing to share," I said. "I never said a word."

He did it. He told them the entire story. The locker room. The beating. The pictures and videos. Neb's viewing party. All of it. No one interrupted. No one ate more pizza or closed the cap on the soda bottle. They listened like he was a podcast host.

"You're not angry?" Pedro asked, sitting crisscross, using his knees to support his elbows. "Man, I would've been so fucking pissed knowing that after all the shit he put you through, he ended up being gay himself."

"I wanted to stick it out," James said. "I really did. So did Brian. His parents are ministers at that place, after all. It's their entire livelihood. My parents share the same financial condition, only they travel for their money. They also have books and DVDs and all these teachings that they sell. I understand the weight, you know. I feel sorry for him." He shot me this puppy-eyed stare. "At least I found love. I found friends. I get to live out my truth. He's still struggling. Hopefully this awkward situation will inspire him to be who he is." James smiled at me. "And who knows? Maybe he'll also find someone worth loving?"

"Oh." Diana fanned her hands at her teary eyes. "You guys are the gay version of Romeo and Juliet. I swear." She fought a whimper away. "Jesus…"

"Wow, James," Fa said. "You're way more evolved than I am."

"Why?" he asked.

"I couldn't forgive them so easily," she said.

"I didn't say I did," he said. "I said I understand."

"Think you ever will?" I asked.

He smiled. "Enjoy the now, Matty. Enjoy the now."

I grabbed the remote and pressed play on the movie.

Everyone was asleep fifteen minutes later. James went upstairs and returned with blankets and pillows for them. They had decided to sleep over, since the couch reclined enough to serve as a bed. He was also kind enough to bring a tube of toothpaste in case they wanted to brush their teeth with a finger.

"Should we wake them so they can change and clean their mouths?" I whispered, tiptoeing my way to him.

"Nah," he said with a wave. "They won't sleep curled up on the floor like that for long."

I followed him upstairs into his room.

"Mind if I borrow a shirt?" I asked. "And maybe a pair of underwear."

He locked his bedroom door, pressed me against the wall, and kissed me. This one felt different than all the others. I had lost count of how many times we had been down each other's throats. He was intense about this time, determined to prove me something. His breath was heavy and I felt his heart pounding as his chest pressed on mine. He performed his last number—a nibble on my bottom lip. That was always the sign he was ready to look me in the eyes. His were glistening with tears.

"Hey, hey, hey." I cooped his hands between mine. "Are you okay?"

"Still thinking." His voice cracked. "How fucked-up it is that we have to hide. Gay kids. Most of us spend most of our childhood and teenage years and even adulthood pretending, hiding, trying to fit in. We create all these different facts about ourselves so we can be accepted. And then you get people like Neb and Brian. How come people like Pedro don't have to come out? People just assume we like the opposite sex and that's it. Like there's a rule book on who you should love." He sat on the edge of his bed. "If people were more accepting, Brian wouldn't have beaten me up. Neb might have turned out to be a cool dude in high school. Maybe none of this would have happened."

"But you also wouldn't have met me." I joined him at his side. "That would be the same thing as me wishing my parents had never brought me here. Trust me, despite everything, I'm thankful they did. Their mistakes brought me to you and to the Forbidden Fortress."

"Our own slice of hell and paradise," James added in a poetic tone.

"C. S. Lewis? Shakespeare?"

"James Alberte," he smiled sadly. "Might have to get a copyright for that one. Fa might steal it and plaster it on one of her hoodies."

I fell back on the bed, fingers laced on top of my stomach. "I have a request."

"What?" He repeated my gesture, his eyes never leaving mine.

"Give me your phone," I said.

He removed it from his pocket and laid it on my hand. It connected to the Bluetooth speaker in the shower as I navigated my way to the infamous Paradise playlist. The first notes of "Clair de Lune" whirled around the room.

"Been a while since—"

I rolled on top of him, holding his shoulder against the bed. "Don't want them to hear what I'm about to do to you." My lips brushed his ear.

"And what are you planning to do?" He shuddered.

My mouth grazed his neck then nibbled at his chin. It traveled south as I unbuttoned his shirt.

20
THE CATALYST

April 2012

"You're sure you don't mind dropping them off?" I asked, holding onto the towel around my waist as I walked out of the bathroom. "Mr. Oliver will have no one else to cover the registers if I don't show up this morning. I think Patrice is flat-out lying about this cold. I bet she went camping with her boyfriend."

"It's fine." James had an arm behind his head, chest half exposed, the rest of him buried under the blankets.

"Thank you." I let the towel drop to the floor and opened his underwear drawer. "You don't mind, right?"

"I think it's hot," he said with a wink. "You wearing my underwear all day."

"Behave." I put on a red pair, got dressed in last night's uniform—which still smelled like coffee—and kissed him goodbye.

The Forbidden Fortress had made a nest out of the blankets and sheets, sleeping on the couch like a bunch of innocent puppies. No one moved as I snuck my way out the door.

I backed out of the driveway and hooked my phone to Paradise's stereo. The skunk smell was definitely pungent once you got in, but then you got used to it.

I scrolled through my music, searching for the perfect soundtrack for my fifteen-minute drive. It was forty-five degrees after all, which meant a half-open window so the breeze hit my face but not to the point where my cheeks would freeze.

    My phone's screen kept freezing as I continued searching for a jam. But then I stared a second too long. And I missed it. A big, red, stop sign. I clutched the wheel, leaving my body for a hot sec—my spirit searching the street for a cop. And there it was, hidden between trees and bushes. Seconds moved like a snail crossing the road as I gazed at the police car, wondering if the beast would stay asleep or if it would light up.

    The theory that life flashes before your eyes when you're in danger paid off. Every important thing in my life popped in my head as the red and blue lights turned on and the car sped up to drive right behind me.

    I pulled to the side of the road, unclenching my hands away from the steering wheel. He stepped out with his sunglasses. He was tall, over six feet for sure. He strode closer, his every step sparking a pounding thought: this is unfair.

    I rolled down my window.

    "Good morning," said the cop.

    "Mor—" I cleared my throat. "Good morning, officer."

    "Why so fast?" He tucked his thumbs between his belt and pants.

    "My, um, I got a text from my boss and he said he needed me this morning. I didn't really notice how fast I was going." My entire body was cold.

    "You were almost fifty on a thirty," he said.

    "I'm sorry."

    "You realize you missed a stop back there?" he asked, my reflection displayed on his sunglasses.

    "I do—did. Yes, I realized I missed it. Again, sorry, officer."

    He stepped back and scanned the vehicle. "You old enough to be driving alone, kid?"

No matter how much I tried, I couldn't get a cohesive word out.

"License and registration, please."

Fuck. Fuck. Fuck.

I opened the glove compartment and handed him the registration, ready to do the exact same thing Dad had done that day.

"License?" he insisted.

"I don't have one." The sound of my own words were like knives cutting at my throat. Dad's face flashed in my head the entire time.

He removed his sunglasses and gazed at the registration. "And who is this… Helton Silva?"

"The car is under his name," I said.

"Does he know you have his car?" he asked. "He knows you're driving it without a license?"

If I said no, he would think I had stolen the car. If I said yes, Helton was probably going to be in some deep trouble.

"The car is mine," I blurted out. "I saved enough to buy it to get me to work. Helton is just a family friend who offered to register it. Just being honest, officer."

"No permit or license for you?" he asked, puzzled.

"No," I replied coldly.

"Why not?" he asked.

"It's out of my hands," I replied in a shaky voice.

His frown was persistent as he scanned the registration. "Tell you what." He handed me the piece of paper. "Have a parent or guardian pick you up. I'll wait here until they come."

My spirit jetted out of my body again. He wanted a parent to come pick me up. I couldn't even lie. I told him I had parents here. Well, *a* parent, but still.

He returned to his car. I could see him staring at me through my rearview mirror. I grabbed my phone. Mom was going to have a heart attack.

> **Me: Mom, can you pick me up near James's house?**
> **Mom: Everything okay?**
> **Me: A cop pulled me over.**
> **Mom: Filho, está tudo bem?**
> **Me: Yes. He just wants a parent to come get me.**
> **Mom: Send me your location. I'll be there soon.**

There was no way she could miss me and the cop by the side of the road. The few people driving by slowed down and glanced at me, probably judging the teenager that got pulled over. Now there was nothing to do but wait. I didn't even know how to behave while waiting. Music? Text? I sat on the driver's seat, frozen. I contemplated a world where I had left this place with Dad. True, we didn't get along, but I wouldn't have been at risk of going to jail or putting my family in jeopardy because I got pulled over.

I hoped Mom would arrive before James decided to drop off the Forbidden Fortress. I didn't want them to see me like this. I told Mr. Oliver I was going to be very late. Family emergency. Nobody questions you when you say that. Sure, they assume you're just using that as an excuse to cover something up, but they'll never have the guts to say that to your face.

> **Mom: Helton is driving me. See you soon.**
> **Me: Are you with him already?**
> **Mom: He's on his way to pick me up. Be there in twenty.**

Twenty more minutes. I could handle another twenty. But I wasn't going to able to handle the new few minutes. My body froze. I wanted to disappear when I spotted James's Nissan coming up the road.

I hid my face with my hand, hoping he wouldn't stop.

The side mirror was my crystal ball. He slowed down.

"Keep going," I whispered. "Keep going…"

I uncovered my face as he drove past me. Our eyes met. Pedro was in the front seat. Things seemed to move at a much slower pace as I watched them go by. I hid my face again so they wouldn't stare too long. No one needed underage James to get pulled over while driving three undocumented teenagers.

The chat started blowing up a few seconds later. I told them all was okay so far and that someone was going to pick me up soon.

I didn't bother replying to the texts that followed. Any movement suddenly felt forbidden, as if a simple breath could trigger an avalanche.

Time was obviously passing, but I lost track of it. I was numb. Helton's red car finally made its grand appearance. Feeling returned to my body once they parked in front of me. Mom quickly stepped out and ran my way. The officer remained inside his car, watching.

"Tudo bem?" she asked as I opened the door and stepped out.

"Yes," I mumbled. "Let's just get out of here." The officer watched me trudge to the passenger side. I imagined him stepping out and asking Mom for her license. But he just watched the whole thing until we drove away.

"Was Helton mad?" I asked.

"Não, Mateus," she replied. "He was worried about you."

"At least that's what he told you," I said. "He most definitely regretted his decision of registering this car."

"I can't read minds, sweetheart," she said. "So I wouldn't be able to answer."

"It's not like we would need a crystal ball for that one, right?"

"What happened?" Mom asked.

"Just drop me off at the Crusty Pie, Mom," I said, eyes welling up.

I scrolled through my phone, pressed play on the first song that popped up, and turned up the volume, so it was too loud for us to talk.

Helton followed us to the Crusty Pie and parked beside my car.

"He's driving you back to work?" I unbuckled my seatbelt, avoiding her gaze.

"Yes," she replied as I opened the door. "Mateus, wait."

"I'm already late—"

"Exactly," she said. "Five more minutes won't hurt."

I shut the door, avoiding her face.

"I wish I could take this pain away from you, filho. I've spent nights awake, thinking about a life that could've been; one where I walked away the first time he laid hands on me; one where you and your sister weren't here without—" She gulped.

"Papers, Mom," I said. "You can say it. Did you also think about a life where your son wasn't gay *and* an illegal?"

Her hands let go of the steering wheel, falling on her lap.

"We'll talk later."

I spotted Mom and Laila watching TV in the living room from the window when I parked in the driveway. I stayed in the car for a bit after turning off the engine. Driving it back home from work felt like—and actually was—a crime. I ignored all my texts throughout the entire day. I didn't want to talk about what happened, but I couldn't run from it my whole life.

I mustered the courage to face the coming family Q&A and

stepped out of the car. Laila was already at the door when I walked in. She threw her arms around me and held me like I was one of her old teddy bears.

"What's this?" I asked, doing the same thing. "You want money? Is that it?"

I thought she was going to let me go after my question, but she held on for a bit longer. When she released me from her bear hug, I noticed the hint of a tear in her eye.

"Wait, were you crying?" I asked.

"Shut up." She went back to the living room. I followed her, sitting on the opposite couch from her and Mom.

"How was work?" Mom tried to make small talk.

"Busy," I said.

"We texted you," Laila said with an edge.

"I was working," I said.

"And you couldn't spare thirty seconds to reply?" Laila protested. "After what happened?"

"You knew where I was," I replied. "Mom most likely told you that I wasn't arrested after getting pulled over."

"I wanted to know if you were okay," Laila said.

"I am…"

"Are you?" Mom asked. "Are we?"

My sister and I stared at each other.

"There's something we need to talk about," Mom continued.

I braced myself for the Matt-you-are-gay conversation I had avoided for years.

"It's about staying here," Mom continued.

That took a different turn.

"What about it?" Laila asked.

"I remember walking into each one of your rooms. You, Laila, were sleeping with that pink teddy bear you had, the one with the blue heart on its chest."

"Alfonso," Laila said. "I loved him. Too bad our dog destroyed him."

"And you, Mateus," Mom continued. "You slept with your face between the bed and the wall. Your dinosaurs were on the floor along with your notebook and that pen you loved so much even though you had chewed on it."

"What night was this?" I asked.

"The night before your father and I went to the consulate to try our visas," she replied. "I watched the two of you sleep for a few minutes and thought about the future. What would happen to us if we got those visas? I cried every night before the interview and every night after we got them. I didn't know what to expect. I didn't know how long we were going to be apart, since your father and I were coming first." Mom fought hard against the tears, but they won the battle. "I went to your rooms every single night until we left and kept thinking about life and how it would change once we got here."

"Are you proud, Mom?" I asked. "Are you proud of us?"

"So proud of every single part of you both," she said. "The part that overcame so many obstacles. You're yourselves, or at least working to be."

"Are you proud of your son being an undocumented gay boy?" I blurted out. "Both are such an inconvenience, no?"

She tapped on the empty cushion beside her. "Sit here, Mateus Franco."

I joined them on the couch. "Listen," she continued. "You can't put those two things in a blender. You have to separate them. You weren't born undocumented. That was a fate decided for you by someone else's decisions. Now, being gay, son, that's part of the package of being you."

"Then how come you never said anything?" I asked with a

shrug. "Dad saw me kissing James, and I know he told you." My chin quivered. "He beat you for it."

Her head jerked back. "You think your dad put his hands on me because of the kiss? Filho, he did that after I told him that if I caught him drinking again, I would ask for a divorce."

I broke down. I didn't even try to hold it back. "So, he was okay with it?" I asked after I regained the ability to speak. "I mean, he couldn't. He said…"

"No," Mom replied with tear streaks down her cheeks. "Your dad projected too many of his own dreams on you—things he wanted to do but never had the courage to. He was never going to be okay with any decision you made outside of what he wanted. That included being gay. When you were born, he already talked about being a grandpa and seeing you marry the daughter of one of his friends."

"And you?" I wiped my face with the back of my hand. "Are you okay with it?"

"Okay with you finding someone you care about?" she asked. "And someone who cares about you? I am."

There was honesty in her eyes, but I still needed to hear it.

"Then how come you never asked me about him?"

"I could ask you the same thing," she said. "How come you never told me about that side of you?"

"I thought you would think I was weak," I said. "You and Dad had so many problems that I didn't want to be another one in the pile—"

"No part of who you are is a burden." She shifted her eyes to Laila. "Same goes to you, filha."

"Did you always know, Mom?" Laila asked. "About Matt?"

"I suspected," she replied. "But a mom has to give space to her kids to live their truth, not impose one. And that ties into the next part of the conversation." Mom shuffled in her seat and took a breath, like someone on the front seat of a roller coaster that's about to plunge. "You two didn't get a say in moving here. It was something your dad and I decided. I feel it's only fair that we decide something together."

"Decide what?" I asked.

"To stay here or to leave." Mom's voice cracked. "I want to be honest with the both of you. What you went through today, Mateus, is a little taste of what you'll always have to live with if we stay. Unless the laws change, that will be your reality. It breaks my heart that you're in this situation, but there's no going back. I want us to keep on moving forward as a family."

"We have to decide this now?" Laila folded her legs on the couch.

"No," Mom replied. "We can take our time, but I feel it's fair to give you both a saying in what happens next."

"The next thing should be James coming over," Laila suggested. "He seems really cool. You should bring him around."

I smiled. Out of all the things I thought I'd hear, I didn't expect to have my sister want James over.

I told them everything about us. Well, not everything—the stuff that was appropriate to share with the family. The first time James and I met; the way he made me feel; what happened after the kiss.

After gushing over James for about half an hour, I headed upstairs for a shower. I stood under the hot water, thinking about time. Ignoring everyone's messages wouldn't help me go back in time—the one thing we never get back. I only had the now, after all.

So much wrong had happened in my life. My mistakes and the mistakes of other people that affected me. But it was in the disaster that I found Fa, Diana, Pedro, and James. It was because my parents decided to cross the ocean that I met the most incredible people.

I decided to text them back when I was done showering, but found them all in my room instead, sitting on my bed, looking angry-slash-concerned-slash-happy. Thankfully, I had left the bathroom with a towel around my waist.

Fa wanted to punch me. I knew it. Her face was too flushed, and her eyes screamed anger. Diana, on the other hand, looked at me like I was an abandoned kitty from the internet. Pedro's face was serious, probably thinking about how things could've been worse than they actually were. Then there was James, who rushed my way as soon I walked out of the bathroom. He hugged me, and when he did, my immediate reaction was to scan around for my family. Then I realized I didn't need to hide anymore; that it was okay to have him here. I hugged him with one arm while clutching my towel with the other.

"Were you never going to reply?" Pedro rose up with hands on his waist. "Were you planning on leaving us all in the dark after what we saw?"

"Can I get dressed first, and then we can talk?" I walked into my room, James behind me. He reclined a shoulder on the doorway, folding his arms.

"Yes, Mateus Franco." Fa stabbed a finger at me. "But I hope you're ready for an earful. I am so mad at you right now. Puta que pariu."

I ordered them out with a wave.

"We'll be out here." James closed the door.

I had honestly thought this was going to be the shittiest day of my life. Things were actually turning out okay.

My vintage *Jurassic Park* shirt and old Hollister shorts were the first things I found in my closet. I opened the door and invited them back in. Diana and Fa took the bed. Pedro folded his arms and reclined against the wall by the window. James closed the door and used it as his own resting spot.

"I'm not in prison," I said with a half-smile. "Hooray."

"That's not funny," Fa said, slapping my arm. "Listen, you could've said something."

"Your mom already told us what happened," Diana added.

"I know," I said. "I'm sorry. I just couldn't face you guys after you saw me like that."

"Like what?" Pedro asked. "A driver who got pulled over?"

"A criminal." I sat on the chair in front of my computer desk, facing the founding members of the Forbidden Fortress. "And the thing is that it could happen to any of you three. Who knows if you'll be as lucky as I was…"

"Matt," Diana said. "Stop suffering for something that hasn't happened yet. We're here now. You can't just cut us off every time something happens."

"Dude, I thought you were going to leave me for a sec," Pedro said. "I was like, I'm going to lose my best friend."

"And if one day the same thing happens to any of us," Diana started. "Then we'll worry about the aftermath then."

"So all of you are in the same situation?" James asked awkwardly. "As in, no papers?"

I glanced at James over my shoulder. Suddenly, he was the foreigner in his own land. He would never have to go through any of this.

"You're the only person not committing a crime with their every breath, James," Fa said with a smirk. "Your friends are badasses though, right?"

A knock on the door. James answered.

"Hey, kids." Mom's smile was huge. "Pizza?"

"Tia." Pedro clapped. "You know I won't say no to pizza."

"Sim!" Diana said.

"And you?" Mom put a hand on James's shoulder.

"Yeah," he said. "I'm starving."

"Don't disappear on us when shit gets hard, Matt," Fa said when Mom left.

"Don't pull that crap anymore," Pedro said. "Please."

"I'll try to be better at it," I said. "I promise."

We all flocked to the dinner table when the pizzas arrived. Laila conducted her own personal Q&A with James. Mom told everyone embarrassing childhood stories about me. Since it was Sunday night, Mom advised everyone that they had to be out by ten. She didn't want to be blamed for everyone's tardiness tomorrow. James talked and laughed with everyone the whole night, but his eyes reflected that his mind was somewhere else.

Me: Thank you for the surprise visit. :)
James: Always.
Me: Was something bothering you?
James: Aside from my boyfriend getting pulled over without a license today?

Shivers. He said "boyfriend."

Me: I'm serious.
James: Can I give you a ride to school tomorrow?
Me: Of course. Dunkin' stop?
James: Absolutely.

21
I LET YOU GO

April 2012

I waited by my window until he pulled up in the driveway, parking next to Paradise. The weather screamed spring. The flowers were in full bloom and there were birds everywhere. I darted downstairs like I was about to go on a first date with James, nearly stumbling over my steps as I walked to the door. Thankfully the house was empty. I picked up on the song he listened to as I approached his car: "Clair de Lune."

"Good morn—"

A kiss. He unbuckled his seat belt without parting ways with my face and pulled me by the shoulders. I grabbed the nape of his neck and pressed his lips even closer—if that was possible. His hand slid away from my face and over my pants. We looked into each other's eyes, breaths heavy, heart racing.

"What's this?" I asked.

"This is what I wanted to do yesterday after I saw you," he said with a shudder. "But we had an audience. And I wanted it to be private. The thought that I could've lost you, Matty, or that your mom could've been arrested when she picked you up…" My thumb followed the outline of his bottom lip. He kissed my hand away. "We should really get going if we want Dunkin'." Half of James's lips pulled up into a smirk.

"You started it!" I slapped his thigh, squeezing it like it was a toy.

"And I have to be mature enough to finish it," he said with a laugh.

I held his hand as he drove away. The last progression of "Clair de Lune" ended and the soft intro began again.

"You been listening to this song on repeat since you left home?" I asked.

"Closest thing I had to having you next to me," he said.

"Wow," I said. "Maybe I should get pulled over more often. Everyone starts acting so nice."

His face went rigid at my comment, knuckles going white over the steering wheel.

"All right, what was on your mind yesterday besides my cop encounter?"

"I'm assuming what happened will lead to a discussion about you staying or leaving."

"It already did."

I told him that part of yesterday's conversation. The frown on his face persisted as I shared every detail. He never interrupted me. He didn't say anything after. We drove into the Dunkin's drive-thru. He placed our orders and remained quiet after doing so.

He wanted to burst the silence bubble with something while we waited. I could tell. I sensed his hesitation. He squeezed my hand a few times, letting go each time he opened his mouth. "Clair de Lune" kept on playing and neither of us changed it. The song at this point was like oxygen. You knew you needed it. You knew it was there. Your lungs were drawing it in. You just didn't remember.

They handed us our coffees. He put his coffee on the cup holder and grabbed my hand as we drove away, his eyes going misty.

"I want you to know something," he said, eyes on the road. "If we're still a time bomb, I don't want you to be afraid of letting it explode."

"What does that mean?" I jerked my hand away, but he snatched it.

"If you need to go," he said. "I want you to know that I'll support your decision."

"Why are you saying this now?" I squeezed his hand. "We haven't decided it yet."

"Because it's true. I wanted you to hear it. You're incredible, Matty, and I don't want you to be held back by anything; papers or even me. I heard you guys talking yesterday and how what happened to you could happen to all the others. You know, it never had really sunk in, how bad you guys have it. It got me thinking about the things I take for granted. And I just want you to know that I don't want to hold back the Elder Wizard in case this is his time to run away from this castle."

"Holding me back…" I was done hiding my tears. "Jamie, you've helped me move forward in every way. You inspired me to own up to the part of me I hid away for so long."

"And for that I'm glad, but if my part in your tale comes to a close anytime soon, I'll still be thankful that I got to be in your life."

I imagined what it would be like to kiss him one last time; to have coffee at the Crusty Pie with him before flying across the ocean; to see the dimpled chin in person before jetting off to Brazil not knowing when—or if—I'd ever be back.

We all know there will be a last time for the things we love. We cope by going through life not really thinking about those. But the moment a timer is set, you begin to measure every second, minute, hour, and every breath you take, and every laugh you share.

I could keep on hanging out with the Forbidden Fortress and loving James, but sooner or later, even being the Elder Wizard wouldn't protect me. Whether by getting pulled over again or by missing out on a job because I didn't have the proper documentation, the truth was bound to find me now or a few years down the line.

It was time to face the truth, even if the cost was a one-way ticket.

James dropped me off at the Crusty Pie for my evening shift after school. We were quiet the whole way there. Not because we didn't have anything to say. On the contrary. We had too much and not enough time to say it.

It was a Monday shift like every other, slow most of the time if not for the casual dinner rush. It also sucked that there had been no scheduled visits from the Forbidden Fortress today. Pedro was on a date and Fa and Diana were having a dinner with their families. James's parents were also flying in tonight. Muffins, bagels, sandwiches, and Mr. Oliver's jokes were my only company and entertainment.

I was getting ready to lock up for the night when Neb showed up. I had never seen him that way. He usually had this way about him where he walked inside a place like the whole thing belonged to him. Not this time. To him, the Crusty Pie was a torture chamber and he was the next victim.

"Hey." He stood a few feet away from the counter, rocking his body back on forth on his tiptoes.

"You can come closer, Neb," I said, wiping the counter. "I can control my urge to punch things."

He took a few short steps.

"You want to order something?" I asked. "We'll be closing soon."

"No," he said, shoulders contracted around his neck. "Just want to talk, if that's okay."

"No punching this time?" I asked.

"Please, Matt," he whispered.

He had probably planned the time to show up. I was about to close, so I would have a few minutes to spare, and there was no way I would've been able to run from him. But there was something about him—a vulnerability I had never seen before.

"Let me finish a few things here," I said. "Pick any table you want."

He slugged his way to the back, sitting where James and I had sat when he showed up with Brian that day. I observed him as I cleaned the counter and replenished the napkin and straw dispensers. He stayed in the same position, keeping his eyes on the ceiling, bopping his legs up and down, acting as if any other move was bound to trigger a catastrophe.

He was a jerk. An asshole. What he did to James was pure evil. But I was surprised at myself suddenly. I could see what James had brought up that night, the way he had to live his life. The things he probably had to do to survive.

I had Googled his family. They were the heads of one of the largest churches in Massachusetts. They also had other smaller campuses around the country. There was a picture of his parents on the church's website. They were under a tree laughing. They seemed happy. I mean, they had to look the part if their job was to sell the idea that their religion was pure bliss. But Neb didn't reflect the joy in the picture tonight.

I made us hot chocolates. Even someone like Neb needed a little sweetening up.

"You look like you need a pick-me-up." I set the paper cup on the table.

"Thanks." He grabbed the drink with a shaky hand.

He ripped a hole in the peelable drink lid and watched the steam rise like it was the most entertaining movie ever made.

"So?" I asked. "What brings you here?"

"I wanted to explain," he said. "To talk about that day."

"I never knew you played for the team." I hoped to lighten up the tension.

"Oh, I don't," he said sharply, looking me dead in the eye. "No, no. It's just a temporary condition. Brian and I are working through it. This won't last. That's what I wanted to tell you. I was out of line that day. But I spoke the truth. This is not who I am."

A lion would never grow wings. Just like an eagle would never grow a mane. What did Neb mean? "Go back to that temporary condition thing you just said."

"I'm on the road to recovery." He forced a shaky smile. "I'm going to be going to this therapy center in Texas. They're going to set my mind straight." He took a sip. "Pun intended."

Some identities could be changed. I could go from undocumented to documented the moment a law was signed. I could go from sick to healthy by undergoing treatment. Now, going from gay to straight?

"I would've laughed at that joke, but I'm still thinking about something you said." I folded my arms on the table. "All right, Neb. I don't agree with a lot of the things you did, but listen, like I said before, if you're gay, then that's a part of you. You can be bi, if anything."

He snapped each of his thumbs with a finger, eyes on me. "I used to have these thoughts when I was younger. I managed to tuck them all away with prayer. But seeing you and then seeing James… I'm now the result of my environment," he said, so sure of himself. "Which makes sense. That's what my parents said. I spend most of my days in school surrounded by negative influences."

"But you have your table at lunch," I said. "If that was the case, then having them around would've helped you with your 'condition.'" I air-quoted the last word.

He rolled up his sleeves and dragged his chair so close, his chest touched the table. "The Texas thing will be good for me, Matt. It has to be. I can't be gay or bi."

"Hate to break it to you, Neb," I continued. "But the world will not always believe like you. You can't pull away every time someone sees things differently. And you can't keep ignoring what's inside of you. The real you. The part of you that will never change."

"And that's why I have to be stronger so I can face the world without leaving my faith," he said. "I wanted to talk to you—"

"Neb, it wasn't that big a deal. So you had your hand on the legs of a guy you liked and he liked you back—"

"It's not a big deal to you, Matt. Because you don't know. You don't know how my world works. My parents could lose their reputation. My congregation would be ashamed of me…"

"But Neb, things—"

"I'm not asking for your opinion. I wanted to talk to you in person because you saw everything in person and you won't see me in school anymore."

"Why not?"

"I'm transferring schools," he said proudly. "My mentor encouraged me to do it; told me it would help me clear my head and stuff. I need distance from the secular."

"And you *want* to transfer?" I asked.

"It's not just about what I want anymore," he said. "I came here to apologize. For showing you those texts from Brian and James and for anything else that I may have done—"

"You showed me the texts because you wish it was you with James," I said. "Come on, Neb. You got pissed that James joined our table on his second day because you wanted him around. And not to help him overcome his—" air quotes "— 'condition,' but because you liked him. And now you like Brian. And I hate his guts. I do. I hate the guy for what he did to my boyfriend, but this is about you and your future. Don't go down this path."

He lightened the frown on his face. He smiled briefly, most likely imagining a future where he belonged. His explicit joy lasted seconds. "Matt, if you only knew the price I'd pay if I gave in." He ran his hands down his face. "I have to make it right. I know how ashamed James's parents are of him."

"Ashamed?" I scoffed.

"You can't really believe they're happy with him," he said. "After everything I told you. James and I come from the same world. You do understand that, right? In our world, people need our lives to be aligned with scripture. That's the way this goes."

"What happened to free will?" I asked. "Isn't that something you guys talk about all the time?"

"Free will is a knife," he said. "In the right hands, it can be used to cook. In the wrong hands, it can be used to kill."

"Fuck, Neb, what do you think you're doing with *your* knife?" I asked.

He gazed at the paper cup like it could save him from this conversation.

"There are things you're born with," I said. "And there are things you're taught. You're born being fully yourself. No judgment from others. No outside influences. You're, like, this rough diamond and it needs polishing. Sometimes a lot of polishing. But being who you are comes with the package."

"You wouldn't understand—"

"I think I would," I said. "You didn't choose to be born in

this religious family. I didn't choose to be undocumented in this country."

His head jerked back.

"Yeah," I continued. "I was brought here. That was something imposed on me. I didn't get a say in the matter back then. But then life gives you chances to decide things on your own. Neb, the pain you experience now might just be worth it in the future."

He lowered his head with a sniff. "Do I owe you for the drink?"

"No, it's on the house," I said.

"Have a great life, Matt." He left the table before I could say anything else. He rushed out of the coffee shop like some creepy stranger was after him. He was, to some extent, being pursued by the stranger he had ignored his entire life: his true self.

22

A LETTER

April 2012

The cafeteria didn't seem at all that interesting this morning. I texted the group and told them I wanted to get a head start on this week's shop project. James's parents wanted to keep him for breakfast. His absence from the bus gave me a whole lot of time to think about Neb. Yes, Neb. I went to bed thinking about our conversation and woke up with him lingering in my head.

I had realized the strangest thing last night. Neb and I shared a talent: hiding our true selves from the world. We had both done an excellent job. We both had to adapt to survive. We both had to create a character within ourselves that wouldn't bother people so much. It was fucking weird having something so common with him. And then I figured something out. While you're adapting and covering the truth with a whole bunch of layers, someone barges in and then boom, all the layers are gone. Just like that. They disappear as fast as snapping a finger.

James had been my catalyst. Brian his. All the comments and the way he had acted since freshman year, all those things were just a reflection of how he felt about himself. I felt bad for him. He had fucked up, but no one deserved to live in a cage. The irony was that Neb and I were still both in cages. My paperless cage was locked shut from the outside and Neb was behind fundamentalist bars.

Walking into the empty shop and seeing Neb's seat was weird. I knew he wasn't coming today or any day after this one. I stared at his chair. Empty. Probably like him, wherever he was.

I gazed at the chair. Suddenly the past two years flashed through my mind in a few seconds. All the times he had used his sarcasm. All the invitations to attend youth service at his church. Maybe all these things were a cry for help.

I walked to the supply shelf at the back of the shop and grabbed a few sheets and took a seat, pulling my art box out of my backpack. My sketch pencil scraped the paper. I looked at the blank sheet and at the chair as I sketched the first lines of what was meant to be the chair's metal legs covered in paint blotches.

I could've done better by him. I could've seen the signs if I hadn't been so judge-y of his attitude. People build barriers for a reason. His had always been high. And maybe, just maybe, he had invited me to sit at his table freshman year because he thought he'd eventually get to talk to me about his truth. Maybe he noticed the gay in me before I ever did. I was yet to know if a gaydar was a real thing. What if it was and his had picked me up from yards away?

He had always seemed like one of the other kids who were in this class because they didn't know what they wanted out of life. He wasn't the best artist, but if I had paid attention, I might had seen a red flag. Pastor's kid. He'd talk about his mission trips all over the country, but maybe it wasn't the mission that mattered to him. It was the trips and getting to explore a world beyond his own.

I had never heard him say he wanted to take over his dad's

place. I wasn't that close with him, but still, I had never seen him show a real interest in anything.

Maybe it wasn't too late. I grabbed my phone and looked for his Facebook account. Gone. I texted. The message didn't go through.

My mind was like a pressure cooker as I sketched the details of the chair's green seat. The door opened. James. He smiled and walked my way.

"Morning, my Matty." He pecked me on the lips.

"Hey. What happened to breakfast with your parents?"

"That happened for five minutes," he said. "And then they had some meeting at the church." He glanced at the sheet of paper on my desk. "And an empty desk? Is that what we're drawing this week?" He sat down.

"This is just me thinking about… stuff…"

"Stuff?"

I sighed.

"You've been quiet since last night. Your texts were short. And you usually FaceTime me to say good night. I missed our little banter."

"Neb isn't coming today," I said.

"Oh? That's what's on your mind?"

"He isn't coming today or tomorrow or ever…"

"What happened?" he asked. "How do you know this?"

"He visited the Crusty Pie last night, right before it closed." I sketched one of the legs of the desk, trying to get it to look as close as the real thing. "He wanted to talk about what I saw that day. Him and Brian."

"In person?"

"Yes. Weird, I know. He told me he was leaving Joseph for good. Something about not being surrounded by temptation. He's sticking to those sessions at his church. And I can't help but think that I could've, I don't know, helped him." The pencil strokes were harder. "I could've helped him somehow. If I hadn't been so—"

"Helped him? How?"

"I could've been less judgmental, I could've sat at his table and he could've talked. Something. He felt like a piece of shit. I could see it in his eyes. I knew that look...."

He slid the pencil out of my grasp and laid it on his desk. "I love your heart, Matty. You see the good. Even when people make these huge mistakes, you still have a soft spot for them. But you can't fix everyone around you."

"But I could've—" He walked to the empty chair, dragged it in front of me and sat down so his eyes were level with mine.

"He could've treated you better as well," he said. "He could've treated many people better. He made his choices, Matty. And sometimes, no matter how much it hurts, we need to let people choose." He kissed the top of my hand. "And we need to let them live on so we can go on. All we can do is be there for them."

It was like being on a seesaw. In front of me were all the fucked-up things Neb had done to me and to those around me. And on the other side was my suddenly merciful heart.

"I feel so shitty," I said. "Here I am, feeling sorry for a guy who ruined your life. I keep bringing him up. Fuck..."

"You give people chances, Matty," he said. "That's a good thing to do."

"Not everyone deserves a chance, though," I said.

"Very true." He grabbed the sketch in front of me and held it up. "And sometimes, not even the past serves to be remembered. We also have to let the past go." He placed the sketch back on my desk. "Sometimes life has a way of working itself out." He smirked.

"Why do I feel like you're about to give me some good news in the middle of all this?"

He rubbed his hands fast. "My parents want to have you over for dinner tomorrow."

I was an anchor that had been dropped unannounced into very dark waters.

"Re—Really?"

"Yeah. They were the ones to bring it up, actually. Would you be down to come?"

From everything I had heard about his parents and the congregation they belonged to, I doubted this was the kind of dinner James had dreamt of. I didn't have the heart to break his hope that it could be.

"Count me in." I hoped he didn't notice my hesitation.

"I know it might end up being super awkward, but it's something, at least, right?"

"It's more than something, Jamie," I said. "And if it does end up being awkward, we'll come up with a plan to make it interesting."

Mr. H walked in with a coffee in one hand and a binder on another.

"Morning, Mr. Franco; Mr. Alberte. No breakfast for you both today?"

"Needed some peace and quiet," I said.

"Well, I had to rush out of the house, so I'm going to go to the cafeteria to grab me a bagel. You guys want something? Just don't tell the other kids. I'd become their bagel delivery guy if they ever found out."

"A bagel sounds great," I said.

"I'm okay," James said.

Mr. H wasn't long. The bell rang a few minutes after he returned with not only a bagel but some chocolate milk. Fa, Diana, and Pedro were some of the last to walk in.

"How was your early morning?" Pedro said after he had settled at his desk.

"Productive," I said.

"I bet it was," Diana said. "Just the two of you in here. It must've been very productive."

"Hey, babe," Fa said. "Let's get an early start tomorrow? I really need to work on this assignment." She winked.

"Such dirty minds so early in the morning," James said with a chuckle.

"All right, kids," Mr. H said, standing in front of his desk. "Let's settle down. I have an announcement."

"Another donut competition?" someone shouted from the back.

"Very funny. Settle down," he repeated. "Settle down, please."

The class got quiet.

"I wanted to let you all know that Mr. Hamwinter will no longer be attending Joseph." Pedro, Fa, and Diana jerked their heads my way. I pretended to be as shocked as they were. James kept his eyes on Mr. H. I should've probably done the same. "He's transferring to a different school. I know his transfer was pretty sudden, so if any of you guys feel like making him something or writing him a letter, I'll make sure it gets delivered to him."

Most of the class chuckled.

"Write a letter?" Pedro said. "Mr. H, it's 2012. Neb will be freaked out if he gets a whole bunch of letters from us, no?"

"Well," Mr. H said. "I know your generation is used to texting and emails and social media, but a letter is more personal." Mr. H looked at me. "Maybe that's what Mr. Hamwinter needs right now. Some honesty in his life for once."

He then told us to start our assignments. Human anatomy. No references, though.

"Mr. Franco, mind staying for a few minutes?" Mr. H asked when the lunch bell rang.

The rest of the class, along with the members of the Forbidden Fortress, left.

"Everything okay?" I asked.

"Oh, yes. You're not in trouble or anything. I want to talk to you about Mr. Hamwinter, if that's all right."

"Yeah, yes, of course."

"Planning on sending him something?" he asked. I could sense it in his voice that something was up.

"I don't know, Mr. H," I said. "We weren't super close. Neb could be an ass—" I cleared my throat. "—a jerk sometimes."

"I know, Mr. Franco," he said. "Why he left Joseph. I know."

"You do?"

"I was a part of that congregation for years," he said. "Neb was probably five when I joined. I had to leave a few years after. Talk about life teaching us all important lessons."

"Why?" I asked.

"A divorced man with a queer daughter doesn't really fit in," he said.

I chuckled.

"Neb talked to me right before he started his freshman year here at Joseph," he said. "He came to my house. Very unlike him. He told me the truth about himself. He said he was looking forward to coming here so he could be around different people."

"Mr. H, that's some bullshit excuse—sorry for cussing."

"You're good, kid."

"When he wasn't in shop," I continued, "he was still hanging out with kids from his church. And he was always around them at lunch—"

"It's hard to leave what you know behind. We try and try,

but it isn't easy to be who we truly are when who we are offends those we love."

Mr. H had gone from art teacher to therapist in seconds.

"Why are you telling me this, Mr. H?" I asked.

"He came to me yesterday," he said. "Right before he went to see you. I know what he decided to do, Mr. Franco. You and I both know that won't work. Maybe receiving a letter or something from you might help him remember that."

"We talked at the Crusty Pie. I think that ship sailed for him. He was set on his decision."

"Give it one more try?" he insisted.

"I'll think of something," I said.

"It must be a letter, Mr. Franco. They keep an eye on his phone and emails. Don't try anything there. I can sneak a letter in. I know someone at that Texas facility. Think of them as an undercover advocate for queer people. I can get them to deliver the letter."

23

ALL THINGS MUST END

April 2012

I thought about the letter while driving home from school and kept thinking about it while cooped up in my room. What would I even say to him? My guts had been spilled already. Maybe Mr. H knew more than he let on. To ask for letters in front of the entire class? Was I missing something?

Mom was working. Laila was cooped up in her room as well. All the members of the Forbidden Fortress were busy tonight. I thought food, music, and art could keep my mind off Mr. H's words. But I was very wrong.

I grabbed my phone and FaceTimed James.

"Hey, you," I said.

"Hey," James said, hair dripping.

"Oh, in the shower?"

"I just got out." He smiled.

"I need to ask you a weird question," I said.

"I love those." He dropped the phone on his bed.

"Yeah…" I gazed at his ceiling.

"Is this about the Neb letter thing Mr. H said today?" His head popped back on the screen as he towel-dried his hair.

"Yeah," I whispered. "Are you writing something?"

"My Matty, you know I love you, but I won't answer that."

"Oh?"

"I don't want to influence your decision."

I stared at his face and said nothing. He did the same. I tried reading what was behind his eyes. Maybe I'd pick up on his opinion.

"Just so you know," James said, "you have a way with a pencil. Why don't you use it to draw something that will help him in some way?"

"Won't that be weird?" I asked.

"It'll be much cooler than a handwritten note," he said.

"I'll think of something," I said.

"You always do," he said. "Baby, I need to get dressed. Parents want to go out for dinner."

"Yeah, yeah. Love you."

"I love you, too," he said.

I scanned the page of the sketchbook in front of me. Monsters, crooked trees, hands, and eyes. Four pairs, actually. A drawing wouldn't be as awkward as a letter. Or would it? At least it'd be different in case anyone else decided to send him something.

I tried to remember Neb smiling. Not the snarky smirks he gave people. His actual smile. His laugh, even. Like someone had just told him a funny story. I realized I had never seen him do such a thing.

Thankfully I had stared at his empty chair long enough to draw it from memory. I sketched him sitting down; worked on the legs and the hands. But his eyes got me stuck. If I drew the eyes I remembered, I'd draw the Neb I had always known. I could get creative with this part; even come up with an expression I had never seen on him before.

I erased his face a few times because it didn't look real. After a while, I realized that it wasn't that the eyes were off or that the smile was too broad. A real smile didn't fit him. It didn't look bad. It just looked different. This is what he needed to see. A smile didn't look so bad.

But eyes, eraser shavings, and smudges later, my stomach reminded me I hadn't eaten since I had gotten home.

I went downstairs to make a sandwich and found Laila in the living room, lying on the couch, scrolling through her phone. I had lost track of time and hadn't even noticed that it was already dark outside.

"Matt," she said.

"Hey." I opened the refrigerator and grabbed the ham and cheese. "Want a sandwich?"

"I'm okay." She joined me in the kitchen. "I wanted to talk to you about something."

"Sure." I grabbed the bread from the pantry. Her face was serious, the kind of serious where I knew she wasn't about to make a funny comment about a random topic.

"Remember that decision stuff Mom talked about?" she asked. "You know, going back and stuff?"

"Yeah."

"Have you decided?"

"I don't know," I replied, setting all my sandwich stuff on the dining table. "I think about it some days. Then other days I forget. Then it hits me hard and I imagine what it'd be like to actually leave everything behind."

"Been thinking about it," she said, watching me put two slices of cheddar on a slice of bread. "Today more than any other day."

"Something happened?" I put the ham and squirted some mayo on it.

"Remember Italo from Christmas?" she asked.

"Yeah."

"His dad got arrested."

"Oh, Laila…"

"He was part of some gang that gave social security numbers out to people. It's probably going to be all over the news by the weekend. It was pretty bad. He told me in secret because he was so embarrassed. But once this is on the news, then there's no hiding anymore."

"I'm sorry."

"He's leaving. Italo. He won't even get to finish the school year."

"That's…"

"Fucked up?" she said. "I think it's the right time to say that, right?"

"I'd have to agree," I said.

"Parents and their fuck-ups," she said.

"I mean," I said. "We all make mistakes, right?"

"I hope parents don't use that excuse to feel better about theirs," she said. "Especially his dad. And how he has to leave because he ended up being some crook." Her eyes glistened. "It's so unfair that he has to pay for his dad's mistakes. He probably had plans to go to high school and graduate. Maybe he even had a college in mind. And now he won't get to do any of those things because of his dad."

"You and I are pretty familiar with that situation," I said. "But we make the best of it."

"I'm tired of making the best of it," she said. "I'm tired of living like this. I can't help but feel that the longer I stay here, the more I'm going to have to pay for Mom and Dad's mistakes," she said. "Dad doesn't even live here anymore and we can't escape what he did. Avoiding his calls is one thing, but…" She sucked in a breath. "He left, and you and I got to stay behind in the mess he made."

"I get it," I said.

"And then you're going to be eighteen soon. I'll be eighteen at some point. And then everything will just come crashing down. You had a taste of that already. You got pulled over. I was so scared you were going to go to jail that day."

"But I didn't."

"Still," she said. "I don't want to stay here like this. I'm tired. We don't belong back home. We don't belong here. It'll be tough going back, but at least we'll have some stability, I think? I don't know. I'm just tired of not knowing how long people will stick around for. How long I will stick around for."

"That's life in general," I said. "You never know how long you have with someone."

"I get that," she said. "But you expect people to stick around for at least a while, right? You go to middle or high school expecting to finish with the people that started with you. You were so brave in starting something with James. There was always the possibility that we could leave and you just threw yourself into it. I can't do that."

I hugged her.

"Hey," I said. "Can I give you some advice?"

"Yeah…" She wiped her nose.

"Enjoy whatever time you have left with Italo," I said. "He's probably lonely enough at this point. Even if you guys won't be together for long, at least he'll carry that memory across the ocean."

"Thanks," she said with a sad smile. "You feel the same way about James?"

My entire life flashed through my head in less than a second.

"I feel so many things," I said. "I'd probably be able to write a book if I were to jot them all down. Mind if I leave you with that one?"

She kissed my forehead and headed upstairs to her room.

I grabbed my sandwich and sat on the couch in the living room. Dad had many flaws. He had hurt us. He had hurt himself. But in his messy pain, maybe there was an echo of truth. Staying here like this would be too damaging. No matter how much I loved this place. It didn't matter that I felt like I belonged. The truth was, I didn't.

I didn't agree with Neb's decision, but I was doing the same thing: hoping to change something that couldn't be changed. In my case, the more I delayed my decision to face the truth, the greater the damage would be to my life and to those around me.

I returned to my room after finished my sandwich, but instead of returning to sketchbook, I sat on my computer desk and Googled immigration news.

There was news. Many articles. From consular amendment fees to global entry stuff, things were moving for some people. Not for me or my sister or my mom. There was nothing on the horizon for the so-called "Dreamers." There were articles about the DREAM Act and plenty of Facebook posts on why it should pass, but nothing solid.

I found a group on Facebook called "Dreamers Are Meant to Stay." I was pulled into the rabbit hole of reading their comments and looking at their pictures and reading their stories. There were thousands like me and Laila, and most of us shared the same feeling. We were getting tired.

Many had it much worse than we did. There were Dreamers being scammed by fake immigration attorneys who promised they knew a loophole to get a green card. Others had been here for such a long time that their undocumented parents ended up having American babies who were now too young to be left behind. And then you had those who swam across the Rio

Grande and lost loved ones during their crossing. Seeing their faces, reading their words, and comparing them to what the media portrayed us to be angered me.

Hearing my sister say she didn't want to stay here anymore hurt. Bad. And yes, I wasn't her dad, but if she and Mom decided to leave, I wasn't sure if I would actually have the heart to stay behind. What would they go back to? If I were there, I'd be able to help them.

My sketchbook and my bed were my destination after I got tired of feeling like crap. My willingness to work on this drawing for Neb only lasted so long.

I put the sketchbook next to me and reached between my mattress and frame until I found the brochure for the Art Academy in Boston. I stared at the building on the cover, imagining me walking inside. That would never happen; proof that the damage would only get worse if I stayed. Yesterday I was pulled over. Today I lost a scholarship. I didn't want to risk tomorrow.

A knock on the door.

"Hey, filho." It was Mom.

"Mom, you're early." I tucked the brochure inside my sketchbook and closed it.

She sat on the edge of my bed with a curious frown. "How was your day?"

"Average," I said. "And everyone was busy tonight."

"You look busy, too." She pointed at the sketchbook.

"Working on a little something for someone," I said.

"Mind if I see it?" She extended her hand.

"Yeah." My voice was a weird mixture of a croak and a whisper. She was bound to find the brochure and I was bound to tell her.

"Wow, Matt." She reached for it. "This is really good—" She grabbed the brochure. "What's this?"

"Just some information on a school…"

"This looks amazing, filho," she said. "Why do you have this?"

I could lie. I could say that I had simply found it at school and kept it because I liked the design. But I needed to face my many truths. Including this one.

Her face grew sadder and sadder as I shared what had happened. Mr. Vine. The scholarship. The missed opportunity. She didn't give in to her tears. I knew she wanted to. It broke my heart. She looked at the brochure and at me like my words were a really messed-up dream.

"Congratulations, Mateus." She laid the brochure on top of the drawing and stared at it. "And I'm sorry—"

"Don't be, Mom," I said. "Don't. Hey, I got it, right? I can't have it, but I got it."

She put the brochure on the bed to look at the drawing.

"This is incredible," she said. "This isn't James, though."

"It's a gift for someone," I said. "He left the school, so I wanted to give him something."

"I'm sure he'll love it." She handed the sketchbook back and walked to my sister's bedroom door.

"Laila?" she asked while knocking.

"Yeah?" Her muffled voice replied.

"Pode vir aqui, filha?" Mom returned to my room and sat back on the edge of the bed.

"Tudo bem, Mãe?" Laila joined Mom at her side.

"I want to ask you if you're okay, Laila," she said. "I heard about Italo's dad."

"Oh, Mom, I'm—" she cleared her throat. "I'm… all is…" Laila broke down. She wasn't much of a crier. "It's okay."

"No, it isn't." Laila wiped the corner of her eyes with a wrist. "None of this is."

Mom sat in a heavy silence. I didn't need to be a parent to

know that a storm tormented her mind.

"I get it, Laila," Mom said. "I do. I still stand by what I said. You have a saying in what happens now." She looked at me. "You both do."

"I know it's unfair," Laila said. "Especially for you, Matty. You have James. And you're so brave. You also have the choice to stay—"

"I'd never leave you and Mom like this," I said. "I could never leave you two and not know when I'd be able to see you."

Truth hurts. My every word proved that fact. I was with Mom and Laila in person, but my mind rushed to the future: the goodbyes, the tears, the last kiss. But I could no longer avoid my time bomb. It was time to let it explode.

24

SOMEONE ELSE'S MISTAKES

May 2012

Dinner with James's parents. The big day was finally here. Mom had agreed to drive me. I wanted to look good but not too dressy so they wouldn't think I tried too hard. I tried on five shirts and eventually set on a black button-down—always a safe choice when in doubt. Gray jeans and Converses were also solid territory to meet the parents, even the ones that weren't too fond of their son having a boyfriend.

Laila had offered me some advice on my outfit before leaving for the movies with her friends. It was sweet of them to be spending more time with her now that Italo was gone. At least Laila and Italo had a shot at seeing each other when we were all living in Brazil again.

I tried to see tonight in a good light. I had nothing left to lose if I didn't make a good impression, because I would be out of the picture soon. Not that James knew. It killed me that he didn't. Well, no one knew, actually. I just couldn't bring myself to find a good time to break the news.

Fa, Diana, and Pedro knew something was off. They hinted many times. James most likely thought I was acting a bit distant because of this dinner. I went along with it because, honestly, I wanted to forget my goodbyes for a little while.

A knock on my door. "Pronto?" Mom asked, the collar of my shirt the invitation she needed to come in. "You look so handsome, Mateus."

"Thanks, Mom," I said as she fixed it.

"Is there a reason why you look this good?" she asked. "Is it a special night?"

"I'm meeting James's parents for the first time." I let out a breath like I had just finished a jog.

"Tão animado," she said snidely.

"I mean, they don't really agree with James being gay. They're very religious, but they invited me over. I agreed since we… well… I wanted to do this for James, but we won't be here much longer. So whatever happens, happens. He'd be so bummed if I canceled."

"I think it's a brave thing," she said. "To stand for what you want like that."

"I'm doing it for him." I shrugged. "Even after I leave, he will at least have gotten his wish."

"You should it for you as well," she suggested.

"What do you mean?" I asked.

"Always stand up for yourself. When people don't see eye to eye with you, let them share their truth, but you also share yours. Our truths matter just as much."

"Thanks, Mom."

"No matter how these people treat you tonight, you let them know where you stand."

"Will do," I said.

"Just like you did with Neb," she said.

"Yeah."

"You did it?" she asked.

"Yes," I said. "I sent it."

"Good." She smiled. "Now, let's go. You don't want to be late. You know Brazilians already have that to our name."

James waited for me by his front door. Walking up his steps usually felt like paradise. Today it felt like walking into a courtroom. He looked fucking handsome in his red button-down. It was hard not to kiss him. He looked startled, confused, and excited at the same time. How could I blame him?

"Hey, you." I tucked my hands in my pockets once I was next to him.

"Hey." He leaned in for a kiss but hesitated. "Sorry, I don't know. I don't even know how to act—"

"It's okay," I said with a chuckle. "We didn't discuss how this part was going to go down."

"Sorry." He pulled air through his teeth and looked up as if searching the stars for answers. Fa would be proud. "I've never done this with them… with anyone. You're literally the first."

"Me neither, but I think it's safe to say that standing outside while they're inside isn't a good thing," I mentioned. "They might find it very awkward. I don't want them to think of me as gay *and* rude."

The house I knew so well felt like a different place. His dad's coat hung by the door. There was a Bible on the table by the stairs. The kitchen was actually being used. James and I had never cooked in there. The long dining table was also properly set.

James led me into the living room. They were on the couch, both dressed in black. Had I missed the memo? Was this the funeral of their hopes of ever having a straight son?

"Mom, Dad." James slapped his hands on his thighs. "This is Mateus."

"Pleasure meeting you, Mr. and Mrs. Alberte," I said while shaking their hands. "You can call me Matt."

"Pleasure, Matt," his mom said, looking me up and down like I was about to go through security at the airport. "Call me Sophia, please."

"Call me Daniel." The smile on his dad's face was so forced, it deserved a Raspberry Award. "So you're the special friend."

My body clenched. Even someone oblivious to his beliefs would've noticed how he emphasized the last two words.

"I… sure…"

"He is special, Dad," James said.

"Come." His mom waved as she walked to the dining table. "We don't want the food getting cold."

I was usually able to read James's expressions. I had gotten very good at deciphering the smirks, frowns, and puckered lips. They were all over the place tonight.

There was chicken parm, salad, garlic bread, and soda.

"This was James's favorite when he was a kid," Mrs. Alberte said. "He asked me to make it tonight. It's nothing fancy, but I hope you like it."

"Really?" I asked, surprised. Had I gotten a slight hint that his mom was enjoying this?

"Yes," James said, the huge smile on his face melting my heart. "But I like Mom's chicken parm only. I refuse to eat it anywhere else."

"I was about to say, I've never seen you order it, like, ever."

"I would've grounded him if he did," she said with a laugh.

This was good. The tension was breaking. This could be a good night.

"Good to know some things never change," his dad blurted out. "If only other things stayed the same."

And there was the tension again. James frowned at his dad's comment.

"Matt." His mom beckoned for my plate with a wave. "Please let me."

"Thank you." I handed it to her.

"What do you want to drink?" James asked. "Coke? Sprite?"

"Coke is fine," I replied. "You know, in Brazil we have this soda called Guaraná. It's *the* thing to drink at any dinner party," I said as James poured my drink. "I should've brought it."

"Next time," Sophia said.

"James told me you were Brazilian." Mr. Alberte watched his wife grab the salad servers and mix the veggies and lettuce. "But I don't hear an accent."

"I was nine when my family moved here," I said.

"Mom, Matt and I can skip the salad, right?" James asked. "That chicken parm is begging to be eaten."

"No, James," I protested. "Let's enjoy every course of the meal. That would be like eating dessert before the entrée."

"Good advice," Mrs. Alberte said.

"What made you leave your country?" Mr. Alberte asked. No matter how much I wanted to call them by their first names, even in my head, I couldn't bring myself to do it.

"Family left. I followed," I replied. "I was too young to decide."

"Here you go." Mrs. Alberte handed me my salad plate.

"Thank you," I said.

"There must be more to that story," he insisted.

"Oh, absolutely," I said. "The classic American dream tale. We came here searching for a better life."

"Came in through the front door?" he asked.

"Dad," James whispered.

"I don't get the question," I said.

"We read about people crossing through Mexico all the time." He handed his plate to his wife, who started serving the salad immediately. "I'm wondering if you had to swim across a river to get here, too."

"It's crazy," Mrs. Alberte said. "I read stories about these people crossing or staying here without papers and I wonder how on earth can a parent do that to their child?" Mrs. Alberte handed her husband his salad.

"It's the end of times, Sophia." Mr. Alberte grabbed a fork and a knife to cut the lettuce. "Just like the Bible says. People are losing their ability to love and are willing to put anything and anyone at risk."

I was ready for a different kind of judgment.

"That depends how you look at it," I said, heart racing a little faster. "Sometimes people need to be bold enough to leave a situation so their lives can change. Sometimes the only way out is to take a risk."

"So you did cross the border?" Mr. Alberte insisted.

"No," I replied. "No, no, we came with our tourist visas."

"Oh, see?" Mr. Alberte pointed his fork at me while chewing the lettuce. "There are ways to do things right. Seeing these Democrats talk about immigration reform—I mean, they want rights for the LGBTY-plus…whatever letters you add. And now abortion. And now, what, papers for criminals? This is what happens when a nation forgets God."

I kept my gaze on his face. James's eyes burned me from the side.

"God is there for the afflicted," Mr. Alberte continued. "But there are laws. We thought about starting an outreach program for the undocumented at church. We're still researching the best way to help them. They did break the law—"

"Dad, Matt is great at drawing as well," James said, trying to change the subject. "You should see his stuff."

"Is that what you want to do in the future?" Mrs. Alberte asked.

"That's the plan." I struggled to keep the anger away from my voice. "We'll see what the future holds."

"You plan on moving back?" Mr. Alberte asked while

munching on his food. "James here wants to go to college in Texas. That's why you should always enjoy high school. Everyone drifts apart after graduation."

"What are you doing, Dad?" James asked with an edge. "Huh? What's going on?"

"We're just having a conversation, son," Mr. Alberte said.

"You know I don't want to go to school in Texas," James said. "You want that. I never agreed to it."

"You have the talent, James." Mr. Alberte wagged his head. "Stop being so modest. You know you'll get into that school. You can't neglect God's calling in your life forever."

"Daniel here wanted to do art before he started his ministry." Mrs. Alberte nudged her husband with an elbow.

"That I did," he agreed. "But no regrets in choosing the ministry path. Sometimes we have to make sacrifices for our family and for ourselves." His eyes were on James. "And when we do, we hope the other party is willing to do the same."

James was frozen on his seat.

"You know." I knew I was going to regret what I was going to say, but fuck it. "Sometimes the sacrifice can be respecting people. I know religion can make people feel entitled, but you don't get to put this weight on other people's shoulders. You also don't get to talk about things you don't understand."

"What do you think we're doing here, Mr. Franco?" Mr. Alberte dropped his fork and knife by his plate. "You think this is a meet-the-parents situation? We agreed to this so we could be loud and clear about one thing." His face flushed. "To Mrs. Alberte and me, you'll always be James's friend. Nothing more. And both of you need to understand that whatever you two are doing is an abomination in God's eyes."

"And the way you judge things you don't understand isn't?" If I were on my feet right now, my knees would've buckled.

"Talking about things you don't get; things that aren't written in your precious little book."

"Dad prefers us lying." James's eyes glistened with disappointment. "Lying is more acceptable because people won't know. He believes in fighting the gay away until it's gone. But can we talk about how—"

"You gave up on your sessions at church, James," Mr. Alberte insisted. "You gave up on trying. You want to be persecuted your whole life? Looked down upon? Whatever you and this boy are doing is a sin. Plain and simple. There's no in-between. There's no gray line like the world says now. There's only good and evil, and right now you're standing on the edge of something very dangerous. I don't get it. Brian is doing so well. You should see him now."

"Brian?" My heart went wild. "You should—"

James grabbed my wrist and shook his head as a sign that I shouldn't continue.

Mrs. Alberte was like an audience member at a live show. Quiet. Observant. I hadn't expected things to go this south this fast. James couldn't hide his disappointment even if he tried. The scene cut through my heart.

Fuck being polite.

"Mr. Alberte," I said. "I'm no stranger to what you people believe. Answer me this, though, since you're, you know, this great speaker. Us pretending to be something we are not—"

"This world has fallen so far from the light," he said, puffing his chest a bit. "You don't pretend to be straight, if that's what you mean. You're born straight. I know this is a choice my son is making. You're also choosing this for a reason, kid. I'm not sure why any of you would choose this path. Maybe it's you trying to be different. Maybe it's you craving attention. I don't know."

"You're right," I said. "We shouldn't pretend to be what we are not, but I do think the Bible talks about mercy and forgiveness somewhere, right?"

"It also talks about choice," Mr. Alberte said. "You and my son are also choosing this lifestyle." His eyes met James. "A choice, son."

"You think I chose to be gay?" James slammed a fist on the table. "You think I'd keep choosing to be treated like this? You think I'd choose the embarrassment this night has become?"

James stormed out of the dining room. I followed. We rushed out of the house and ended up on the dimly lit sidewalk, walking through the darkness. James paced faster and faster with his every heavy breath.

"Hey." I was beside him. "Hey, hey…" I grabbed his wrist.

He threw his arms around me, burying his face on my shoulder, his tears leaking through the fabric of my shirt. I held him under the lamppost, his house behind us. His parents were on the front porch. His dad didn't linger, but his mom remained still, watching.

"I'm sorry," he repeated in muffles.

I wasn't willing to stick around. I was sure he didn't want to either.

"I want to take you somewhere," he said, head on my shoulder.

"We can go anywhere you want," I said.

We walked a few minutes until coming to a pathway disappearing into the trees. He grabbed his phone out of his pocket and turned the flashlight on. Yes, dinner had been a disaster, but why were we going into the woods at night? If this had been under any other circumstances, I would've asked him his reasons. I followed him instead, trampling over what I assumed were twigs and leaves and hoping was nothing more.

He seemed to know the landscape well. He never stopped to look around to make sure we weren't going in the wrong direction, regardless of how dark it was. The trees made way for a lake. The moon reflected over the water, and the lights of the town were in the distance.

My eyes slowly adjusted to the moonlight as he led me to a fallen tree. It was long, its tip disappearing under the water and its branches stretched out like hands begging for help.

He climbed up, using one of the branches for support as he walked across the bark, taking a seat so his feet had enough height to dangle above the ground. I followed his act. I didn't look as savvy, but I managed.

"I used to come here before the sun rose and after it set when that whole thing with Brian happened." My eyes were now friends with the dark. The outline of James's face was visible under the light of the moon. "I'd think about those sessions with that guy at church and how I could choose to be different." He laid a head on my shoulder. "What a stupid thing to believe. Some things can't be changed. It's like asking a lion to be a bird or something."

And that was the reason I had to let him go. Because I was the bird, and my wings had been clipped by choices outside of my control. Tonight wasn't the night I'd tell him, though. I wrapped my arms around him and rocked his body back and forth, humming the melody to "Clair de Lune."

"I know tonight sucked." He broke my melody, trying to find his voice again. "I'm so sorry. I don't know why I thought this was going to be good. How could it be good? A part of me knew why they had invited you. I wanted to believe things could be different."

"Don't beat yourself up for it." I held his hand. "You took a shot. It was brave."

"At least this happened with you before you moved back," he said.

I wished the moon was brighter so I could see his face better. "How do you…"

"I know you well enough by now," he said. "You grow distant when there's something on your mind. I knew it was pretty big this time. Especially in the last few days."

I squeezed his hand, biting hard on my lips.

"Do the others know?" he asked.

"No," I said. "But can we not talk about that tonight? There's still time before the fuse ignites."

"And because of the mistakes of other people," James said, "I'll have to say goodbye to the best thing that ever happened in my life."

"Nothing lasts forever, James Alberte," I said. "No matter how much we want to hold onto it."

"One thing will," he said. "The pain of your absence."

25

GOODBYE

May 2012

The entire crew jetted to the Crusty Pie after school. Yes, I spent my days off at the same place I worked. Honestly, I wanted to enjoy every mundane thing, because once I was gone, they would no longer be the simple things in life. They'd be the things I missed.

Mom had bought the tickets. On July thirtieth, Mom, Laila, and I would hop on a plane and return to Brazil. At least we weren't going back to my old town. I had an aunt living in Rio. I barely remembered her. I had also never been to Rio. We were going to stay with her for a few weeks until Mom found a job. Oh, and going to school there after all these years was bound to be an experience I wasn't looking forward to having. I'd probably need a private tutor to help me improve my Portuguese writing skills.

I was breaking the news to the Forbidden Fortress today. It was time. I needed to rip off the band-aid and get this over with. Easier said than done, obviously. I thought about the best way to break the news while driving Paradise to the coffee shop. Ever since the cop incident, I had started curating driving playlists to avoid glancing at my phone while behind the wheel. If my coming out was any example of how I broke important news to people, I would most likely just blurt it out at a random moment. Paradise was also going to officially belong Helton once I was out of here. It was only fair he got to keep her after registering her.

Mr. Oliver worked the counter today. "Matt!" He spread out his arms. "I take it your people are coming as well?"

"Hey," I said. "You know it. Can't stay away from this place no matter how hard I try. The muffins are too good."

"Tell them their food is on me today," he said. "A little gift since they're always here."

"Appreciate it, Mr. Oliver," I said. "We'll all order when they get here."

"Okay." He fixed his glasses. "Your table is empty, by the way."

The memories I had shared in this place struck my eyes. No, I couldn't cry yet. Not now, at least. I sat down, hands in my pockets. They were late. I didn't care. I wanted this moment to move slowly.

I observed the mugs on the shelves, the roasted coffee bags for sale, and the plants hanging on the ceiling. I was so distracted that I missed Pedro, Fa, and Diana's grand entrance. I only noticed they had arrived when Diana slapping the edge of the table snagged me back to reality.

"Wow," Fa said, pulling a chair. "He waited for us. I'm so proud."

"I can be a gentleman when I want to," I said.

"I've got news." Pedro sat in front of me. "Major news."

"Funny, because so do I," I said.

"No, no." Pedro's mouth gaped wide. "It's big."

"That's what she said," Fa said.

"Well, in my case, *he*." I chuckled.

"Okay, Matt." Pedro shrugged. "TMI."

"Where's James?" Diana asked.

"He's not coming today," I revealed. "It's just the four of us. By the way, Mr. Oliver said food and drinks are on the house today."

"Oh, today is the day all my dreams come true." Pedro rubbed his hands and headed to the counter.

"Love, do you mind getting me a cappuccino and a peanut butter and jelly?" Fa asked Diana.

"Of course not." Diana stood to her feet. "Matt, want anything?"

"I'm okay."

"Be back," she said.

"Everything okay with you and James?" Fa asked.

"I should ask you if everything is okay." I pointed at her plain black hoodie. "No major statement today?"

"Decided to keep things simple." She gave me the side-eye. She knew I was up to something. "Everything okay at home?" she asked, trying to scout for answers.

"Yeah," I said.

"Talked to your dad lately?"

"Not since his surprise visit before he left," I said.

"And James isn't coming on purpose?" she asked.

"I asked him not to."

"You're scaring me," she said. "Is this good news? You don't even want coffee."

"Let's wait for them." I scratched my head. "And for someone so in tune with her inner self, you should learn how to be more patient."

"We all have our weaknesses," she said. "Mine is that I'm *too* in tune with myself that I don't have time to be patient."

Pedro and Diana returned with the coffees and a few PB&Js.

"All right." Pedro sat down. "What's your big news?"

"So…" I cleared my throat while trying to find words that would make them hurt less. "Well, um, so there's—"

"You got James pregnant?" Diana said.

"Strangely, I wish that was it," I said. "Um, so we bought our return tickets. July thirtieth." Their faces were rigid and cold. "So, two more months and the Forbidden Fortress will lose one of its members."

Their eyes remained on me, maybe hoping I was going to laugh and say it was a joke.

"What happened to us living together?" Pedro finally asked. "What happened, Matt?"

"I can't, Pedro. No matter how much I want to stay, the truth is, I can't. I can't leave Mom and Laila."

"Well, *we* are staying here," Fa said. "We don't have papers either. You can if you want."

"All right, I don't want to stay here like this," I affirmed. "I won't."

"Fuck, Matty." Pedro puffed air. "And I had all these plans in my head. A two-bedroom. We each would have a sign on our door so if we were getting laid that night, we'd just flip it to avoid any awkwardness."

"Was there a sign to avoid that comment?" Diana frowned and held my hand. "I can't believe you won't be in shop next year."

"Save my chair for some new student," I said.

"No one will ever be as cool," Diana said.

Here was the part where someone normal would say, "Don't worry. We'll see each other soon." I couldn't say such a thing. I was leaving not knowing when I'd ever be allowed back. They wouldn't be flying back anytime soon either. This was it. This was the big finale I avoided thinking about; the match was lit that would lead to the big explosion of my time bomb.

"Why is James not here?" Pedro asked.

"You three were there in the very beginning," I replied. "I wanted it to be just us when I broke the news of our big final season."

"Tell me this is another one of those times where you're leaving but you end up staying," Diana insisted.

"Not this time," I said.

"Fuck, Matt," Diana said. "Fuck. Fuck. Fuck. I don't cuss, but fuck…"

"We still have two months," Fa said. "We can't let the future burden us today. Otherwise we'll waste the time we have left together drowning in pain."

"What if we all go camping when school's done? Get a cabin somewhere?" Diana said. "Oh, we could sit under the stars and build a fire. Instead of looking forward to Matt leaving, we could look forward to an amazing trip."

"That would be pretty sweet," Fa agreed. "I could bring my Tarot cards for midnight readings."

"And here I thought you were going to say cookies or something we could eat." I shrugged. "And that sounds incredible. We're nearing the end of our movie, and I really don't want to think about the credits."

"So we're going camping when school's done," Fa affirmed.

"Sounds good," Pedro said.

"Imagine a Tarot reading at midnight," Fa said. "God, that's got to be something, right?"

"I guess we'll find out soon." I wiggled my fingers as if casting a spell. "Oh, Pedro, you said you had something to share." I laced my fingers behind my head and used my foot to lean my chair back. "I hope I didn't kill the mood."

"Thank you," he said. "You actually did. But it's okay. You're forgiven already. For a minute there, I thought we had forgotten about my news."

"Just spill it, Manga Boy," Diana said.

"I may be officially off the market by the end of the week," he revealed.

"Mayyy?" Fa frowned.

"Yes, mayyy. I haven't asked Tiffany yet, and I don't know if she'll agree." Pedro scrunched his nose. "Okay, witch, where are your superpowers? Anyway, I'm taking her out tonight."

"And if she says 'yes,' you can't bring her to our camping trip," Diana protested.

"What, so I'll be a third wheel in the woods?" Pedro grabbed one of the PB&Js. "So unfair."

"The unfair thing was you waiting until now to find a girlfriend," I said. "You need to have a certain level of friendship to go camping with someone—or go on any trip at all. Not to mention that no involved parents would let their daughter camp with a new boyfriend. Good luck trying."

"James barely made the cut," Fa said. "Just saying."

"See?" Pedro waved his sandwich at Fa. "I should've gone with that girl with the weird nose ring. I should have…"

Their voices and faces and jokes were the soundtrack to my private thoughts. The laughing and the coffee and hearing Pedro talk about his maybe-maybe-not girlfriend confirmed that they were going to be okay without me. No matter where I was, I would always remember them. Because that's life. It moves on and moments turn to memories. At least you carry those with you wherever you go. If only you could bring along the people that matter to you the most. But life isn't that willing. That wasn't a choice we got to make.

26

THE UNIVERSE BEYOND OURSELVES

June 2012

"Hey, at least our parents agreed to split the cost of the cabin," I said from the passenger seat of James's Nissan. "And were also okay with us skipping the last Friday of the school year."

"Of course they would be okay with all those things," Pedro said. "We're going to Hopkinton Park. When we talked about camping, I thought, I don't know, New Hampshire or Vermont."

"This is still a cool place." James glanced at him through the rearview mirror. "And it's not like they're going to check my age at the gate when we drive in. We just pay the five dollars and go to the cabin."

"But aren't you supposed to camp at least an hour away from home when you go camping?" Pedro continued.

"Who established that rule?" Fa said with an arm around Diana.

"No one," Pedro answered. "But it's pretty logical. This is twenty minutes away. It breaks the illusion of it all. And we're staying here for three days. I can literally ask my dad to drop off toilet paper if we run out."

"Speaking of illusion, how's Tiffany?" James made kissing

noises. "Been smooching a lot? Are we going to get to meet her soon?"

"We were together last night." Pedro's eyes lit up. "She's so fun, you know. She's sweet, and when she is finally allowed to go camping with us, fingers crossed we find a place that's not in our backyard."

"Nothing you can say will make me regret my decision," Diana said. "She needs to earn her place to come on a camping trip with us."

"I can literally call her and she could be at our cabin in less than half an hour," Pedro said. "See? Not a camping trip. We can call this our time in the woods."

"God, that sounds so wrong," I added.

"I would've been fine with her coming," James said. "As the newest member of the Fortress, I would've even knighted her…" He hummed. "What would be a good name for her?"

"Sailor Moon," Pedro mumbled. "Manga Boy and Sailor Moon."

"A match made in heaven," I said. "Wow."

The tall pine trees popped up ahead. They surrounded a wide lake that could be seen from the road. We drove under the wooden sign that read "Hopkinton Lake: Make Memories. Inspire Dreams."

We paid the fee to a guy who pointed us toward the Wild Turkey camping grounds. Our cabin was supposed to be secluded and a short walk to the lake.

The road led us through the trees. James lowered the windows once the vegetation got thicker and blasted the *Jurassic Park* theme. It was things like these that reminded me why I had fallen in love with him.

To our relief, the pictures on the website were accurate. The cabin had a lot of trees around it and it was far enough from the screaming children on the other side of the lake. There was a table by the entrance and a grill.

"Okay, I can live with this," Diana said. "This is cool, right?" She pointed at the door. "And look. 'Enjoy That Cabin Life,'" she read the little wooden sign. "How sweet."

"Happy, Pedro?" James asked.

"Seventy-five percent." He popped the trunk open. "I can still call my dad for toi—"

"Do not say 'toilet paper' again or I'll throw you in that lake," Fa said. "I swear I will."

The floors of the cabin creaked as we walked in. The floor-to-ceiling windows faced the woods. There was a stone fireplace and a chandelier made of warped elk horns.

"They do have a microwave, right?" I asked. "This all looks fancy, but none of us can really cook, so…"

Diana rushed to the kitchen and yelled, "Confirmed!"

Our parents had been the official chefs for our long weekend. There was a lasagna, stroganoff, cheese-bread, cornbread, pizza, and I had bought stuff to make spaghetti and meatballs. The crew went upstairs to check out the rooms while I put the food in the fridge.

We unpacked and changed into our bathing suits so we could go canoeing. Summer was literally five days away and Fa insisted on wearing a black bathing suit with "I Know You're Staring" written on her ass. It was the first time I had seen James wearing swimming shorts that were, well, so short. They were red and sat way above his knees. Pedro decided to wear an Indiana Jones hat that matched the brownish color of his shorts.

The four of us followed the gravel road. Diana wanted to see a deer at some point, but our screaming and laughing shattered her hopes. It was hot, in the upper eighties, but the breeze didn't let us melt to death. The road took us around the lake, leading to a launch dock.

The dude who got our canoes ready talked about these scattered islands throughout the lake. He said one of them had been the home to this couple in the 1800s. He told us to follow an arrow that said, "Parkers Island." Fa got way too excited about the revelation that remains of the cabin were still there, and suggested that she should've brought her Tarot cards along.

Most of the visitors in the park were on the opposite side of the lake, swimming and barbecuing. Aside from us, there was only one other couple in the water, and they were already a little dot on the horizon.

"Make sure your life jackets are nice and tight!" Fa shouted, paddling away from the shore. "We all know how to swim, right?"

"A bit late for that question," Pedro replied, sitting behind Diana. "But I can swim well enough. If only Ariel was around."

James sat in front of me. The muscles of his back were a slight distraction as we paddled away from the shore. We all remained pretty close as we ventured farther.

"Signal sucks here," James said, holding his paddle with one hand and scrolling through his phone with another. "Jeez."

"You brought your phone?" I asked. "So brave of you."

Silence.

"Who are you calling now?"

The intro to "Clair de Lune." He set the phone beside him and remained still. The others gazed at James's face, a sight I wasn't able to see now. They paddled a little farther while looking confused. James's shoulders moved up and down. A whimper escaped him. Then another. A sniffle. I laid my paddle on the floor of the canoe and touched his arm.

"Hey." I knelt, holding onto one edge as the canoe wobbled.

"Sorry." He looked over his shoulder, a tear stain on his cheek. "I didn't mean to ruin the moment."

"It's all right." I hugged him from behind. "You're not ruining anything."

"I guess there's a reason why we're oblivious to when we're going to die," he said, facing forward.

"Why?"

"Because then we would only think about the day we were going to die. We would forget to live." He risked a glance over his shoulder, the boat rocking. "All I can think about is losing you, Matty."

"I guess it's no use pretending, huh?" I asked.

"I'm not pretending to have fun with you here. I'm definitely not pretending that I love you. I'm pretending to ignore that soon we won't be able to do this anymore. I won't be able to touch you or kiss you…"

"Tick, tick, tick…" I said.

My arms tightened around him. I closed my eyes, resting my chin on his shoulder while listening to the song. We remained like this until the song finished echoing down the canoe. When I opened my eyes, the rest of the Forbidden Fortress were a few feet away, doing a terrible job of pretending not to stare.

"Are we done?" Fa shouted.

"Yes." I waved them closer with an awkward chuckle. "We're done."

They paddled fast. Too fast. Diana looked at us like we were her enemies in a battle. War had been declared against our boat.

"You can swim, right?" Diana shouted.

"Fuck you!" I yelled back with a laugh.

"Hold on to your butts!" Pedro shouted when they crashed into our boat and tossed us out.

My eyes were open when we plunged into the lake. Time slowed as I watched James's hair, chest, arms, his dimpled chin. It seemed accurate to have been thrown into the water with him. It was even more accurate that he got to swim up while I stayed under.

"What the hell, guys?" He wiped the hair out of his face when our heads popped out of the water. "What was that?"

"No super-sad-this-is-goodbye allowed this weekend." Fa pounded on the edge of her boat. "We still have the Elder Wizard for a few weeks. Let's save our tears and sobs for the going-away party."

"You think I want a going-away party after this?" My teeth chattered. The water was fucking cold.

"Don't worry, it'll be Titanic-themed." Pedro clicked his tongue. "Like the temperature of the water?"

They held one side of our canoe so James and I could climb back on. Thank God the paddles were still there and James's phone was intact.

I grabbed Fa's life jacket and pulled her into the water. She plunged, flailing her arms in the air.

"Now we're even, Rose," I shouted.

"Excuse me!" She latched on to the edge of their canoe. "It was Pedro's idea." She grabbed his arm and pulled him in. Diana needed no convincing at this point. She simply plopped into the water.

We weren't pretending. None us were. We were enjoying time—even if it was going to expire soon. Seeing them laugh and joke and be horrible at paddling made me realize that the most important thing wasn't the end of something, but the everything that happened in the in-between of the good and bad.

"I'm going to feel my arms tomorrow," I said as we neared the cabin. We had been the last ones to return our canoes and had arrived back a few minutes before sunset.

"Lasagna tonight," Pedro said. "What do you guys think?"

"Yes, please," James said. "I'm starving."

"And a hot chocolate after," Diana suggested. "Oh, we have cookies, right?"

"We would never come to a cabin without them." I typed the code on the door.

"Shotgun for the shower!" Pedro raced inside and grabbed a towel from the closet.

"Wow." Fa put her hands on her waist. "What happened to girls first?"

"Still a thing. I just need to shit." He blew her a kiss and rushed into the single bathroom we had in the house.

"Disgusting," she said.

James and I went into our room. Something was on his mind. I assumed what it was. The weight of my departure was becoming heavier by the day. I didn't bring up the subject. I didn't want to risk more tears. Not now. Not this week.

"Jesus, to think we're all going to have to shower after Pedro destroys that bathroom," James said as I sat on the edge of our bed near the nightstand.

"Shit." I grabbed my phone. There were five missed calls from Mom. Shit. Something was wrong.

"What?" James asked.

A text message with a link.

"Matty?" he insisted.

I clicked it.

"Mom called a whole bunch of times." I glanced at him. "And she sent this article that says, 'Hope for Dreamers.'"

A video of Obama popped up, but an ad about pimples showed up on top of his face. How dare they? I had always been curious about his skincare routine. I scrolled down the page.

"You okay?" James asked. "Matt, you look pale…"

I kept on reading.

"What is it?" He sat next to me.

"The best news I've ever read," I said. "I have to Google this… make sure it's real… DACA…" I mumbled the last word. It was brand new. I had never read about it before. There was a chance this could have been some major fake news. I visited other websites and realized that I had just been given a very, very early Christmas gift. DACA was all over the news.

"Matt!!!!!!!!!!" Fa screamed from the living room.

"What's going on, guys?" James asked. "Tell me."

"You guys read it?" I grabbed James's hand and ran down the stairs, nearly stumbling on the last step. Diana set the phone on the coffee table of the living room. A speech from Obama.

"My aunt just sent me the link!" Diana yelled. "Is this real life?"

He was behind his podium in front of the White House.

"*Good afternoon, everybody. This morning, Secretary Napolitano announced new actions my administration will take to mend our nation's immigration policy, to make it more fair, more efficient, and more just—specifically for certain young people sometimes called 'Dreamers.'*"

My heart was beating fast.

"*These are young people who study in our schools, they play in our neighborhoods, they're friends with our kids, they pledge allegiance to our flag. They are Americans in their heart, in their minds, in every single way but one: on paper. They were brought to this country by their parents—sometimes even as infants—and often have no idea that they're undocumented until they apply for a job or a driver's license, or a college scholarship.*

"*Put yourself in their shoes. Imagine you've done everything right your entire life—studied hard, worked hard, maybe even graduated at the top of your class—only to suddenly face the threat of deportation to a country that you know nothing about, with a language that you may not even speak."*

"My God, it's real," I said. "It's fucking real."

"Effective immediately, the Department of Homeland Security is taking steps to lift the shadow of deportation from these young people. Over the next few months, eligible individuals who do not present a risk to national security or public safety will be able to request temporary relief from deportation proceedings and apply for work authorization. Now, let's be clear—this is not amnesty, this is not immunity. This is not a path to citizenship. It's not a permanent fix. This is a temporary stopgap measure that lets us focus our resources wisely while giving a degree of relief and hope to talented, driven, patriotic young people…"

"Wait, so you're all getting papers?" James's eyes circled the room.

"Yes, and no?" Diana replied.

"I'm just fucking happy that we aren't getting kicked out of here!" Pedro raised his arms. "My God!"

I did some more digging. DACA would shield Dreamers brought to America as kids from deportation. We'd be allowed to work and have social security numbers and work permits. By no means was this a final destination, but it was still something. No more living in the shadows. We'd be able to breathe.

The four of us stared at each other like this had all been a bad dream. Their eyes screamed relief. Mine probably did the same.

"So, college?" Fa asked. "Vermont? Los Angeles? New York?"

"I need to take driver's ed." Pedro nodded. "I mean—"

"I think for the sake of humanity, you do," Diana said.

My phone buzzed. A message from Laila.

Laila: Did you read it, Matt? I just watched the video. OMG-GGGGG!!!!
  Me: I did!
  Laila: What do you think?
  Me: Not thinking at the moment. You?
  Laila: Down to stay? :D

27

ONE LAST TIME

June 2014

I was the driver for today, and it was my duty to pick up everyone for the big event. Everyone had agreed that even though parents were coming, we were all riding together in Paradise one last time.

Suits and black dresses were required for today. James looked like James Bond in his. He said I looked like a mixture of Jon Snow and Keanu Reeves with my hair gelled back. Fa had picked a dress all right, one with a plunging cleavage. Diana had surrendered to the black dress, but protested the school's decision on the color by pinning an orange brooch shaped like a pumpkin on her chest. Pedro had a suit on, but his famous once-white Converses graced his feet.

Our gowns, tassels, and hats waited in the shop, staring at us from the left side of the class. Mr. H looked extremely sharp in his black suit, but he had added his own touch to the attire; a blue ink blotch on his thigh.

"All right, all right, all right!" he said as we walked in. "Are we going to the Oscars? You all look sharp!"

"If only," Pedro replied. "Then that would mean I was a millionaire who was buying a penthouse in New York instead of going for school."

"Like you haven't been dreaming about the one hundred dates you're going to go on in a year," James mentioned.

"Too bad things didn't work out with Tiffany," Pedro added. "She would've loved New York."

"You would've broken up regardless," Fa said. "Glad it happened before we all got to be neighbors."

"Remember." Mr. H clapped to get our attention. "Your main goal is to study. Mr. Franco turned down a scholarship here in Massachusetts."

"And got offered another one in NYC." My comment earned a high five and a cheer from the Forbidden Fortress.

"I'm going to miss you guys," Mr. H said. "And quick reminder that you can only put on your gowns and hats fifteen—"

"Fifteen minutes before we leave." We all finished the sentence together.

"They said that one million times during rehearsal," I said.

"All right, I'll save the speech for when the rest of the students get here," he said. "Meanwhile, help yourselves to donuts in the back."

There was a table with four dozen donuts. I grabbed a Boston cream once we encircled one of the tables. "Everyone, get one, get one. Donut toast."

"Are you sure Pedro can handle donuts in a suit?" Diana grabbed a glazed donut. "He might squirt."

"Because it is graduation," Pedro said, ensnaring a strawberry frosted, "I will ignore that comment."

"Cheers to the future." I held up my donut.

"Fuck yes!" James agreed.

"Cheers to being together," Diana said.

We bumped our donuts in the air and practically inhaled them.

I looked over my shoulder. Neb's chair. A new student had claimed it during junior year. He was all right. He definitely didn't make a statement like Neb did.

"Never heard from him?" Mr. H asked, standing next to me.

"No," I said. "Radio silence."

"Me neither," he said.

"I hope he's okay," I said.

"You're a good kid, Mr. Franco," he said. "I'm glad you stuck around."

"Me, too," I said.

Once everyone was in class, Mr. H reminded us that we only tossed the hats in the air after all names were read, and only then was the tassel moved to the left. Mr. H snapped the fingers of his left hand for those who lacked any sense of direction. He had allowed parents to see our shop thirty minutes before the ceremony, but before they stormed in, he insisted on a class picture.

Parents started trickling in, marveling at the art on the walls. Diana's aunt arrived, trying to run in heels because, apparently, they needed an Olympic moment in front of the entire class when hugging. Fa's mom followed, wearing a lipstick so red, at first glance I thought her lips were smeared with blood.

Mom and Laila showed up with balloons that read "Happy Graduation." She had one for me and one for James.

"Can't believe this will be my school next year," Laila said.

"You'll love it here," I said.

"And you guys have a vending machine inside every shop," she added. "I'll have to be careful."

"Filho, que legal!" She scanned the shop.

"Are you proud, Mom?" I asked.

"Always."

"You don't feel bad we stayed?" I asked.

"I'm glad we did."

"But DAPA didn't go through," I said. "You need to be protected as well."

"Son," Mom said. "Everything will work out. Seeing you and your sister doing well, that's what matters to me."

"Tia," James greeted her.

"Oh, James." Mom kissed him on the cheek. "You look handsome, James."

"Thank you," he said.

"You look sharp in a suit, Alberte," Laila said.

"I trust your fashion eye," James said.

"Are your parents coming?" Mom asked.

"I may be going to college," James said. "But it's still not what they wanted for me. I better get used to the absence anyway, right?"

"Sorry, honey." Mom hugged him. "Are we all still on for lunch after?"

"Absolutely," he said.

Mr. H clapped his hands again and asked all parents to go to the auditorium so we could put on our graduation gear. We were finally allowed to put on our gowns and graduation caps.

The bell rang one last time, our cue to head out. Mr. H tried to keep us in a single line, but his plan failed miserably. At least we made it to the auditorium on time.

Our seats were reserved on the first floor. Parents and guests sat on the upper level. Our seats had been assigned according to our last name. James was close to the first row. I recognized the nape of his neck from where I was. I would've recognized every part of him anywhere.

He was bummed his parents had decided not to attend. It had taken months for me to get another dinner invite, but people can be like rocks sometimes. With time, even a little consistent drip of water can break one.

I searched the upper level. Mom promised to sit on the first row so James could see his surprise. It had taken an in-person meeting to talk them into coming. It had been extremely hard to keep it a secret. At least they had agreed to show up. I finally spotted them to my left. Mom waved frantically, Laila next to her, and James's parents on the other side. They were as still as statues, but hey, at least they were here.

Me: Turn around and look up until you see my mom waving. Text me when you see her.
James: Is she okay?
Me: Just do what I'm telling you.

His eyes searched the upper level. His face went from curious to surprised in less than a second. I was glad he didn't know I had a front seat to his expressions. I wanted to see the unblemished look on his face. He burst into laughter, waving like a kid at a preschool play. He scanned the crowd, trying to find me. He succeeded. His smile was so broad, people probably thought he was modeling for a toothpaste commercial.

James: I love you, Matty.
Matty: I love YOU, Jamie.

I looked at Mom again, but another face pulled my attention. Neb. He waved. I did the same. He sat a few seats away from James's parents. He smiled—the kind of smile I had never seen on his face before.

Standing here felt like a dream. At one point, I was caught up in the nightmare that this moment would never come. Not like this, anyway. But then they called my name. I got to walk up that stage to get my diploma while Mom and Laila watched.

I was worthy of the title the media had given me. Dreamer. We found the courage to believe even when the odds were against us.

This truth—the one related to documents—this was the truth I could change. I knew this was only the beginning. DACA wasn't forever. Parties still debated if being a Dreamer was constitutional. Some said that we had no right getting the relief we did. But while they debated on my worth, I decided to focus on who I truly was, and not what they made me out to be.

Even if having DACA was like being on a rocky boat, I decided to paddle until I reached the other side of the ocean.

Acknowledgments

This book was written during a worldwide lockdown. In the lonely hours of both day and night, I poured my heart and soul into it while undergoing weekly therapy sessions. One could never finish a book like this without support. Beyond the art of writing, I had to revisit memories of events that happened to me and around me—some of which had been locked away for quite some time.

To my family: Thank you for encouraging me to face the shadows and write this novel.

To my agent, Susan Velazquez: You believed in Mateus and James before so many others.

Thank you for helping me tell the story the way it should be told. Fingers crossed that many will join Forbidden Fortress!

Mariana Novaes, you read the very first words I ever put on paper for this book. The world will finally meet the crew.

Flavia Duddey, you are and will forever be the OG "Biblical Whore." I love you!

Sasha Alsberg, you were a cheerleader when I was so close to giving up on this book. Thank you for encouraging me to finish the race.

Elizabeth Sagan, your passion for this book—even in its rawest state—inspired me to press forward. Thank you for making space for Mateus and James in your reader's heart.

Lilly Santiago, you listened to me rant and dissect every motive and action of these characters for hours. We finally have them on paper. Thank you for listening and believing Forbidden Fortress to be worth your time and attention.

To my alpha and beta readers: Your honest feedback made these characters all the more real.

I cannot conclude this section without aknowledging the need for a fair and compassionate immigration system in the United States. May this book inspire readers to approach these matters with both kindness and reason. My hope is that we look back on this moment in American history and learn from our triumphs and missteps as a nation and a community.

About the Author

J.D. Netto is a multi-faceted bestselling author. His first fantasy series, The Whispers of the Fallen, became an underground phenomenon when first published. He's also the founder of Saved by the Page, a movement that invites readers to share stories on how books saved their lives. A few of these heroic tales were compiled into an anthology, published in 2018. He's also known for *Henderbell: The Shadow of Saint Nicholas*—a speculative fiction novel that follows the cursed bloodline of Father Christmas. His latest work, *The Broken Miracle: Part One*, is a fictional biography inspired by the life of acclaimed pianist Paul Cardall and his journey living with half a heart. The novel also spawned an album featuring Paul himself alongside David Archuleta, Thompson Square, Tyler Glenn, among others.

Find J.D. Netto on his website at www.jdnetto.com or Instagram at www.instagram.com/jdnetto.